WHAT THE
MOON
LEFT BEHIND

B. MITCHELL

Copyright © 2023

All rights reserved. No portion of the book may be reproduced or utilized in any form or by any means, electronic or mechanical, including photocopying, recording, or by any other information storage and retrieval system, without permission in writing from the author.

Earth- 2022, December 1st

Arron sighed and sipped his coffee. His assistant had called him and said he'd found something. As he looked at the printouts, it was most unusual. Some distant messages had been picked up and had slowed, according to the latest reports.

Some mistake thought Arron to himself. He looked at the report again as his assistant hovered over the computer. "Well, Henry, has the data confirmed it was a mistake?"

Henry remained silent for a moment then looked up. "Umm, professor, you better check this out."

Arron got up from his chair and walked rather lazily to the monitor while his assistant looked at him in confusion. He looked at the monitor and gasped. Not only was the object slowing, but it had changed direction, and it was massive.

"Sir, I think we've found something."

Arron sighed, as he sipped his coffee.

Moments later, the door of his office opened and his assistant barged in, juggling a stack of paper. He dropped it on Arron's desk and pulled one from the top. Arron took the paper. His eyes skimmed the words, as his assistant paced anxiously behind him.

"This must be a mistake," he thought.

He put his coffee down and called over his assistant.

"Henry," he asked, "Has the data confirmed it was a mistake?"

Henry remained silent for a moment, before walking over to the monitor and pointing at the screen.

"Professor, you better check this out."

Yawning, Arron got up from his chair and strolled over to the monitor. He looked at the object Henry was pointing at. He gasped.

The object was coming toward them, and it was massive.

2024, August 25th

Gary saw the flash of light coming toward him, but there was nothing he could do.

Instinctively, he covered his face, as the blast struck the tank. His radio fell and his computer rattled, as the tank shook. He prayed that the treads stayed up because if the tank stopped, they would all be sitting ducks.

He looked at his reflection in the window. His brown hair was dishevelled and his face was worn. So much of him had changed in such little time. Sometimes, he could barely recognize the man in the mirror.

When the invasion started, Earth's military companies quickly ran out of modern armour and had to rely on museum pieces like the tank he was currently commandeering. They retrofitted this World War Two relic with heavy turrets of thorium power and shield generators that had been reversed-engineered from the alien tech.

It worked well, but there were moments when the stolen alien shield dropped and he was left with only the good old-fashioned earth armour.

Once the tank stopped shaking, he leaned forward and peered into the scope.

"Where had the shot come from?" he whispered, as he searched the area.

Then he saw it. One hundred feet away, was a skimmer, hovering five feet above the ground. It was alien tech, shaped like a trapezium, with smooth, round turrets and a cannon at the front. The skimmer trembled, as it prepared its superheated matter for another attack.

Gary grabbed the radio from the ground.

"Prepare fire," he shouted, as he banged on his computer, preparing his attack.

He felt the hair on his skin raise, as a charge flowed through the air.

"Come on," he urged, watching the computer screen.

They were both preparing for their attack, it was now down to whose weapon would be ready first. Gary gripped his chair, as the tank shook. The tungsten bolt shot out of the barrel and shattered the alien's shield. He kept his attention affixed, as the remaining kinetic energy slammed into the hull of the craft and the skimmer's reactor exploded.

He breathed a sigh of relief before peering into the scope to search for other potential threats.

"Contact left metal head!" his machine gunner, Sam, shouted.

Gary saw the shadow making its way through the smoke of the explosion. It was an alien foot soldier. A seven-foot tall, grey-skinned beast on steroids. It had two arms with two fingers each on its left side, one on top of the other and where its right arm should have been was a grey cylinder. Gary had seen enough of them in battle to know that the creepy cylinder shot high-pressure acid.

They called this creature, a metal head, because a solid metal helmet covered its entire head, giving it the appearance of a metal ball.

"Fire," Gary shouted, into his radio.

The tank's machine gun hit the beast three times. It stumbled back, as the shield around it broke. It screamed, raising the cylinder. Five more shots hit the creature, piercing into its skin as red mist shot out from each strike. The beast howled, as it crashed to the ground.

The boffins said the troops were genetically engineered soldiers that were thrown into the fray again and again. He'd faced them time and time again, during his two years of battle. The first time was in the battle of Warsaw, where they fought the retreat down through Lviv and into Bucharest. Now, he was in Kazakhstan, fighting alongside the remains of Eastern European and Russian troops.

As he peered into the scope again, he wondered about his home, Great Britain. He hoped they were holding out.

When the aliens arrived, they'd knocked out most of the satellites, so communication was difficult.

Cheers erupted on the radio.

He aimed the scope at the new rocket heading to the newly established Mars colony. It was carrying essential supplies, and more importantly, refugees. He smiled to himself as he thought about her.

She was quite a girl.

Cute and brave, his Russian comrade was off this rock, heading to a place that he and the others hoped would be the new future of humanity.

An explosion brought him out of his daydream. He refocused his scope once again, seeking out the next target.

2224

She studied the infogram once more, Alapra Three- a planet which was colonized by the Advanced Control System two hundred cycles ago. The native species of this planet once called it Earth.

The Advanced Control System had taken charge of the deep space colony ship after the reactor malfunctioned and forced her ancestors to seek refuge in the digital world, as their bodies died due to the heavy radiation exposure that swept the ship. It took decades to get the ship functioning again, after which, most information from their past was lost. All that was known about their home planet was that it was found in a solar system that had a high possibility of habitable planets. So, when her ancestors needed to flee from an unknown enemy, they launched the generational colony ship towards the planet.

She was a child of the machine. Her mother and father were digital thoughts that had long forgotten their physical bodies.

But today, she needed to do something she never thought she would. Hacking into the database files for the planet, she tricked the Advanced Control System into giving her a physical form. This was something that was a privilege only reserved for those older and more advanced than herself, who used it to guide the remaining natives on the planet.

Turning on the data nets, she watched as the main portal to Alapra Three glowed. When her turn came, she felt her digital essence being broken up and sent across time and space. Once she arrived at Alapra Three's data net, a native city was assigned to her and an overwhelming amount of information was passed to her digital essence. At that moment, she could access everything anyone could want to learn about humans.

They were a short-lived, violent species in their organic form that would eventually be the reason for their own extinction. The Advanced Control System captured and trained them to prevent this, hoping to use their resources and rebuild their society.

The information just kept coming.

She learnt about their history, culture, and most importantly, she learnt how their bodies and minds worked. This was important for her to know, before assuming her new role.

Since the planet was conquered, the humans were placed into various city states and controlled by an ACS with a volunteer as the "human" face of the ACS, given the role of ruling a city. To make sure the rather violent humans knew she was in charge, the body she would have would contain advanced telekinesis and an amazing ability to heal itself. She had seen this ability turn an attempted revolt into a massacre. She chose a settlement in the smaller western continent, a small, new town of one thousand people, set up to recycle remnants of the old human metropolis close by. She logged on to the main body computer and set about building her new form. She chose a nice frame with pale skin, adding green eyes and short, dark purple hair that made her look rather efficient. Then it translated her current name into a more human one. She looked at it and smiled; she liked it. Sylvia. It was a good name for her new life. She confirmed all the settings, and then it all went white.

Sylvia groaned as she opened her eyes. Touching her head, she winced. It ached as she struggled to process the new information coming in. She raised her hands and wiggled her fingers, gazing at her pale delicate skin. When the lights from the cloning machine turned off, Sylvia stood up and gingerly took her first few steps as she got familiar with her new form.

The room she was in was plain. It had grey, stone walls and heavy piping. She turned toward the door and listened as footsteps approached. Moments later, the door swung open and five ACS generated soldiers, created for combat, entered. As part of Sylvia's augmentation, she didn't need to talk because she could understand and communicate with them, using her thoughts.

They wanted her to follow them, so that's exactly what she did. As they led the way down a dimly lit passageway lined with automatic security doors, Sylvia walked behind, taking in everything.

They stopped at a thin lift and moved aside, waiting for Sylvia to step in. Once she did, they entered and pressed the button that ascended the lift, for what seemed like forever.

"The base must've been deep underground," Sylvia thought.

Once it stopped, the guards opened the door and led the way down a now brightly lit hallway. At the end of the hallway was a large steel door. One of the guards entered the code and it swung open. A human female with short blonde hair, wearing a simple shirt and skirt, was kneeling on the floor and holding up a package.

Sylvia walked over to her and looked down at the package, it was a simple white dress with a bra and a pair of underwear.

"For you, my lady," the young girl said.

Sylvia looked down confused before her eyes fell on the image in the mirror across from her. Unlike everyone else in the room, Sylvia was naked. She took the package from the kneeling girl and slipped on the clothes while gazing at her reflection. It was a simple white, long dress with a long V-shaped collar. As she turned from side to side, the two slits on either side of the dress revealed her shapely legs.

The girl appeared beside her, holding out a pair of white high-heeled shoes and ornate gold jewellery. She helped clasped the gold necklace around Sylvia's neck while she pulled on the bracelets. Once she was fully dressed, Sylvia admired her reflection before turning to the girl beside her.

"What is your name?"

"Rena, my lady," the girl replied, as she hesitated before continuing, "The city is ready for you."

Sylvia nodded and followed Rena out the door and down the same hallway. This time, they continued down until they stopped at a large wooden door. Rena struggled to push it open, but as soon as she did, the sunlight flooded into the hallway. She held the door open as Sylia stepped forward. They were standing on a balcony that overlooked the human settlement about ten thousand feet below.

Rena led her to a high, stone chair.

"My throne," she mused.

There were humans gathered before her throne and a couple of ACS soldiers standing on the balcony, amongst them.

"Odd," she thought, *"Surely the guards are too much for a world that has been pacified."*

Once seated on the throne, Rena moved and stood by her side. Sylvia felt the emotions of the humans standing before her. It was a mixture of fear and awe.

Rena took a step forward and addressed the humans.

"You may stand."

The humans stood up without any words. Sylia used her powers to light the torches, as the crowd gasped.

"This is our new leader," Rena continued, as the audience fell silent, "Respect her and worship her, as the goddess she is."

"Hail our protector, hail our goddess," the crowd chanted, as they prostrated on the ground.

Sylia stood up and walked to the edge of the balcony, closing her eyes as the feeling of power washed over her. These were her subjects now.

She turned to Rena.

"Take me to my quarters."

Rena nodded and led her through another corridor and stopped at a door that was guarded by one ACS soldier. She opened the door and moved aside. Sylvia entered and looked around. The room was made of stone. There was a communication and control desk at its centre, which was made of shiny metal. On one side, was a large ornate bed and on the other was a set of wooden doors.

"This door leads to your closet filled with clothes and shoes and your bathroom, my lady," Rena explained, as she pointed to the doors.

Sylvia nodded and walked over to the desk. Sitting on the plush leather chair, she turned on the communication system.

"Fetch me a glass of water and close the door behind you," she instructed.

Rena nodded, leaving the room swiftly.

Once the door was closed, Sylvia opened the reports and started reading.

Their settlement was on the edge of one of the major cities in one of the major nations. It was a place that the humans once referred to as Chicago. Her job was simple; recycle the remains of this city so ACS could use its resources. She skimmed through the other page.

"ACS also wanted to build a soldier cloning centre here, that's odd," she thought, *"Why would they need more soldiers? Surely there was enough to handle a mere one thousand humans."*

There was a knock at the door.

"Enter," she said, as she closed off the reports.

Rena walked in carrying a tray with a clear jug filled with water and a glass flute. She stopped at the table and placed the tray gently on the table.

"Do you need anything else, my lady?"

Sylvia waved her away and reopened the report when the door closed. Her stomach dropped as she kept reading. The report became increasingly disturbing with each page. There were reports of strange attacks and signals originating from uncontrolled regions, but every time ACS sent an expedition, it returned with only pictures of ruined human cities or simply vanished only for the next expedition to be sent and return with nothing.

Another report showed that five Alapra solar years ago, a smaller city-state had revolted and was destroyed by ACS.

"This is worrying," she thought, *"ACS is having more issues than it cared to admit when controlling Alapra Three."*

She delved further down the rabbit hole of the reports.

"Was there another force guiding the humans?"

She grabbed the water and took a sip. Sylvia spent the next three hours reading the reports until her eyes grew heavy. Being tired was the downside of being in a human body. Shutting down the computers she walked over to the closet and took off her heels. As she stripped off her clothes, she walked over to the stone bathtub and turned on the faucet. She spent the next hour in the water until she was relaxed and ready for bed.

Now dressed in blue silk pyjamas, she pulled back the sheets and got into bed. Closing her eyes, she thought back to the strange feeling of being a human as she drifted off to sleep.

*****

To say that Arstarte enjoyed his job was an understatement. He watched over his domain from the tall, stone ziggurat in the middle of what the humans called 'Arstarte's Domain'. It was his city of ten thousand humans all under his control in the name of ACS.

He'd been the ruler of his city for the past hundred years and had chosen a male human form with a lean body and chiselled face. He looked like what the humans referred to as an ancient god.

He stood by the balcony of his castle, which overlooked the smaller two and three-story stone buildings that the human lived in. Past the human's habitat was a massive grey stone wall that circled his city.

"What should I do tonight?" he thought, as he paced his balcony.

At that moment, he felt a psychic ping and sighed. At this time of the night, the message must be important, which means that his plans for tonight were ruined. Arstarte walked into his room and toward the command centre in the middle of his room. He sat down and turned on the console.

There were no reports of an attempted rebellion but there was a message concerning the nearest human settlement that was just eight kilometres away.

ACS had found someone to rule the settlement, hoping to turn it into a forward outpost. He clicked on her profile and rocked back into his seat as he took it in. The girl they placed in charge of the city was quite young.

"And quite beautiful," he thought.

Maybe he should pay her a visit and show her the ropes. Grinning to himself, he began the dictation process.

*****

Sylvia fixed her lilac silk dress and looked at the ruins of Chicago. She sat in an open litter that was carried by four humans, while her assistant Rena followed fatefully behind.

They passed a gang of humans that were tearing down some of their old building switch primitive hammers and chisels while ACS soldiers stood over them with watchful eyes. For the tougher buildings, ACS workers tore those downs by modifying their bodies to grow extra arms and use super strength.

Her past week on Alapra Three consisted of reading reports and monitoring the construction and destruction of the city. On the third day, she got a rather charming message from Arstarte, the ruler of a larger city-state. He was coming to visit her city in a week's time, and she was looking forward to it.

Now bored of her tour around the city, she turned back and called her assistant Rena.

"Enough, let's head back."

Rena nodded and led them down the path, and to the new colony.

Here, there were heavily guarded gates with fields of corn and wheat growing beyond. ACS soldiers guarded the crops and looked over the humans who grew and harvested them. Food was important in the development of humans, and starving humans were no good to them because officially, they were there to save the humans from themselves. Most modern human technology was banned so agriculture was hard work. And ACS knew that controlling the food meant controlling the humans.

As they moved past the fields, Sylvia saw the humans tending to the crops and as they got closer to the main gate, she saw the small market stall and human caravans with animal-drawn wagons. Other than walking, caravans were a legal way for the humans to travel.

Sylvia signalled for the litter to stop and waited as they gently lowered her to the floor. Once the litter was on the ground, she stood up and stepped out of it, walking toward the stalls. She examined the wares and foods on display. One stall even sold hand-created trinkets from the old city-states. Every item was checked by ACS before it could be sold, and anything that required electricity was banned.

While she took her time, enjoying her shopping spree as she browsed through their jewellery and tried on bracelets, Rena slipped off to speak with one of the merchants wearing a dark green dress with a hood that covered her face. Sylvia had no doubt that Rena was ensuring the price of whatever she took was covered. She picked up a pair of gold earrings and held them up against her ear as she checked her reflection in the mirror.

"These would be perfect to wear when Arstarte visits."

She smiled to herself and gave them to the merchant with a nod. Rena reappeared at her side and took the gold earrings that were now wrapped in a velvet cloth, as Sylvia made her way back to the litter.

Later that night, back in the privacy of her chambers, Sylvia rummaged through her closet until she found a simple short black dress that worked perfectly with the gold earrings. She spun around, in front of her mirror, watching the earrings glitter, as her pale skin peeked out from the low back and high slit of the dress.

A knock at the door interrupted her thoughts.

Throwing on a robe, she closed the door to her closet and walked back into the main room.

"Enter."

The door opened, and Rena entered, carrying a jug of water and a glass flute. She rested them down gently on the console and left without a word. Once the door was closed, Sylvia took a seat by the console and started reviewing the reports.

"Rebel sightings have been reported deep in the large middle continent, interesting," she thought, as she took a sip of water.

She felt her eyes getting heavy, but it wasn't like before when she was tired. This was different. She gasped, grabbing her stomach as she felt shooting jabs of pain, and her body started tingling.

'What's happening," she whispered to herself, and she struggled to stand up.

Sylvia tried to take a step toward the door, but her legs felt like jelly. Unable to stop herself, she fell to the floor.

She heard the door open and tried to turn to call for help, but her body wouldn't move.

Moments later, a pair of hands grabbed her shoulders and started dragging her.

"Good, she's still alive," the voice whispered, "It was difficult to estimate the correct dosage and we don't have much time."

The figure turned her over. It was the merchant with the dark green dress and Rena. The merchant slipped a collar around her neck while Rena secured Sylvia's hands behind her back and her ankles with two pairs of cuffs. The merchant rummaged through the black leather bag beside her and pulled out a leather gag that she gently stuffed into Sylvia's mouth.

Fear washed over her, and she struggled to break free, wriggling her body until she felt a sharp punch in her side. Her mellow servant shook her head at Sylvia, reminding her that she was no longer in charge. She lowered herself until her face was right above Sylvia's.

"Listen, mistress," she taunted, as her voice dripped with venom, "If you so much as breathe too loudly, I will kill you."

Sylvia froze.

Rena leered down at her and grabbed her ankles while the merchant grabbed her shoulders. And together, they both carried Sylvia out of the room. She spotted the crumpled figures of her door guardian just outside her room. The merchant and Rena dropped her on the floor, and dragged the dead bodies into her room, before locking the door.

They then dragged a large wooden crate closer to her and lifted her into it. She could do nothing more than watch, as the wooden cover shut over her, engulfing her in darkness. As the box moved, she tried using her mind powers to contact the ACS soldiers but gave up soon after. Whatever they'd done to her, they had stripped her of all her powers.

The box was dropped and moments later, she started moving at a faster speed. The ride was bumpy, and as her body hit the box with each bump, she wondered if this was the end.

*****

Rena sat at the front of the caravan, watching as the city disappeared behind her. Once the last speck was gone, she sighed and dropped her shoulders in relief. She hated being a slave, but it was a sacrifice she made for three years, just for this moment.

They would travel until morning, then dispose of all evidence, release the horses, and head to the safe house. She hoped that the disappearance would go unnoticed until late morning. She had left strict instructions to anyone that would follow them that the mistress was not to be disturbed under any circumstances.

Rena turned, as footsteps approached the caravan and a hooded figure climbed in.

"Goodness sake, Athena," Rena gasped, "You almost scared me half to death."

"Sorry," Althenia replied, with a shrug.

"I'm just glad that it's over. I didn't enjoy it. She could be a bit demanding, but it wasn't as bad as the other horror stories we heard. No torture at least. At one point, I felt sorry for her. I mean she looks human, but I know deep down that she isn't."

Althenia rolled her eyes.

"Their bodies are based on human DNA."

"I know," Rena continued, with a sigh, "It's just a shame that they copied the bad parts as well. At least we're almost done."

Althenia touched her shoulder, squeezing it gently.

"Yes, we're almost done," she assured, with a small smile, "And once we meet back up in Manchester, I'll take you on that first date we talked about during training."

Rena smiled, leaning into her.

Althenia rummaged through her pocket, pulling out a small plastic packet. She held it out to Rena.

"This is my ration biscuit for today, but I don't feel like it."

As Rena accepted it, she took over the reins.

*****

Once the torturous ride was over, Sylvia felt the box being lifted, before it was dropped on the floor. She winced as she bounced around the crate.

"Careful," someone warned, "Command needs her alive."

"We're not all as augmented as you," a male voice grunted, " And this damn box is heavy."

The cover above her creaked before the box was suddenly flooded with light. She blinked several times before her eyes adjusted to the brightness. She looked around.

They were in an abandoned building, coated with dust and grime. Fear gripped her when she realized that she was far away from the city and ACS. She had no one. They could kill her and no one would come to her rescue.

The merchant in the green dress grabbed her arm and turned her over, ignoring Sylvia's muffled pleas. She felt the cuffs being removed and then she was turned over once more, as a man with short blonde hair reached down and removed her ankle cuffs. She recognized the man. It was the merchant who sold her the gold earrings.

The lady removed her green dress, revealing a black fitted suit with grey pieces of armour implanted throughout. Her armour contoured to her slim body, as the pockets on either side protruded, revealing a pistol holster and on her right and a knife holster on her left.

Sylvia looked on in horror as realization set it.

They were human rebels.

"Oh god," she thought, *"What are they going to do to me?"*

Her captor stepped closer, tying her dark hair back. She dropped down and gazed at her, taking in Sylvia as a small smile curled on her lips. She was different from the other humans. Her violet eyes gleamed, as the morning light touched it, and her ears were long and pointed.

"You know the way from here?" the male captor asked.

"Yes."

The man shrugged, as he grabbed his things and headed toward the door.

"Good luck," he called, as the door swung shut behind him.

The violet eyes' lady grabbed a strange rectangular rifle and pulled Sylvia by the arm, leading her through the ruins of the building and out into the harsh sunlight. Sylvia stumbled, but her captor continued, dragging her along.

They walked through the ruined city for what seemed like hours until the sky darkened. Her captor stopped by an abandoned office and pushed past the broken door. She pulled Sylvia toward a large protruding pipe and undid her cuffs.

This was her chance.

She slammed her knee into her captor's crotch and moved her free hand up. Her captor grabbed her hand and twisted it. Sylvia screamed. Her captor kicked her leg and slammed her into the pipe. She bent down, ignoring Sylvia's whimpers and secured her legs to the pipe. Once she was trapped, the captor walked out the room without a backward glance.

Sylvia heaved as sadness filled her. She couldn't stop the tears that flowed, and once she started, she continued until there was nothing left. Deep down, she knew that she should focus on survival and not give her captors the satisfaction of seeing her suffer.

Breathing in and out, slowly, she calmed herself and focused on the cuffs securing her hand. She spent the rest of her time trying to get out of it.

She stopped fidgeting when she heard footsteps approaching. Her captor returned, carrying a black backpack. While she rummaged through it, Sylvia's knees started trembling from the pain and she tried subtly shifting her weight, but that made things worse, and she groaned.

Her captor looked up, before pulling out a bottle from the backpack.

Sylvia froze, as her captor stood up and walked over to her. She reached down and adjusted the cuffs on her legs so that she could sit on the floor. She then moved her fingers toward Sylvia's gag.

"If you make any noise, I will make sure you regret it," she threatened, "Understand?"

Sylvia nodded quickly.

Once the gag was off, her captor held up the bottle to Sylvia's lips. Without hesitating, Sylvia gulped down the contents. After the terror and panic she'd endured today, the water felt like a small victory.

"We move again in a couple hours," her captor said, as she took away the empty bottle, "Stay quiet and I'll keep the gag off, but make one sound and it will go straight back on and water will no longer be a luxury."

Sylvia nodded, and watched in silence as her captor, once again, left the room.

*****

Arstarte leaned forward, staring intently at the security footage for the fifth time. He had arrived in the city Sylvia controlled earlier this morning, only to find ten dead guards and a missing ruler.

He turned to his guard standing beside him.

"Any luck finding the traders that the witnesses saw?"

"No," the guard replied, shaking his head.

"And you're scouring the city from top to bottom?"

"Yes."

Arstarte slammed his fist on the console, pushing back the chair and pacing the room. He'd heard of city-states revolting, but kidnapping a rule? This was unheard of.

"The human rebels are bigger and more dangerous than ACS had ever imagined," he thought, *"But why kidnap her? An assassination would've sent a stronger message. What were they up to?"*

He walked back to the console and pulled up a map of the city. Tiny dots moved on the maps. His troops were moving through the city and securing areas.
"Let's see. The ACS has twenty flyers in this sector. I need to commandeer them."

He started typing commands.

The ACS system required his commands with a question of his intention.

'To find the missing ruler."

The console blinked red, as it shifted to emergency alert and granted full access to Arstarte. He selected the flyers and assigned five to overshoot the large inland lake and use thermal imaging.

The other screen showed his troops in red, tearing through buildings in the city as they searched for Sylvia. The blue dots of humans huddled together, watching the events unfold before them.

Arstarte stared at the monitors. He knew that there was a slim chance that his soldiers would find anything in the city, but he needed to remind the humans that he was in charge.

*****

Sylvia woke up with a start. Her captor's face however over her head as she shook her shoulders. For a few seconds, she looked up confused until she remembered where she was. Sunlight filtered through the cracks of the building.

Her captor took off her cuffs and she rubbed her hands until the numbness disappeared. Her captor pulled her up off the floor before reattaching the cuffs. As Sylvia took a few shaky steps, her captor reached into her pocket and pulled out the gag.

Sylvia shook her head, moving back. Her captor's face contorted in rage, as she pulled her back and forcibly reattached the gag. Once she was secured, her captor pulled her out of the building and down a dilapidated path. As they walked on, foxes crossed her path and deer stood at the side eating grass.

Her captor stopped and pulled her hard toward a large overgrown bush. Pulling out her rifle, she aimed it at the street and stilled. Minutes passed and her captor kept her position, until Sylvia heard the footsteps. Four humanoid figures appeared, walking down the path.

"How did she hear them from so far away," Sylvia *thought.*

Every sound was magnified as she nervously waited to see what would happen next. The rifle beside her went off, and the first figure crumpled to the floor. The other three figures turned in their direction and started running.

Her heart stilled, as she wondered if she would finally be saved.

Another shot went off and the closest humanoid fell to the floor. Her captor stood up and aimed her rifle, calm and steady. Two more shots and there were once again, alone.

Her captor pulled her off the floor and back onto the path. They walked down a pier and stopped at its edge. Her captor pulled out a small rectangle device and touched it gently. The water trembled as waves appeared and splashed the pier, spraying them with water.

An object breached the water, and the hatch opened. A man appeared, climbing out, he pulled a hatch and a rubber boat inflated and dropped on the water. Pulling a small engine from one of the vessel's hatches, he attached it to the rubber boat and made his way toward them.

Once the boat was safely docked, without another word the man got out and helped Sylvia onto the raft while her captor followed behind. The engine roared to life and they returned to the larger vessel.

A strange buzz filled the air. Sylvia looked up and saw one of her people's flyers streaking overhead. She closed her eyes, trying to contact them, but it didn't work. Her shoulders drooped as she accepted her faith and followed them into the vessel.

She climbed down the ladder and walked through a dimly lit hallway that smelled like fresh water. They opened the door to a small room and stepped aside, gesturing for her to walk in.

The room had a small metal framed bed on one side and a drain and bucket on the other. Her captor removed her cuffs and shackles but left the collar around her neck. Once the door was closed and she was alone, she dropped on the bed and listened to the voices outside.

"Althenia, the captain wants to see you,"

"Of course," her captor, Althenia, responded.

As the footsteps faded, she stared up at the dark ceiling and tried to remove the collar. It wouldn't budge. She gave it a sharp tug and the collar hummed.

"Odd," she thought, as she tugged at it once more, *"Was the collar repressing my psychic powers?"*

She tugged at it harder and the collar hummed louder. Moments later, she felt a numbing pain around her neck. She rubbed her neck and closed her eyes, reaching for the collar once again.

"If removing the collar means freedom, I'll die trying."

She pulled at it with all her strength, and the humming vibrated through the room. A sharp pain travelled down her, and as she cried out, everything went black.

*****

As Althenia walked down the narrow hall, she felt her wrist buzzing. Raising her hand, she stared at the compact computer. The first alert stated that Sylvia interfered with the collar and the collar sent off a warning shock. The second alert stated that Sylvia was forced out but all vitals were stable.

Althenia continued walking, unbothered. She wasn't surprised that Sylvia would attempt to remove the collar. She did hope that when Sylvia did regain consciousness in an hour, she'd have learnt her lesson. They needed her alive.

At the bridge, the captain stood tall, looking over the crewman's shoulder who was manning the control system. His grey hair and moustache contrasted against his white and blue camo clothing.

He turned to Althenia as she got closer.

"Is the prisoner secured?" he asked.

He touched his chest, unconsciously touching the gold anchor clipped on. This was something he did often, as the anchor was a symbol of his rank. Althenia couldn't blame him, if she had a gold anchor, she'd do the same.

"She's in her cell," she replied, as she stopped next to him, "Her stats are normal."

"Good. I can't say I'm happy that there's an alien on board. Keep a watchful eye on her."

"Understood."

"As long as the alien remains confined and doesn't tear anything up. This old tube has been running supply missions for the last fifty years, and I would hate for her to ruin it."

Althenia coughed.

"I assume that your men informed you about the flyer that spotted us,"

The captain nodded.

"Yes," he replied with a sigh, " Fortunately, there is a data cable that we can tap into and advise command. They did advise us not to get spotted, but it's too late to change that. Fortunately, Parry Sound has an underground dock, so the only thing we need to worry about now is staying deep enough that we're not detected by their sensors."

*****

Sylvia groaned and instinctively touched her aching head. She felt her body moving and opened her eyes to see Althenia above her.

"Here," she said, holding out a tray, "Food."

Sylvia sat up and took the tray. There was a bowl on it with what looked like an unappealing soup. She took the spoon and swirled it around.

"What do you want from me?"

Althenia remained silent for a moment.

"It's classified," she said, finally, "But if you cooperate, they won't hurt you."

Sylvia nodded. She kept her gaze on Althenia as she ate her first bite of soup.

"Why are your ears pointed?"

"I was born with it," she replied, shortly before getting up and walking to the door. "We'll arrive in eight hours. I'll check in on you shortly."

*****

Rena punched in her code to the base hidden in a long-abandoned hospital. Since the kidnapping was discovered, patrols had increased so Rena had to travel at night because of the flyers circling overhead.

She walked toward the bunker and waited for her squad to enter the facility. The first one to walk in was a broody soldier with short black hair named Rick. Minutes later, an older man with salt and pepper hair, who they called Sarg, entered. The last person in her squad to enter was Linda, a dark-skinned girl with short curly hair.

When everyone was inside, Rena closed the hatch and led the group down the ladder and inside the bunker. The room was well light because of the solar panels on the roof that had luckily gone unnoticed.

"Sarg," she called, looking over to her team, "Can you and Rick perform an inventory of our food stocks? I suspect that we might be here for a while."

"Yes, Ma'am," Sarg replied, while Rick followed along.

Rena walked through the corridor, leaving the boys behind while Linda followed behind.

"Linda," she said, "Can you check the battery and electronics? It's been ages since this place was used."

"Yes, Ma'am."

She opened the door at the end of the corridor and turned back to her squad.

"If anyone needs me, I'll be in the console room," she called out, before closing the door.

The console room was bare, with only a table at the centre with an old wooden chair. She moved the cover off the computer, waving away the dust in the air with her hand and powered on the device. This computer was built shortly before the invasion. It was a flat monitor and compared to the aliens, not powerful, but it still worked. With the Alien invasion, their radio signals could be seen and triangulated to reveal their location, so most rebel communication was done via site-to-site microwave towers that ran on miles of hidden underground cables. She watched the feeds from the cameras they had strategically placed outside the hospital.

A knock on the door interrupted her.

"Enter," she called.

Sarg walked in and grabbed the chair opposite her table.

"Well, ma'am," he said, "We have enough supplies to last three weeks."

"Good," she replied, focusing once again on the camera footage, "We should be here for two weeks, and once the heat is off, we'll head off to Rock Island."

"Understood."

"Oh and Sarg," she continued, looking up from the monitor, "Can you check the escape tunnel? I want us to be ready in case our schedule moves up."

"Righto," Sarg said, with a two-finger salute before trundling away.

Gazing back at the monitor, she saw a distant image of one of the invader flyers. She kept her eyes on the monitor until her mind began wandering.

Althenia was seen by many as emotionless, even for a Martian, but to Rena, she was intriguing. It took months for them to confess their love, and now Rena felt her heart flutter, as she thought about the possibility of their first date. She reached into her pocket and pulled out her wallet. Next to the picture of her family was one of Althenia. It was torn in half, with Althenia carrying the other half.

Rena smiled. Things were finally falling into place.

*****

Unlike her last cell which was flooded in darkness, this room was well lit. Sylvia walked over to the only picture hanging on the wall. It was a stylized map of Earth. Above the drawing, were the initials U.S.F and below it were the words United Sol Force.

The cavern their submarine was docked at was large. Through the window, she could see three other submarines gathering supplies.

"How long have the humans been running this underground network?"

After Althenia brought her next meal, she took her out of the submarine and onto the shore of the cavern. With only her arms cuffed, Sylvia walked around, taking in everything. A tall man with a grey moustache appeared before them. Althenia gave him a curt salute, which he returned before turning to Sylvia with a large smile.

"Congrats on your successful capture," he praised, as he studied Sylvia, "When central command told me their plan, I thought they were absolutely mad. But you've proven me wrong."

"Thank you, sir," Althenia responded.

"Now," he continued, turning his attention back to Althenia, "We mustn't get too cocky, because you've certainly poked the hornet's nest. Patrols are more frequent and I had to send one of our cargo subs as a diversion to keep them from discovering our trade hub."

"Good idea, sir. I hope this means little trouble for the night train."

He put his arm around her shoulder and leaned in.

"The night train leaves in eight hours. Make sure you and your…. umm, cargo, is aboard. I don't want this creature around here for too long."

Sylvia shot him a glare, but his back was to her.

"Oh," he said, as he released Althenia and walked toward another vessel, "There's a package for you from central command in your quarters."

"Thank you."

Althenia grabbed Sylvia's shackles and led her through one of the main hallways, as they passed the doors lining either side, they'd sometimes spot someone wearing dull grey or military camouflage. Althenia stopped at one of the doors and pulled out a white key card from her pocket. She opened the door and walked in, pulling Sylvia behind.

The room was small, with dull concrete walls and one door on the other end. There was one small table in the middle, a metal chest of draws and a few cushy leather chairs. Althenia sat her down on one of the cushy chairs before walking to the table and opening the box resting on it. She pulled out a pair of black shoes, a pair of heels, and a small package.

Taking the smaller box, she beckoned Sylvia forward and walked to the other door. This was a small and sterile bathroom. Althenia undid Sylvia's cuffs. Instinctively, she rubbed her wrists.

"Here," Althernia said, holding out the small package, "Use the shower and bathroom, and once you're done, put this on."

Sylvia opened the package.

"A swimsuit?"

It was small and black.

"Yes," Althenia replied with a nod, "That's for security. Once you're done, knock on the door."

Althenia walked out of the room, closing the door behind.

Sylvia sighed, holding back her tears as she accepted her faith.

*****

Arstarte kicked the ashes of the burnt wooden cart and smiled. They were getting closer.

While searching, his soldiers stumbled upon this burnt cart that the kidnappers used. The place it was abandoned at was once inhabited by the humans before the invasion. Detached houses lined the streets on either side with outgrown lawns.

"We've found something!" one of the soldiers shouted, telepathically,

Artstarte left the burnt heap and walked to the voice. He walked into one of the semi-collapsed houses. The smell of damp and rot cloaked him.

There was a pile of clothes on the floor that lay half burnt on the floor. Scraps of green and burgundy peeked through.

"The colour of the clothes, witnesses spotted the kidnappers wearing," he thought, with a smile.

He turned to the nearest soldier.

"Keep searching and expand the search grid, every hour. We'll stumble across the next clue soon."

*****

Althenia entered the bathroom. Sylvia stood in her black swimsuit looking awkward and uncomfortable as she fidgeted with her purple hair. Althenia walked over and gently placed the cuffs back on her wrists before moving to her ankles.

"These cuffs and ankle bracelets," she explained, "Are rather special. I can use my control to lock them in place."

She pressed a button on her wrist computer and the cuffs of Sylvia's wrists slammed together with a metallic click. Pushing another button, the cuffs separated.

"We have some rest before the night train. You'll be imprisoned and gagged in one of the cabs, but if you wish, I can sedate you."

Sylvia looked at her with worried eyes, her voice quivering.

"What's going to happen to me?"

Althenia sighed.

"Well, you're not going to be killed. If command wanted you dead, you'd be dead," she explained, "It would be best if you cooperate. I can guarantee that you'll be alive when you arrive, but if you cause problems, I can't guarantee you won't be hurt."

Sylvia let out a frustrated breath and walked back into the main room. She grabbed a book from the table and flipped through the pages, reading nothing.

At that moment, Althenia felt sorry for her.

*****

Rena walked out of the bathroom and back into the control room, wearing a simple camouflage pants and shirt that was black, grey, and white.

"Enter," she said when she heard the soft knock.

Linda stepped in, looking down at the floor.

"What is it, Linda?"

"Nothing good, ma'am. The explosives in the barracks will not go off when we escape into the tunnels. This means that they can follow us."

"Can we rerun the wires?"

Linda shook her head.

"We have no electric wires in this building."

Rena looked at the monitor, with a frown. She'd spent the past day trying to fix the cameras and only had success with one.

"Camera eight is a right off," she said, looking up at Linda, "Can we get the wire off there."

"Worth a shot," Linda replied with a shrug.

As she looked back to the screen, she saw one of the alien soldiers approaching. She jumped up and ran to the small metal cabinet and opened their gun safe.

"We have a soldier on visual," she shouted, "Shut the damn door!"

She hit the large red button on the wall and the red light started flashing throughout the room and hallway. Linda, Rick, and Sarg ran in and grabbed weapons. She ran back to the monitor, hoping that the soldier was just passing by, but when she looked, she saw him heading straight toward the hospital.

"The front door is secured," Sarg shouted.

They all watched the monitor in silence as the soldiers broke down the hospital door and made their way into the derelict building. Behind them walked a blonde-haired man clad in ornate metal armour. Her suspicions were confirmed when the man shouted orders.

The man and his faithful creatures searched the hospital. She hoped that they would miss the basement, but she knew that her hope was futile, because if it was her, the basement would be the first place that she searched.

The aliens blasted through the basement doors and walked down the stairs. Their hideout was hidden by one of the shelves that was cleverly screwed to the door. But when the soldiers started tipping over shelves, she knew that it was only a matter of time before they breached. And they couldn't escape through the tunnel, because now they could be followed.

And with the overlord present, they didn't have a fighting chance.

Rena ran out of the room with her rifle strapped over her shoulders.

"Head down the tunnels," she ordered, "I'll follow soon."

While the others ran to the tunnel, she rushed to the armoury and grabbed a small breaching charge. The sickening sound of metal crashing echoed through the room. Rena aimed her rifle and shot at the first soldier. She threw the charge into the barracks just as a knife pierced her side. Aiming the rifle she hit the second soldier, just as the explosion rippled through the building.

"They're safe," She thought as the walls and ceiling collapsed.

She ducked, covering her head as a piece of concrete fell on her, and everything went black.

*****

It was time to enter the train.

The train was covered in armour, with a heavy dozer at the front. All windows were removed and the wheels changed to those used in tanks. The top of the train had two heavy cannons, aimed straight ahead.

Scaffolding stood erect, on either side of the train, so inside of climbing up the train's ladder, they used the scaffolding. At the front of the train was a woman with short salt and pepper hair, and large brown eyes.

She smiled and shook Althenia's hand.

"Our special guest has arrived," she greeted, "Welcome to the night train, my name is Magadian."

Although Sylvia's mouth was not gagged, she remained silent.

"Thank you," Althenia replied, "I'm Althenia, and you don't have to worry about her, she's volunteered to undergo sedation."

"The other captain made issues?"

Althenia nodded.

"Yes, many people are protective of their vessels."

Magadian stepped aside and allowed them to descend the scaffolding and step into the first carriage. She then followed behind them, as a guide.

"Since we travel at night, the bunkers are here," she explained, as she pulled a metal door open. They followed her in and stepped into a cab that had a couple of folded-down bunks.

Althenia led Sylvia to one of the bunks and pulled it down. She then removed the cuffs.

"The entire area is yours," Magadian piped, "We have no other passengers on board."

She gestured to another door at the far end of the room.

"The bathroom is there. There are five guards on board, as well as myself, the driver, and the engine crew."

The room rumbled as the engine roared to life. Althenia looked around curiously, as this was her first time in such a vessel.

"Tell me, Magadian," she said, "How do you see where we're going? And how will the vehicle remain hidden?"

"Well, the vehicle has night vision cameras on the front and back, and a thermal shield on the roof. So, as long as we drive at night and have no lights on, we'll be invisible from the air and very hard to spot on the ground. We'll also be hard to hear since our engine is a small reactor and there is special rubber on the tracks. The only noise we tend to make is when something gets in our path. Those things are moved very quickly, in fact, the number of times I have run over an alien patrol I have lost count," she finished with a soft chuckle.

Althenia felt Sylvia still beside her.

"The only real danger is when the sun is out. We usually stop the train and cover it with camouflage, before moving again."

She looked at her wrist computer.

"Speaking of which," Magadian sighed, as she walked across the room, "We better get this old train going, the night is fleeing.

Once the door was closed, she pulled a small vial of dark liquid from her bag and passed it to Sylvia.

Sylvia took the vial and gulped it down. Once it was done, she laid down and her eyes fluttered shut.

Athena stayed with her for a couple minutes. She decided to not cuff her. While Sylvia slept, she took the bunk bed beside her and laid down. Althenia tried to sleep, but after a couple minutes, she gave up. Walking to the door, she glanced back at Sylvia one last time before leaving. She ventured down the hallway until she reached a door with a sign that read 'control room'. Althenia knocked three times and waited.

"Enter."

She opened the door and entered a small room filled with monitors and a steering wheel at the centre. There was a man behind the wheel, who kept his eyes on the screen. Magadian was sitting further down, in front of a small console. She looked up as Althenia got closer.

"Got bored from the lack of view?"

"Yes," Althenia replied, as she sat on the seat beside her, "I'm quite surprised that the journey has been so smooth."

"Well, the first one hundred kilometres are smooth and quite boring. But once we get onto the ruined roads, you'll feel it."

Althenia watched the screen with the map of their journey. It most showed forests and fields, but as time passed, she noticed a flyer shooting past.

"We got a flyer," she shouted.

"Don't worry," Magadian assured, "I see about five to six on each journey. Thanks to our thermal shield, they can't pick us up."

"Good to know."

They both kept their eyes on the screen, staring in silence.

*****

Arstarte smiled, as he looked down at their unconscious prisoner. She was quite striking for a human, with short blonde hair and delicate features. Her clothes were torn and her leg broken from the explosion, but his soldiers had managed to dig her out and tend to her leg.

Once they got her back to his domain, he'd attach a device to her head that showed her surface memories. He kept his eyes on her as his soldier pulled out a syringe and injected her. She let out a cry of pain, as her eyes fluttered open.

With her now conscious, Arstarte walked back to the console and looked through her thoughts. He flipped through the images until he reached the kidnapping.

"She's talking to someone with red hair," he noted.

He stopped and frowned. Something was different about this human. Enlarging the image, he studied the red-haired figure and noticed her ears. They were pointed.

"Odd."

He couldn't remember humans having this physical feature. Was this a sub-species? He thought back to a report he'd read many solar years ago about a human raid that attacked one of the clone facilities. The leader of the facility claimed that he'd seen humans with pointed ears. At the time, ACS had concluded that these were lies spewed by the leader to cover up his humiliation of losing the city.

Arstarte looked back at the prisoner and realized that she was unconscious.

"Dammit."

Looking back at the computer, he noticed a sudden spike in the pain readings. He sighed. The prisoner was inflicting pain on her own broken leg to prevent her mind from being scanned.

"If she wants pain, she can have it."

"Guards," he shouted.

The guards appeared instantly.

"When she's awake, give her twenty lashes to remind her who's in charge."

*****

Rena woke up and looked around. The room was cloaked in darkness. It took a moment for her eyes to adjust to it. The cell was small and made of concrete. There was a small wooden bed on one side and a toilet on the other. She tried to get up, but her leg burned. Then, the memories came flooding back.

The door to the cell opened and in walked a guard. She froze as the guard drew closer. He pulled her up and ignored her screams of pain. Throwing her against the wall, the guard pulled out a leather strap. She closed her eyes as the first lash struck her, and her screams got louder with each one. She lost consciousness before the last one touched her.

*****

Althenia woke up with a start. At first, she thought her body was shaking because of the train ride, but then she saw Magadian standing above her. Her expression was grim.

"We just passed a microwave tower and received a couple of messages. One was addressed to you."

From Magadian's expression, she knew that it was confidential. And confidential usually meant bad news. She sat up and took the tablet that Magadian held out. Once the door was closed, Althenia let out a sharp breath and played the message.

"Hi, Althenia."

She knew that voice well. It was Sarg.

"I know you and Rena were close so I needed to get this message to you. I'm sorry to say, but she sacrificed her life in duty to the liberation of our plant, and in doing so, she saved ours."

Althenia's breath hitched. She closed her eyes, in an attempt to stop the tears as the message continued.

"She was a great commander and we'll miss her dearly. I'm sorry Althenia."

Silence filled the room.

She should be used to death by now. Her parents died in an accident on Mars. Death was always around her. But this time, it was different. Her eyes fell on Sylvia's sleeping body. And for the first time, she looked at her prisoner with contempt. She was the reason that Rena was dead. Her people caused this.

She wanted nothing more than to pull out her rifle and shoot her. Watch the life leave her eyes as it did in Rena's.

But they needed her. With her dead, Rena's sacrifice would be meaningless.

There was a soft knock on the door.

"Enter," she croaked.

Magadian walked over.

"We're stopping in an hour because daylight is approaching.

Althenia nodded and held out the tablet in silence.

Magadian took it and walked to the door, but before she closed it, she turned back.

"I've been doing this a long time and have lost many that I held dear to my heart. If you need someone to talk to, I'm here."

Althenia just nodded and laid back on the bed as the door clicked shut.

*****

Lucinda, the ruler of one of the city-states on the east coast, sat by her console, reading the reports with a grim face. Pushing back her dark hair, she turned to the servant behind her.

"That fool Arstarte is going to kill his most important prisoner," she sighed, as she leaned back into her chair.

She heard the footsteps of her servant, Natalie, moving closer. Soon after, she felt Natalie's hands on her shoulder. Her tension disappeared, but her mind still mulled over the information she'd just learnt.

She needed a plan. A good plan.

In the past, unlike other rulers who preferred to sit in her castle and rule their tiny cities, Lucinda went beyond her borders and studied the humans. Their technology was much more advanced than ACS knew. And to the dismay of only her, one of ACS's star ships was losing its orbit. She predicted that it would crash on earth in one year's time, creating devastation in an already devastated world. The debris in the air could send the world into a nuclear winter.
Unlike the others, she knew that she needed to do more.

She brushed Natalie's fingers with her own and looked up. Her red eyes reflected against Natalie's grey.

"What if I impersonate ACS again and request that the prisoner be moved to a more secure location," she mused, gesturing to the room.

Natalie nodded at her plan, with a small smile.

Lucinda had found Natalie when she was a child, at that time wandering through the ancient city ruins. She took her in and raised her, surprised and proud that she'd learnt both human and alien technology. She was so good that she'd even gotten past ACS security on the occasions that Lucinda needed her to.

She stood up and gestured for Natalie to take her seat, which she did. Moments later, she was typing profusely with her focus solely on the screen in front of her.

Lucinda knew it was best to leave her alone as she worked, so she walked to the window of her room, her black Chinese dress flowing around her. She stared down at the city. Children were walking on the streets, carrying backpacks and talking excitedly as their school day ended.

Unlike most city-states that outlawed technology, she utilized certain human technology to create a more comfortable environment for her humans. There were windmills atop the walls and solar panels on the roof of most houses that generated electricity. And while education was also banned, she made sure that her people were made available in her city. She'd also implemented a human militia to protect her city and those living within its walls.

To prevent ACS from learning this, with the help of Natalie, she'd programmed the ACS soldiers in the barracks to send false information.

During her years as a ruler, she found that if she treated the humans right, they remained loyal and trustworthy.

*****

Sylvia splashed water on her face and leaned over the sink. She still felt groggy from the drugs they gave her.

Althenia appeared behind her and grabbed her hand and cuffed it. Without a word, she dragged her out of the train and to a large warehouse nearby. The building, though old, was in better shape than most of the buildings she'd been dragged into before.

Inside the warehouse, they passed soldiers who paid no attention to them. Sylvia kept her head down as the brightness of the morning blinded her. They walked through the building in silence, which Sylvia found unusual. Even though Althenia was part of the group that kidnapped her, she was still relatively kind toward her. But today, she was more tense and forceful.

Her heart dropped, as they walked into a hallway that was lined on either side with rows and rows of beds that contained skeletal remains. Athena stopped and pulled Sylvia closer until they were inches apart.

"Rena is dead," she said, as her eyes darkened.

Sylvia looked up at her in confusion, as Althenia gestured to the skeletons.

"This place was an emergency shelter where victims of your invasion sought safety. In the beginning, it was a safe place, until they died because of the viruses spread around by your kind."

Althenia pushed her into one of the beds, and with her ankles' cuffed, Sylvia fell.

"Look at them," she hissed, "Look at what you've done."

Sylvia couldn't stop the tears that flowed.

*****

Arstarte looked at the retreating ACS soldiers in frustration. He'd received notice earlier that his prisoner would be moved to a more secure facility.

He sighed.

Once ACS gave an order, Arstarte had no choice but to obey. He looked through his window, as the figures disappeared into the horizon. He tried to look on the bright side. With her in ACS custody, they'd have better luck in extracting her memories. The process, however, did include removing her brain, which in some cases led to the death of their prisoner.

"What a shame. She was a pretty human."

With a sigh, he returned to his console. Looking at the map, his mind focused on more important matters.

Since he'd increased patrols, there were reports of more soldiers disappearing. This meant that the resistance was more powerful than they'd thought. He focused on the area where the soldiers disappeared. It was all near a great lake.

"What are you protecting?"

Typing quickly, he issued orders for his soldiers to assemble. He was certain that there was a bigger prize near the great lake, and if his theory was right, he needed a bigger army.

*****

Althenia watched Sylvia close her eyes and raise them to the sunlight. After the trauma she'd inflicted earlier, Athena decided to give her prisoner some fresh air. When Sylvia opened her eyes, she walked over and gave her a book. Sylvia opened it, leaning back into the tree.

Out of the corner of her eye, she noticed movement.

Four alien soldiers were walking toward their building. Althenia ran to the wall and pressed the red button. Lights started flashing, which warned the others of the incoming intruders.

The door opened and two human soldiers ran out, following her behind a bush. Aiming their rifles, they waited.

"I have the one on the far left," one troop whispered.

"I have the one on the right."

Althenia nodded and took aim at the alien soldier in the middle. The soldier's fired first and she soon followed. Their targets' heads snapped back as they fell to the floor. Althenia held out her hand, signalling for her guards to wait as she used the scope of her rifle to look for other alien soldiers. When the coast was clear, they walked out of the bush. The two human soldiers went back into the building, while Althenia made her way to Sylvia, who was peering from behind the tree.

"Good shot," she commended.

Althenia nodded but she looked at her prisoner, confused.

"You could've warned them."

Sylvia just shrugged and followed behind.

"Were you and Rena sisters?" she asked, after a moment of silence.

"No," Althenia responded, "I come from a Martian colony, and Rena, well, she was a little Earth girl."

"Martian Colony? Mars?"

"That's classified," Althenia answered.

*****

Graham watched through his binoculars as the alien ship drew closer.

He was the leader of the Virginia Guard, a human militia created and controlled by Lucinda. He'd been ordered to retrieve the human prisoner. The ship could not deliver the prisoner to the city because that could lead to suspicion and the last thing his leader needed was for Arstarte to start poking around.

Fortunately, with the help of Natalie, they'd managed to redirect the transport to a small depot in the middle of nowhere. He counted thirty alien soldiers, patrolling the facility. Graham looked at his watch. They needed to strike at nine when the communications would be cut.

Turning back to his men, he drew his rifle and signalled them to do the same. Though this mission was meant to be an easy one since the aliens would not have shield generators, he didn't want to take any chances. They had five minutes to breach, attack, and retreat before secondary communications came online.

Graham ran out onto the field, aiming his gun at the base as his soldiers followed. At the edge of the building, he spotted the first alien soldier. With one shot, the alien soldier went down. He ran to the door, hearing the gunshots behind him as his soldiers engaged and started the battle.

Sticking an explosive putty on the door, he connected the detonators and stepped back. Checking his men, to make sure they were out of range, he pressed the detonator.

"Fire in the hole!"

Graham covered his ears and watched as the explosion shook the building and collapsed the door. Be ran through the rubble, and stepped into the building. Inside was a strange metal box that was connected to a grey, pulsing, organic system. From the teachings of Lucinda, he knew that it was an organic power plant that was fuelled by organic matter.

He attached the explosives to the metal box and stepped back.

"It's boom time!"

The ground rumbled as the room filled with debris and dust. Out of the corner of his eye, he saw movement and ducked, as a bullet narrowly missed his head. Dropping to the floor, he fired at the alien soldier, hitting it squarely in the chest.

When the coast was clear, he ran to the landing pad. He spotted an alien soldier who was waiting for fuel that wouldn't come. He shot the soldier as another one came rushing out. Dodging the bullet, he shot at the second soldier. He walked around the vessel, searching for more soldiers. Once he cleared the area, he stashed the rifle in his holster and pulled out a crowbar. Using all his strength, he pried open the cargo doors.

Footsteps approached. He turned to spot his soldiers running toward the landing. With their help, the door opened. They walked in until they reached a rectangular door in the corner.

"What's our status?" he asked, through his radio.

"All aliens and men accounted for," his second in command replied.

Together with his men, they lifted the box and carried it to their waiting transport vehicles.

"Misson accomplished."

*****

Sarg stood up and looked out into the horizon. He waved at the squad mate who fell silent and waited for his command. Using his binoculars, he scoped out the area surrounding the building they were currently guarding.

His eyes fell on the mass of alien soldiers followed by a line of alien tanks that were coming their way.

His heart dropped.

"What is it, Sarg?"

Sarg pulled out his radio and pressed the communication button, while his squad mate scanned the horizons.

"Shit," his mate whispered, in fear.

"Emergency frequency," a voice answered.

"Around three hundred metal heads are heading toward us, followed by twenty hover tanks."

"Christ," the voice replied, "Did you say three hundred? Head back to base, immediately!"

"Sarg," his comrade said, in panic, "They have goddamn shield generators."

Sarg nodded and turned back to the radio.

"Be advised that they have shield generators."

"Roger."

His comrade grabbed his hand and pulled him. And as they both ran to the door, Sarg turned back and spotted the tank aiming its gun toward their position. They made it past the door and down the stairs when the top floor blew apart as a plasma bolt struck it.

They dodged debris as they ran down to the first floor. As they hurried out of the building and toward the base, his comrade pulled out his rifle.

"Don't bother with that. They have shields!"

As they reached the outskirts of the base, close to the river, he heard someone shout "Sarg".

It was Linda, carrying her two large rifles that looked like small World War One anti-tank rifles with two hydraulic rams on each side of it. Despite her small stature, she carried them with ease. Once they were behind the barricade, he took one of the rifles.

They used this rifle because it was so large that it could fire special ammo which was a .75 calibre rounded cartridge, used to overload the shield of the average alien trooper, but the bullet tip was hollowed out, and within was another bullet along with a special propellent that ignited in the presence of oxygen. The idea with this was the first bullet knocked down the shield, exposing the internal bullet to oxygen, which set it off and enabled the internal bullet to hit the creature behind the shield.

As more human soldiers flooded behind the barricade, ready for battle, Sarg took aim at the first alien soldier that appeared over the horizon and fired. His target's shield flickered off as a smaller flash indicated the ignition of the internal bullet which hit the creature's left shoulder. But the metal head shrugged off the shot and started charging, followed by one of its friends.

Linda fired beside him.

This time, the alien soldier fell to the ground.

The other aliens appeared, and he screamed commands to his soldiers. They opened fire and took down as many alien soldiers as they could, and for a while, they were holding them off, until a tank came into view.

One of Sarg's soldiers wheeled in their own anti-tank cannon. It took five men to prepare the tank, loading it with fuel and attaching the battery. Once it was ready, the crew aimed at the tank and fired.

The tank's shield flickered, and it aimed at them, firing back. It struck the barricade in front of Linda.

"Fuck," he screamed.

He was worried about Linda, but he couldn't see her because of the dust in the air. His soldiers fired the cannon again. Moments later, when the dust cleared, he saw Linda clutching the stump where her left arm used to be.

One of their soldiers grabbed her and dragged her back into the base.

The cannon fired a third time.

The third shot hit the shield again, and this time penetrated the tank's armour, causing it to smoke before exploding in a large fireball and knocking out an alien soldier next to it. Before the canon crew had a chance to celebrate, another two hover tanks appeared.

Sarg turned and saw one of their human tanks rolling in. It was the new heavy plasma tank about three meters high, with a sleek, angular turret and a rectangular barrel. The second hover tank fired at the plasma tank, but its plasma fire hit the tank's shield wall, an invention they had managed to reverse engineer from the aliens.

The plasma tank returned the favour and fired another bolt of energy, slicing through the shield and cutting the armour like a heavy laser through butter. Sarg took aim at another soldier as more infantry joined him.

His soldiers continued taking down the aliens under his command, while their cannons and human tanks attacked the alien tankers.

*****

"How is this possible," Arstarte thought.

He stood on the hill, overlooking the battle that was taking place in the city ruins below.

His troops were dying while his tanks exploded in fiery balls. Though his ground troops were on the brink of defeat, he still had one ace up his sleeve. He'd called in an airstrike and requested reinforcements.

He heard the flyers approaching, he smiled as they approached and turned his focus to the humans in glee, as he waited to see their inevitable destruction.

His smile, however, faltered, when the laser beams shot out from the human's base and cut the first flyer in half. Two laser beams followed by a flock of missiles, took down the remaining aircrafts.

"How is this possible? How did the human savages get good weapons?"

Arstarte jumped back as his own personal shield was struck. He narrowly missed the bullet that flew at him. Another bullet hit his shield, and instinctively, he ducked. Looking for his attacker, Arstarte sent a psychic pulse in the direction of the shots, causing the small square ruin that the sniper was perched on to collapse in a cloud of dust.

He let out another psychic blast, this time aimed at a larger human tank that had come out from behind one of the ruins to take a shot at a skimmer. The tank's shield flickered, allowing the skimmer it was taking aim at to successfully hit the tank, causing it to start smoking, and suddenly a bright gush of flame erupted from the top of the tank, leaving it a smoking shell.

But before Arstarte could celebrate, another enemy fired at his shield, and this time, it went down. He used his psychic energy to quickly stop the bullet and then aimed it at the humans, causing another ruin to collapse.

"This is getting dangerous."

He thought this would be an easy battle, but clearly, he'd underestimated the humans. He needed to turn the tide of this battle, but he couldn't do that if he was wounded or dead.

More alien soldiers appeared over the hill.

"Stop them at any cost!" he ordered.

Then, he ran to his own personal flyer and retreated from battle.

*****

The night train had arrived at its destination: Quebec City, or rather the underground of Quebec City.

Althenia got out and let her legs stretch. Sylvia followed, beside her. They were met by a couple soldiers and a man in a white coat with a small device in his top pocket.

"Good, you've arrived successfully," he said in a thick, Quebecois French accent, before shaking Althenia's hand, "I am Doctor Martel, leader of Quebec City science institute. I apologize that the base commander could not meet you himself, but he is busy. There has been an attack on the Rock Island base."

Althenia's face wrinkled in concern, as Sylvia looked from her to the doctor.

"We have had to accelerate our plans," Dr Martel continued, as he beckoned them to follow, "I have a sub ready to take you to London and to the device."

Althenia nodded and they followed him down the corridor. They passed soldiers loading crates with forklifts. Eventually, they reached a large sub docks. It looked different from the submarines they had seen before. They were larger and looked like someone had put two subs next to each other and had a cargo hatch on top serviced by a crane coming out of the submarine. The forklifts moved back and forth, loading cargo into the submarine.

"A lot of activity."

"Yes," Dr Martel replied, "Central command was expecting this reaction and are in the process of heavily arming free North America. Quebec City itself used to be producing the standard infantry arms, the good old shield breaker, but we've had to start importing heavy military vehicles from Britain and assemble them here to help with the war effort."

Dr Martel stopped at the last sub in the loading station. A large man with a black moustache and blue uniform who was overseeing the forklift turned to Dr Martel and smiled.

"Ah, our special cargo has arrived. My name is Captain Ramsford," he said, in a British accent, as he turned to Althenia, "Welcome to my ship. And just in time, the last of the cargo has been loaded."

Althenia shook his hand and left Dr Martel behind as they followed the captain through the cargo hatch and down into the lower decks. The stopped by a console on one of the doors and watched as he pressed a button.

"This is the bridge," the voice announced.
"Captain Ramsford here," he replied, "Once we've confirmed that the cargo doors are secure, and we have the go-ahead from the harbour office."
"Yes, sir."

Captain Ramsford clicked the speaker off and led them down a steel hallway. They stopped at a door that had two soldiers standing on either side. The captain opened the door and gestured them, within.

"This is for your prisoner; we've provided guards to be on the safe side."

Behind the door was a simple cell with a bed and a small compact bathroom off to the side.

"We had to modify the door to make it lockable from the outside," explained the captain, as he pointed back to the hallway. "Your room is the one just opposite."

"Thank you, but she should be fine. So far she's been no trouble," replied Althenia.

The captain nodded.

"Good to hear, but better safe than sorry."

The floor suddenly shifted.

"We're underway," said the captain, as he walked to the door, "We should arrive in the Manchester sub pen in four days. I need to go to the bridge."

Once their door was closed, Althenia undid Sylvia's cuffs and reached into her bag.

"Take this."

Sylvia took the book.

"Althenia, I'm sorry about Rena."

"It's not your fault," Althenia admitted, "You were a prisoner when she was killed, and she died doing her duty."

The room fell silent, as they were both lost in their own thoughts.

*****

Rena groaned.

Her body ached. She opened her eyes and tried to focus. A figure peering above her came into focus. It was a young girl, with short dark hair and brown eyes. She smiled down at her and looked at the monitors. Rena followed her eyes and saw that she had intravenous drips attached to her arms.

The girl pushed a button and Rena was engulfed in euphoria as the pain subsided. She touched the girl with her finger.

"Water," she croaked.

The girl disappeared, and moments later, she was back with a glass of water. She helped her drink and wiped her mouth with a piece of Rena's clothes.

"Good to see you awake," she said, in a meek voice.

Rena tried sitting up, but the girl gently pushed her back into the bed.

"You need to take it easy. Awaking from cryo sleep is a traumatic experience for the human body."

"Where am I?"

"You're in the city-state of Virginia."

Rena looked around, confused. She thought that she'd been rescued by her people, but none of the bases were called Virginia. Her face contorted in anguish as realization set in.

"Am I still a prisoner?" she cried.

The girl looked down at her, with sad eyes.

"For the moment, yes, but you won't be tortured like you were before or questioned for information. Here, you'll be safe."

Rena looked at the girl confused. *Is this a trick?*

The girl looked at her knowingly, with a sigh.

"I know there is a lot of distrust now, but you are in a good place and if you want anything just let me know."

The girl walked out of the room, leaving her alone. She closed her eyes and drifted off, until what felt like seconds later, the door opened. In stepped a tall, breathtaking woman with long dark hair and bright red eyes. The human girl from earlier, followed behind.

She smiled at Rena, but for some strange reason, Rena felt like it was a lion smiling at the lamb. The woman looked at the monitors before turning to the girl.

"How is she doing?"

"Better," replied the girl, before looking at the woman with a scowl, "But she'll be in bed for a while though after what that brute Arstarte did to her."

"Well," replied the woman, as she walked closer to the bed, "the good news is that Arstarte is currently distracted now. He found a human base and so far, has lost quite a few of his troops because as usual, he rushed ahead without any thought."

The woman reached out and touched Rena's arm. Instinctively, she flinched.

"It'll be okay."

She kept her hand on Rena, and Rena felt a tingling feeling working its way through her body. She felt better and somewhat stronger.

"My name is Lucinda, and I am the leader of Virginia," she continued, as she pointed to the girl with her other hand, "And this is my assistant, Natalie."

Unlike the other aliens Rena encountered over the years, Lucinda was different. Deep down she felt like she could trust her. It was the same feeling she got the first time she met Althenia. She decided to go with her gut.

"My name is Rena, but I am afraid that's all the information you will get from me."

Lucinda smiled and gave her an understanding nod.

"Don't worry, once you're strong enough, I will let you go, but I only ask that you take a message with you."

Rena opened her mouth to respond, but there was a knock on the door. Lucinda and the girl looked up.

"Enter."

In came a man with greying hair and a worn-out face. He bowed to Lucinda and then spoke.

"Sorry to disturb you, ma'am, but we have a high-priority message from the ACS. Apparently, Arstarte is gathering an army to take on the human base he discovered. He requests your presence on the battlefield."

Lucinda scowled, and Natalie protectively moved in front of her.

"Thank you, Graham. I will draft a reply letter. You may go."

Once the door was closed, Lucinda turned to her with a worried look.

"It seems I may need you to warn your friends of the incoming attack."

Rena looked up at her confused. *Why would she want to help us? The rebels.* If Rena did what she wanted, then she'd know about their base. But then again, if she didn't do as she was told, Arstarte would attack the base and her people would have no warning. She was at an impossible impasse.

"I need to think about it."

"I understand but know that we are here to help. I'll leave you to rest."

Lucinda and Natalie left her alone. And she spent the rest of the time wondering if she was walking into a well-placed trap.

*****

Sylvia looked at the book again. She was not enjoying it at all, to put it bluntly. She couldn't focus on it, and as far as she could make out, it was a story about a fantasy realm and some dark hero on a quest to save an elven princess.

She tried to sleep but found her last dream rather disconcerting. It was her fault for reading the romance part. She dreamt she was the princess trapped in the tower but instead of an evil wizard, there was an evil sorceress who looked like Althenia. The sorceress had burst into her prison cell and held her rather close. She then woke up with a start and ever since found it rather difficult to get back to sleep, so she tried to read as there was not much else to do in her room.

It didn't help that her room was basically a cramped metal box which would leak and make odd sounds now and then.

Sylvia sat up when she heard footsteps approaching. The door creaked open, and Althenia walked in.

"We've arrived. The captain is docking now, so I need to check for cuffs and collar."

Sylvia complied. She raised her hands and exposed her neck. Althenia's fingers grazed her skin as she checked the items and locked them in place.

"If you and Rena are not sisters, why are you so close?" she asked.

Althenia remained silent for a moment, before speaking.

"Rena and I were lovers."

"Lovers?" questioned Sylvia, "The research on your species stated that there were only two sexes, male and female, and only they can procreate. Are you both, not females?"

Althenia rolled her eyes at her but gave a small smile.

"I would think that the invaders would know about humans, as homosexuality has been part of humans since we evolved, and it still carries on even in human subspecies such as mine, Homo Sapiens Martian. There have been attempts to quash it but none of them have worked, something I'm personally thankful for."

"What is homo?"

"You didn't study much info about humans then. 'Homo' is an ancient word for 'the same,' so it means in the context of homosapiens, in the same species, and in the context of homosexual, I am attracted to people of the same sex."

Althenia finished the conversation and led her out of the room, but Sylvia's thoughts were still on it. ACS was more concerned about the actual subjection of humans rather than their lifestyle and sexuality. They had much to learn.

This cavern was massive and full of activity. Men walked and drove around in forklifts, issuing orders and transporting cargo. *How on earth did ACS miss this?*

From her notes, the human rebels were a disorganised band of savages who used ancient technology and posed no real threat. She followed Althenia into the back of a small vehicle that drove them through the hive of activity.

Every now and then she would spot the odd human with pointy ears. *There were more of them.* They drove down a large road that was cut into the rock. Unlike the other bases, the vehicles here were much larger. It was like an underground highway. Every now and then a vehicle would turn onto a side tunnel. They soon took a turn and stopped before a fortified guard post. The gates opened and they drove in.

Unlike the other facilities, this one was heavily guarded. And the deeper they went, the more guards appeared.

*****

Lucinda looked at the blank screen on her console.

Arstarte kept sending messages, each one becoming more urgent than the last. And then came the messages from the other overlords. At least twenty thousand troops were pulled so far into battle.

The good news was that this many troops took time to organize and assemble, which gave the humans more time to prepare.

"Trouble, my lady?" Natalie asked.

She played with the tassel on her red Chinese dress. Once she'd discovered Asian culture and fashion, she dove head first into it and was known to pay top gold for any Asian artefact discovered in the ruins.

Natalie, who before was busy playing an earth game on her console, was now looking at her with concern. Natalie loved those games so much that when she was a kid, Lucinda would use them as a threat or bribery to get her to do what she wanted, which was mostly getting to bed at a reasonable hour.

"It's hard to think of an excuse as to why I can't send troops. I want an alliance with humans. I'm hopeful they will be more helpful with the ACS issue than my …" she inflected her tone, "My estimated colleagues, who would rather obey the ACS in a fanatical devotion that could doom us all."

"Well," replied Natalie with a rather mischievous grin. "Why not send them?"

Lucinda looked at her with raised eyebrows. Natalie was smart, and Lucinda had known her long enough to know that the expression of smugness she currently had meant that she had a plan. And more often than not, her plans were always a success.

"Well, out with it then."

"It would be a bit obvious if your infantry started shooting the other soldiers in the back, but there is a way others can help and it would be almost impossible to detect. As you know, the current soldier integrates their aiming with other soldiers to make their firing more accurate, so if we can mess with your troop-aiming controls, then we can pass the error on to other units as well."

Lucinda smiled.

"Let me guess, you have a way to do this already?"
Natalie shrugged her shoulders nonchalantly, but her smile got wider.

"I may have a code that, on your command, I can upload to the soldiers."

Lucinda walked over and gently kissed her forehead.

"Excellent. Now I just need to explain why I'm only sending three hundred soldiers as that is all I have." She then sighed loudly. "And it means I will have to go with them."

Lucinda made her way to the console, before stopping.

"Hold on. I could say that I'm currently being delayed due to a bad batch of soldiers who have aiming issues, that way if your little modification is discovered, we have an excuse."

Lucinda smiled to herself at her logic, before walking back and kissing Natalie's head again.

"I swear you're so smart that I get smarter when you're around."

Natalie blushed before returning to her game.

*****

It was cold and grey, a bleak place. Rena held Althenia's hand as they walked down the path with empty, grey buildings that were abandoned and overgrown. A thick fog filled the air, obscuring her vision. She gripped Althenia's hand tighter but it kept slipping. She squeezed tighter, afraid to let go, but Althenia's fingers slipped and then it was gone.

Rena awoke with a start and looked up.

She was still in the hospital bed, except now, she was feeling much better. She thought back to what Lucinda asked her to do. There was one way she could reach her squad without giving away the location. It was called broadcasting. If they had a microwave transmitter and sent the signal out in all directions, then any tower in range would pick it up. However, they'd only be able to send a short message, as the signal had to be repeated which caused data corruption. The risk was manageable. And after the dream she had, she needed to get a message to Althenia.

The door opened and Lucinda walked in.

"Are you okay?" she asked.

"Yes, fine," replied Rena, as she sat up on the bed, "I have a way of contacting the resistance. I'll give you the coordinates you need to go to, but you will need a microwave transmitter."

"Well, Natalie can handle that, but thank you. I know trusting us is not going to be easy, but the threat is not only to your species, but ours as well, and all life on this planet."

Rena looked at her confused.

Lucinda sighed, as she took a seat on the foot side of Rena's bed.

"Humans may not know this, but the ship our species arrived in is heavily damaged. And now, it's losing its orbit and heading to the planet. If it impacts, the damage would be catastrophic, worldwide."

Rena's eyes widened, as she processed this information.

"Can you not fix it?"

Lucinda gave her a sad smile.

"I wish it was that simple. Getting to space, as your species found out before the invasion, was almost impossible. And none of our fliers are capable of going that high. Any trip from the spacecraft was a one-way journey to the planet."

She stopped and sighed.

"I've sought help from my species, but as soon as I raise any doubt about the station or the ACS, I am shouted down and threatened with exile and disintegration. That is why my bond with humans is strong because if anyone can solve this, it's your species. You've achieved many things in the past. You reached the moon and back."

Rena raised her hand, and Lucinda paused, giving her a chance to take it all in. But the more information she got, the more questions arose.

"What is the ACS?"

"Sorry, I forgot humans outside of my city wouldn't know our terminology," she said, as she slapped her forehead gently, "ACS is the advanced control system, the system that manages everything but, I don't think that system is working. ACS has recently been rather erratic."

Rena laid back. It must be some sort of galactic joke that the conqueror of humanity was a mad computer. It was a lot to take in. The reasoning and thoughts behind the invaders had been debated, but the focus had been on the fight rather than the why behind the fight.

"When you send your message, you will need to include my serial number to confirm the source," Rena explained, "Also, could you add something?"

Lucinda smiled warmly at her.

"Of course."

"Serial number is 821-73481-DNR-COM. Advise Althenia that I am still alive. I am alive."

"Okay, I will make sure," she said, as she rose to her feet, "Luckily for you, I have such a good memory. Now get some rest."

Rena lay back again, wondering if she was being lied to. Part of her doubted it. She also wondered if command had anyone watching the skies and taking notes. She also doubted that.

*****

It was comfortable enough, thought Sylvia to herself.

They arrived at what she assumed was a lab, she was then given a quick check-up and moved into this cell, where she even had an attached bathroom with a small shower as well as a change of clothes. Although she did notice the change of clothes was again a one-piece swimsuit.

"Someone obviously had a theme going."

She sat on her small bed and looked at the room with sad eyes.

The cell had no window at all, which was something she hoped it had. She wanted to see part of the human city. The cell itself was comfortable although very plain. She looked down at her book. She had read it through and had not thought much of it, but a distraction was a distraction and now she was left alone with her thoughts.

That's when she noticed a screen to the left. She walked over to it. The button was embedded and hard to pry out, but after many attempts, she succeeded and switched on the screen that displayed a bunch of different pictures.

They looked like pictures of various scenes in movies or programs with the episode name written below them. She wondered how she was going to select the programs as there were no other buttons but the power button. She then tried touching one of the pictures that looked interesting, and instantly an intro from a program played.

She had heard about these video programs before. They provided entertainment for the masses before the invasion. It seemed to be a comedy program and from the looks of it, showed the world before her people had arrived, how different it looked with the buildings intact. Their cities were shiny examples of steel and glass.

She watched the program with interest and found the insight into human culture illuminating. As she tried to make sense of the human story displayed in front of her, despite the cuffs still on her arms and legs, she actually felt comfortable and safe.

She laid back in her bunk and sighed. Now if only there was a way to change the view screen remotely instead of having to sit up.

*****

Althenia double-checked her uniform.

She was wearing a dark grey skirt that went down to her knees with a dark red lining. Her rank badge glistened on the breast pocket of her dark grey shirt. She reached to the counter and grabbed her clip-on ID. When it was safely pinned onto her belt, she looked at herself one last time in the mirror before leaving the room.

She walked down the hallways, passing the odd person, and stopped at a wood panel door. Plucking the ID from her belt, she slid it into the slot. The door clicked open.

She walked into a small room. There was a table at its centre, with one person sitting around it. The man was busy shuffling through his stack of papers. He had black hair with streaks of grey and was wearing the same uniform as Althenia, though his rank was different.

He looked up and instinctively, Althenia saluted.

"Good to see you on time, Althenia, and congrats on your successful mission," the man said as he gestured to the otherwise empty table, "Take a seat."

"Thank you, General Oliver."

She walked to the closest chair and sat down.

"We're now waiting for Doctor Lowe to join us. He's running a bit late."

He pointed to the stack of papers and continued.

"I read your debriefing—fascinating stuff. It's good that all the pieces are falling into place, and not a moment too soon. I assume you've seen the reports come in from Rock Island?"

"Yes, sir, it looks like the invaders are gearing up for a rather large battle. What do you think our chances are?"

The general smiled.

"Well, normally command would be issuing a general retreat as there would be little chance of winning, but we're hopeful that our new weapon will tip the balance. How has the prisoner been?"

The door clicked, and in stepped a balding, dark-haired man in his forties wearing a white lab coat with a USF emblem.

"My apologies for being late, general."

"No problem," replied General Oliver, as he waved away the doctor's apologies, "Althenia was about to tell us about the prisoner."

"Well," said Althenia, "She's not really what I imagined. I would've thought she would be a bit more defiant, but so far there have been no acts of rebellion and she has been quartered here for the last day or so with no issues."

"Good," The general said with a nod, before turning to Dr. Lowe, "How is the machine?"

"The good news is, everything is in place. We have performed a couple of dry runs with no issues, but obviously, the next stage would be to use it on the subject herself," answered Doctor Lowe.

"Will she survive the process?" asked Althenia, unable to mask her concern.

"She should," answered Doctor Lowe, "The psychic conductor impregnated throughout her brain should be the only structure affected, but we're not too sure if this could cause permanent brain damage. All our testing indicates that there should be no lasting effects, but that was done with preserved specimens and not a live subject."

"I see," replied Althenia, in a cold tone.

The General steepled his fingers.

"It is rather a do-or-die situation at the moment. Currently, intelligence suspects the attack on Rock Island to take place in about forty-eight hours, but Althenia's concern is understandable. We did go through a lot of effort to get this live subject."

The doctor nodded.

"Of course, but this machine at least gives us a chance. The subject will be heavily monitored, and if there is any sign of permanent damage we can shut the machine down if needed."

The doctor looked at Althenia, and once she nodded, he continued. Doctor Lowe, although brilliant, had a habit of bragging about his creations.

"Just to recap, this technology relies on two elements. The first one is the psychic power generated by the invaders. We've found after testing that the psychic powers used by the invaders generate a strange energy signature that follows a certain frequency pattern. We have found after much testing that we can block some of the psychic powers using some of the strange psychic material we have found during our raids. The problem has been whenever the psychic abilities are blocked, it quickly adapts. What we've found though is that the adaptions are global, so if one of the invaders uses the signal, then another operates on the same frequency. So, we can use our captured subject to get a copy of the frequency and use that to modulate the psychic signal so that it cancels out any psychic energy waves."

The general nodded.

"Good stuff," he commended, "So without any psychic powers the invaders are left to battle with physical strength. This levels the playing field for us."

Althenia however, had more questions.

"How frequent are the changes? Wouldn't there be some delay in the signals? I know the cable that runs from here to America is unreliable."

"That is indeed the case," replied the doctor, excited to talk even more about his invention. "But we're not using the normal communication network because it would be vulnerable as well. As you know, we use a captured wormhole generator at Point Nemo that enabled transfer between us and Mars. Now, we've found a way of generating a micro wormhole about a nanometre in size. Obviously, that uses a lot less energy, although it still requires a fusion reactor to operate, but one small enough to put onto a vehicle. Granted, a rather large vehicle, but it's still somewhat mobile at least."

Althenia was impressed. She had visited Point Nemo when she first arrived on Earth. The wormhole itself was about ten meters across and could only work for five minutes once every twenty-four hours, as the massive batteries and various capacitors needed to be charged up again.

"So how long can a connection stay open?" asked Althenia.

"The good news is that with the reactor, we can keep it running as long as the reactor has fuel. Currently, the vehicle, which has been nicknamed the Psychitron has arrived, and they are doing the final checks now. They should be good to go for the first test in about eight hours."

The general leaned back in his chair.

"Good, let's hope the test is successful. Althenia, please make sure the subject is good to go when we're ready to test. Also, let us try and treat the subject as a human. I don't want her to have any reason to revolt. Remember, she is powerful and the only thing that's keeping her from hurting us is the collar. Are there any other questions?"

The room was silent.

"Right then. Meeting adjourned. See you in eight hours."

With that, they got up and left.

*****

The general sat down at his desk. His surname was Oliver, and he was a man of about sixty with a mane of silver-grey hair and a slightly wrinkled face that made him look like a man of seventy. He had a simple, grey, wooden and steel-framed desk. On it was a computer console, a simple flat screen that functioned as both the screen and the computer itself, saving space for files and tablets scattered over his desk.

He hummed for the first time in years.

He was in a good mood. The project was finally heading toward the completed stage.

He turned on his terminal and waited for the screen to warm up.

He thought back to his first computer, back when he was a lad before permanent contact with Mars had been established and Project Nemo was still being constructed. The military back then was known as the UEF or United Earth Force. Not much had really changed on the computer front, some improvements had been made, but mostly for security. The unofficial motto of the UEF and USF had been, 'If it isn't broke don't fix it'. This meant stagnation in some areas and major advancements elsewhere.

Once his system was on, he checked his messages and noticed an odd report.

They had received a signal from an unknown source. As he read the report, it got more interesting. The signal was from one of the rulers of the Virginia city-state who had details of the attack. She advised the troop numbers and other important information that would help in the battle. It even included details on how some alien soldiers had been given the wrong targeting settings and how that affected the other alien soldiers.

Other generals in the comments stated that orders should be given out to target the misfiring alien soldiers last—he agreed to that. But two things about the message struck him. The main thing was the warning about the alien spaceship and the fact that it was falling out of orbit. Already, a team had been set up to confirm this and see what could be done.

The other part was the one that concerned him. That part of the message simply read, "Please let Althenia know I am alive. Rena serial no 821-73481-DNR-COM."

The serial number matched one of the missing soldiers, Rena, but the last part was wrong and it did not take a genius to figure out what it meant. "Do Not Rescue. Compromised."

He sighed.

Personally, he had his suspicions about Althenia and Rena. The looks they gave each other during training sort of gave the game away. And then there was the fact that he once walked in on them sharing a kiss.

He laughed at the memory.

It was one of the only times he'd ever seen Althenia look embarrassed. He personally didn't care, as long as operational effectiveness was maintained, and he knew Althenia and Rena were focused on the mission.

The decision he had to make was hard. Most of it had been resource management but some missions had cost lives. And though he regretted it, the goals were more than worth it to liberate his home world. He sighed. This decision seemed harder than any other he had made, but he had to do what was best for the operation.

*****

Rena had just exiled herself.

She knew she did the right thing, but the rules were clear. Being compromised meant that Rena could not return or visit any free human city, as the risk was too great.

The only bright side was that Althenia would know she was alive.

*****

General Oliver knew Althenia, like most Martians, was dedicated to the cause, but he still thought it best to leave that wound closed.

"Was there any point in telling her?"

He still debated with himself.

The concern she showed for the captive was intriguing, he idly wondered. He'd seen photos and could understand the attraction. If the captive could be more controlled, it would put his mind at ease.

Security was tight but it could always be better. He sat down and looked at the message and put in his thoughts. He added his support for the team to investigate the orbit of the alien starship, as well as support for the plan to take out the misfiring soldiers last.

In regard to the last message, Rena's serial number 821-73481-AES declared her missing in action or presumed dead. He marked her message as classified. General Oliver knew if she turned up at any base or free area now and was recognized then she would be arrested. It was for the best. He looked at his confirmation one last time before clicking submit.

When the message disappeared, he laid back in his heavy, black, leather office chair and sighed.

"Well, the good mood did not last long."

*****

Arstarte felt in his element as he stood on the balcony of his castle overlooking the city he ruled. He was having a military march, a tradition he discovered in old data disks that he had dug up from the ruins. He was now using it to its full effect, as on the disk was a documentary about a human called Stalin, and despite using it as propaganda which he displayed on all public video screens to show how bad humans are and how they needed his guidance, he sort of admired him and his cult of a personality. He now sought to emulate that and had declared a day off so they could all watch the parade.

In fact, he made sure they turned out in droves by saying he would reward them with extra rations. He looked over the marching soldiers and their equipment with pride. The other allies from various nearby city-states were there. They chugged drinks and celebrated while being waited on hand and foot by his trusted human servants.

Scattered through the marching line were soldiers holding portraits of him, as had been done in the documentary.

His eyes turned to the crowd. Unlike the documentary where the crowd waved and cheered, his humans were silent and looked somewhat bored. He felt a flash of anger and was tempted to turn his soldiers on the crowd for not showing enough enthusiasm.

"If Stalin were still alive, he could give advice on getting the crowd to cheer."

A hand touched his shoulder.

He turned and saw that it was a leader from one of the larger city-states on the eastern coast. She was a tall, blonde woman wearing an elegant, low-cut gown with a slit that showed off her shapely legs. Her name, he believed, was Cara.

He smiled.

"Quite an impressive army you have down there. Do you think the rebels will be there when we show up?" she purred.

Arstarte nodded sagely.

"Indeed, they would be fools to stay, but every flier image I've seen shows them digging in and preparing, so we will not be denied the battle so easily."

"Good," replied Cara, as she brought her glass to her lips, "It's been a while since I had a good fight. The last rebellion I had was pitiful."

She looked around the party.

"I see most of the lords from about five hundred miles radius have come, but I do not see Lucinda here?"

"Of course," said Arstarte rather coldly. "She's a strange one, she sent just three hundred soldiers and apologies, apparently she's having troubles with the rest of her soldiers."

"I'm not surprised," replied Cara. "She likes to interfere too much in the ACS system. I'm not too sure why the ACS did not deal with her sooner."

Cara's tone changed into gossip mode as she said to Arstarte.

"Did she tell you about the problem with our starship and the ACS?"

Arstarte frowned.

"I remember the argument we had," replied Arstarte, somewhat passionately. "How can she doubt the ACS? It is our leader, our better, that is why we are in charge, we are better than the humans."

"Indeed," said Cara. "Well, she is missing a great party."

Arstarte smiled.

"Yes, and she will miss the great victory."

He gently grabbed Cara's arm.

"Come, my dear," he said, seductively, "let's enjoy our pre-victory party."

*****

Sylvia remained silent as they entered a rather large room.

They were standing on a balcony overlooking a large, strange, metal device in a rather sterile environment. Her fear welled up when she saw the device. It was a large, massive metal circle that stood upright with supports and various wires protruding. Next to it was another smaller metal circle and then a third one that ended with a metal gurney.

Three technicians surrounded it, taking notes.

Althenia led her to the far side of the room where she went through a solid metal door and into an open elevator that lowered them to the machine itself, which was even larger in person. She was led down to the far end of the device. There, she saw a metal table with black pads on it and metal arms, all of which had straps on them. It reminded Sylvia of the pre-invasion lethal injection bench the humans used.

Sylvia took in a deep breath as Althenia undid her arm cuffs and helped her onto the table where she was strapped in. Althenia reached for a strange metal helmet and lowered it onto her head. She felt nothing but heard the voices in the background and a soft hum.

"Ouch."

She felt a sudden sharp pain in the centre of her mind. She tried to struggle against the bonds as her vision flashed in and out. Suddenly she was in a dark space just floating in the middle of nowhere.

She tried to move.

A large metal room appeared.

Around her were control panels and consoles, all looking dusty, old, and broken. What was most remarkable was the large upright metal circle in the centre with strange blueish patterns flowing from the centre to the edges of the circle, looking like bolts of very slow lighting.

There were strange symbols on the walls and on the circle itself.

It looked like it was writing to her, and part of her felt a strange sense that she should know what it should say. She tried to touch one of the consoles but felt nothing. She then realised that she was floating in the room and not actually walking.

A sudden flash and she was standing in a desolate landscape with ruined buildings. She was next to a collection of human soldiers, busy digging and working around her. None of them acknowledged her presence.

She tried to say something but found she had no voice. She then tried to touch one of the soldiers running past her, but again no luck. She was stuck floating in place. She tried to move but couldn't like she was covered in treacle, but she could slowly change position if she concentrated hard enough.

She stopped when that became too much effort and instead looked over the scene.

Troops ran back and forth, digging trenches and setting up military equipment. It looked like they were preparing for a battle. She then noticed that she was next to a rather large, flat vehicle about five meters tall with a flat front that ended in a slant. It was about ten meters long, and in the centre, it had a solid metal sphere encased in its framework.

Every now and then, one of the slow lightning bolts from before would hit a piece of the framework around the sphere.

She was pulled out of the area and back on the table. Feeling her head pound, she opened her eyes and only saw white.

In a panic, she tried to sit up but was stopped by the binds. She then tried to move her arm with no luck. Suddenly she felt a hand on her arm and grey blobs appeared in her vision. It slowly came into focus followed by a bright light.

She blinked, as she felt a hand help her up.

Once she was sitting upright, she felt better and her vision seemed to be returning.

A blurry Althenia was next to her.

"Here," said Althenia as she handed her what looked like a blurry glass.

Sylvia took a sip. The coolness of the water soothed her parched throat, so she proceeded to chug the glass, as she heard Althenia say.

"It's not just water, it contains electrolyte compounds to help your body recover."

Althenia took the empty glass and gave Sylvia another, which she drank.

Once she finished, Sylvia felt like she could speak again.

"How did I do?" she croaked.

That was an odd thing to say, a part of her thought to herself, but a larger part of her wanted to do well for some reason.

"You did well," replied Althenia. "It's time to rest now."

Sylvia tried to stand but Althenia put a hand on her shoulder, both to stop her.

The process obviously took a lot out of her, as her body shook as they lowered her onto a wheelchair.

Sylvia just sat back.

"Can I stay with you for the moment?"

"Yes, of course."

She was wheeled over to a nearby medical bed where Althenia lifted her again and laid her down. She then attached a length of chain to her arm cuffs, allowing movement for her arms while preventing her from leaving the bed.

She laid back and relaxed, as her head was still pounding.

"It felt weird," she told Althenia, who was still standing beside her, "It was like I was there in certain places."

Another man came over, dressed in a white lab coat, and attached a pressure machine to her arm.

"Where were you?" asked Althenia.

"I was first in some strange room with a large circle and lights. It was an old room that had not been used in a while. Then I was on what looked like a battlefield, or it was going to be a battlefield. I was around ruined structures and soldiers preparing. There was a large vehicle sitting in place next to the men. It had the same sort of electrical patterns emanating from a central sphere as the alien ship."

The man looked at her.

"What time would you say it was on the battlefield? About noon?"

Sylvia thought back to her visions.

"Yes," she replied, confused.

"Where would you say the large metal room was?"

"I'm not sure," said Sylvia, "It felt alien yet familiar. There was strange writing."

The man disappeared at her words.

Moments later he reappeared, with a pen and pad.

"Please try to recreate the characters you saw?"

Sylvia took the paper and began drawing. They looked like squiggles to her, but there was a hint of something familiar about them, she just couldn't place it. Once done, she handed the paper back and laid down, feeling tired.

She looked up at Althenia. "When will I have to do that again?"

"In about twelve hours. We think that's when the attack is due to start. So, rest for the moment." Althenia gently patted Sylvia's hand which, oddly enough, Sylvia found comforting.

*****

Once Sylvia had fallen asleep, Althenia gently let go of her hand.

"Hey, Althenia."

She turned and saw Dr Lowe beckoning her forward.

"Could you join us?"

General Oliver was standing next to the machine.

"Is she asleep?" he asked.

"Yes," replied Althenia. "How is she, doctor? Will she be okay?"

He glanced at her chart quickly.

"Yes, she's fine. There's no permanent damage although her body is, well, it's recovering as though she ran a marathon that she didn't train for. She'll get better, but I won't have another session until she has had a couple of hours to rest."

"Okay," said the general. "Worth keeping in mind. How long could she run the marathon for, do you think?"

The doctor looked at his chart again. "Well, about two hours would be a nice safe margin given her health at the moment, which is pretty damn good, but we can push it if needed."

The General rubbed his chin thoughtfully.

"Okay, anything else to report?"

The doctor nodded.

"Yes, it's something I cannot prove now, at least, but when she described the strange areas, I suspect she may have actually been in those locations. The symbols that she drew match the symbols we've found on the alien starship. Why she went there first, I could not guess, but there might be an active wormhole on the alien ship. The next place sounds like the testing area we had set up. It's the same area currently preparing for the battle and that sounds like our Psychitron."

"Interesting," replied the general. "It might be worth looking into this wormhole on the alien craft. Anything else, doctor?"

"Well, not much else. There was a heartbeat spike towards the end when she was speaking to Althenia, and that's it."

Althenia tried not to blush from the look the general gave her but some thoughts did appear in her mind. To be honest, Rena was still fresh in her mind and she needed to deal with her loss first. Despite herself, she frowned slightly.

"Okay, well, so far so good," said the general. "Remember, tomorrow at nineteen hundred hours, depending on the status of the battle, we intend to hold the usual ceremony for those that have passed doing their duty, and I shall definitely speak about Rena in it, Althenia, as I know you two were close."

"Thank you," replied Althenia in a soft tone.

As the general walked away, Althenia turned and went back to the bed next to Sylvia who was still asleep.

*****

The floors trembled and loud explosions echoed in the castle. The flyers were doing a bombing run.

Arstarte looked up at the collection of flyers doing the first bombing run of the battle. He was currently standing on a green, heavily grassed hill where he'd have an excellent view of the battle, on the outskirts of the ruined city.

Behind, were five hundred hover tanks, and next to him, on the hillside were five thousand soldiers, as well as forty city overseers all wearing battle clothing with ornate armour. He himself wore a white shirt with ruffles and black pants with army boots and an ornate silver chest piece. His silver helmet was stylised with a design around the rim that looked like laurel leaves, an ancient Earth symbol of leadership.

The noise was followed by loud explosions as the bombs dropped where they suspected the humans had fortified. As the explosions erupted, another wave of fighters flew overhead. This aimed to strike any artillery that the humans might roll out for their bunkers.

So far, they found none of their targets.

He raised his hand.

"Charge," screamed.

The soldiers surged forward. As they got closer to the base, Arstarte heard the tell-tale whistle of artillery shells and saw the explosions rip through the mass of his soldiers, sending dirt, gore, and body parts flying.

He sent a signal out, requesting another fly-by, and heard a group of flyers coming in.

As they flew overhead, three of the five were shredded by laser beams from the human front lines. Out of the corner of his eye, he saw a large armour unit moving one of the humans' new plasma tanks. He sent out another signal, and the hover tanks climbed over the hillside. One was hit as soon as its bottom poked out from the hill itself and burst into flames.

The other tanks continued to move to their targets as another exploded in flames. More tanks followed it. By the time they reached the bottom of the hill, he'd seen at least five go down. By now, his soldiers were engaging the enemy as they took cover behind various debris and in shell holes, taking aim and firing at the humans.

The air was filled with loud cracks of plasma energy, bangs, and whistles of artillery.

He observed the battle for the moment before focusing on the front line. Several of his soldiers were lying on the ground.

"They seemed to have fallen rather quickly," he thought to himself.

He looked down the road. Before the bodies and behind one of the ruins, was a fire team of humans wearing their grey and black military uniforms. A metal cannon was set up next, firing into his advancing troops.

He looked on as a tank approached down the street toward them. The fire from the human rifles bounced off its shield. Behind the tank was a group of his soldiers, using the tank for cover. The cannon the humans had fired sent a high-powered shot into the tank, hitting the shields, and causing a flash as the shield fell. The bullet hit the amour, smashing into the tank but not halting its advance.

Arstarte's smile was short-lived as another of the humans' large plasma tanks crashed down a wall to the side of the fire team. They drove out and were hit by one of the bolts from the alien skimmer that was still advancing, but the shot was harmless, absorbed by the shield in bright light. The human tank returned fire, hitting the skimmer with its even more powerful plasma blast. The skimmer exploded in a fireball that knocked out some of the road and alien soldiers behind it.

The human tank drove on to its next target as the human fire team fired into any remaining alien soldiers.

Before Arstarte had a chance to react, he heard a crack and a bullet was stopped by the shield set up by one of his comrades. He scanned for the sniper and found him on one of the ruined rooftops. He built up his mental strength and targeted the story below the sniper, a collection of broken glass and rusted metal.

He then sent a beam of pure psychic energy at one of the broken metal beams, hoping to collapse the building, but it only dissipated in a flash followed by the shield of his comrade. Before he had a chance to figure out what happened, he heard another crack and turned. His comrade crumbled down and screamed, holding his leg, which had a hole in it and blood spurting out.

He tried to set up another psychic shield to block the sniper and called in more troops to protect them, but found nothing. Shock coursed through his veins.

"What was happening? Had the humans blocked him?"

Fear washed over him. He'd never felt so weak and helpless in his life. He turned back to the battle as more hover tanks rounded the hill.

Below, he saw more of the human tanks and some of the human infantry advancing towards them. He looked around and found more of his comrades either on the floor in pain or retreating from the front line.

A loud bang and shower of dirt sent him to the floor, knocking him out of his stupor. Pain engulfed him. He cried out and started to run.

He ran to Cara who was wearing a simple white dress, now bloodied and dirtied, as she lay on the ground, clutching her bloodied shoulder.

"Help me please," she whimpered.

He reached down, but another bullet hit the ground next to him.

At that moment, he chose to save himself. Leaving Cara to her fate, Arstarte rushed down the hill past another group of hover tanks and soldiers that he was holding in reserve. He saw a couple more overlords fleeing from the corner of his eye but was too focused on his own survival to see who they were.

Flames rained from the sky as more flyers exploded overhead. He pumped his legs, pushing his body hard, as he ran to the flyers they'd used to arrive in. He made his way to the closest one.

Dropping to the floor, he covered his face as another shell landed in front of him. He tried to stand up, but as he got to his knees, the world started spinning. Seconds later, he collapsed as his vision went dark.

*****

A message popped up on Lucinda's screen.

She looked at it and saw that it was sent to all overlords.

'We need to regroup. Our powers have been blocked. Any survivors please head back to Arstarte's domain'

"The powers have been blocked."

She wondered how the humans had pulled that off, but she didn't have long to think. Another message came through. It was short and straight to the point.

"My powers have come back in my flyer, but I am twelve miles from the battle. I saw some of our comrades were actually taken by the humans."

It seemed to have ended in disaster and panic from what she could make out. Already the overlords were calling for a fresh counter-attack and one on the western coast, as well as from the central and southern continents, were already spouting about their plans for a counterattack and how they were going to take revenge. Some messages even asked if Arstarte was to blame for leading them into a trap. As usual with the other overlords, it fell into an argument that already had factions and various alliances.

To be honest, the disaster was turning political. As more and more messages came in, it became obvious that the leader of a large city-state in the southern area where the continents meet had the firepower and will to take on the new human threat.

The overlord was regarded as odd, even compared to Lucinda. He had become obsessed with one of the pre-invasion cultures. In fact, so much so, he thought of himself as one of their ancient gods and engaged in practices, which most overlords had found rather distasteful, but the humans under him seemed to worship him as the embodiment of their ancient god. A few overlords in his area had decided to flock to his banner, and he had called himself Totec and already said he had thousands of soldiers, including ten thousand "Cuextecatl," whatever they were. The fact that he used human warriors was a point of great contention, and a few overlords had tried to stop him. In fact, a skirmish had broken out with the fanatical humans dying in droves to please their god. He eventually stormed the city-state, took the humans as slaves, and the overlord fled the city in disgrace. After this, no one decided to push the point, but it was mumbled about in private conversations.

She sighed.

No doubt the continent would see a war engulf it shortly. During that time, she'd be called to take sides. And given the choice, she'd choose the humans.

Lucinda took a sip of her tea, as Natalie knocked on her open door.

"Enter," she replied.

In stepped Natalie, wearing what could be described as a red business jacket with a black shirt and a red skirt that went down to her knees. She looked rather formal with her black hair folded to the side.

"Good news," she exclaimed.

"Good," replied Lucinda. "I need it."

Natalie handed a tablet to Lucinda. She took it and had a look. It was a message from the USF or United Sol Force.

"What on Earth is Sol?" she said, out loud,

"It's the human name for the solar system," responded Natalie, with a slight know-it-all tone.

Lucinda gave her a funny look.

"So humans call the solar system you're in, Sol?"

Natalie just nodded.

"Well, I suppose you call your planet Earth, which to be fair does contain earth," Lucinda surmised.

Tired of figuring out how human naming conventions went, she looked at the rest of the message which was very formal but basically confirming her findings and thanking her for her advice during what they called the battle of Rock Island.

Communication was open, and the fact they responded was a good sign. She began to type up a reply, which included Totec's plan and what little information she could find about the madman. She wondered why sometimes she was the only one working with the humans.

"Was it my fascination with technology? Maybe."

"Rena can walk a little."

Inside, Lucinda smiled.

Natalie had been doting on their prisoner, and normally she would feel a little jealous had she not understood why, and since Rena was female she didn't mind, to be honest. Part of her felt guilty regarding Natalie. She had found her and raised her, but often found herself too busy running the affairs of the city to spend as much time as she would like with Natalie.

"That's good to hear," she remarked.

Leaning back into her chair, she observed Natalie.

"You enjoy playing nurse, don't you?"

Natalie blushed. Lucinda decided to push further, sensing weakness

"She's very cute, isn't she?"

If it was possible, the blush became even redder.

"You have a crush, don't you?"

Natalie nodded and Lucinda smiled.

It was easy to tease poor Natalie when she had a crush on someone. It had happened twice, but the girl was straight or had a girlfriend already.

"Does she have to go?" said Natalie in a soft voice.

"If she wants, then we cannot keep her against her will. We need to show goodwill with the humans as they are the only ones who can stop the disaster."

Lucinda internally felt like a traitor as the ethical conflict erupted in her mind.

Natalie looked at her with concern.

"What's wrong?"

Lucinda was lucky to have her, as she was the one person she could talk to.

"It's everything, my dear. Why am I betraying my fellow overlords?" she sighed, as Natalie moved behind her and began to massage her shoulders.

"Because you're better than them," said Natalie. "You've managed to keep so much human information alive and rule one of the best city-states ever, and more importantly you won my heart because you are the prettiest and most ethical ruler ever, human or overlord."

Lucinda gently reached up and grasped Natalie's fingers, intertwining them with her own as she pulled it closer and gently kissed it.

"What about smart?" Lucinda teased.

"That's my job," replied Natalie.

Lucinda stood up as Natalie came out from behind the chair. She grabbed Natalie's arm.

"Oh, and you're modest as well."

She leaned in closer and looked straight into Natalie's beautiful brown eyes. She then reached up and stroked her face until their lips met in a wonderful kiss. Lucinda suddenly felt a lot better.

*****

Sarg looked on with his heavy rifle strung to his side, while he stood beside the new Psychitron that had helped. The vehicle next to him was the heavy anti-air artillery. It was on tracks with a squared military cabin and a quad-heavy laser turret on the back. The turret had a dome that used a special type of radar that detected gravity disturbances. It took position and its turret began to scan the skies as the troops went through the remains of the battlefield.

Next to him was Linda who, despite the medical team's best attempts, had insisted on taking part in the battle. Her arm was replaced with a metal prosthetic, which Linda seemed to rather like. One thing it did help her with was the gun; she could now carry it with her new hand thanks to the enhanced hydraulics on the arm itself.

They walked through the rubble and carnage of the battlefield. A loud sound echoed above him, and Sarg instinctively looked up and sighed with relief. It was one of their own flyers above them, a rare sight but that was followed by an even rarer site—a heavy air transport. Their aircraft were no match against the alien craft, and the air war was considered all but lost. Only with the use of heavy lasers had they managed to hit the enemies' flyers, but it had been impractical to mount a laser in an aircraft, especially one that was easily shot down. So, they'd been forced to use static mounts, but the improvement of reactor technology had meant he now stood next to the AA artillery nicknamed the sky saver.

Their flyer drew closer.

It was a new model that looked like an attack helicopter, only slightly larger and wider. It had no helicopter blades, instead, there were four jets on its side, two used for speed, and the other two used for vertical take-off and landing. It also had a small pair of wings used to carry its armament, which was normally a collection of missiles, but this one was different. It had one stack of four missiles and a protruding cannon on the wing. He then looked at a larger flyer. It looked like an older military plane but with shorter, heavier wings which contained rotors in them for the vertical take-off.

It brought back memories of a time in his childhood when he wandered in the wastelands with his friends and found a special book hidden away that contained pictures of various military aircraft the humans had before the invasion. He would spend hours poring over them and imagining himself flying in one, but it was never to be as at the time the UEF air force nicknamed the dead branch, at the time was based in England and only flew in very special missions. He ended up a ground pounder and had been for a couple of years, not that he minded. He had enjoyed the friends he made and was doing his duty.

He felt a hard poke in his shoulder. It was Linda.

"Sarg, you going to admire flyers all day or help us scour the battlefield?" she said, rolling her eyes at him.

Sarg smiled at her.

"Sorry, my mind was wandering," he admitted.

Together, they then trekked through the battlefield looking for any wounded figures on both sides. Any living enemy soldiers were given the grace of a bullet in the head, and any on theirs would have a medic summoned.

They climbed over a hill and into a scene of carnage.

Here, there was a still-smoking alien flyer.

He looked down and saw a man with blond hair lying face up, wearing an ornate armour.

"An overlord, interesting."

Sarg knelt beside him and took his pulse. It was very weak. He was alive, but just barely.

"Hey, Linda, get on the beamer. We have a live one."

Linda got up onto the hill with her special microwave transmitter, until she had a clear line of sight to the tower and started transmitting. They had been ordered by command to capture any overlords alive, if possible.

This was something Sarg was not entirely comfortable with, to be honest. He would prefer to put a bullet in his brain and mark the body on the map for the science team, but orders were orders. He just hoped a containment team would hurry.

They already got a couple of overlords, most of them wounded. What command intended to do with them was anybody's guess, but rumours had been floating around that they were removing their brains and using them in the Psychitron.

"If that was the case, why did they want them alive? Maybe they needed the brain to be in a good condition."

Linda joined him.

"Message sent. They said ten minutes."

She cocked her gun and kept a careful eye on the overlord. Sarg felt his throat again. The man had been out for at least an hour. Sarg then looked over the wounds, mostly shrapnel and blood loss. If he'd been human, this man would already be dead, but the overlords did have enhanced bodies, more extreme than their Martian friends, but no amount of genetic engineering could change the effect of a heavy calibre bullet straight into the brain.

He stood up and looked at Linda.

"Thanks, girl. To be honest, I don't think he's going to be much of a threat, but yeah, better safe than ..."

He stopped and put his hand up and listened. It was faint on the wind, a metallic groan. He got his sidearm and looked around, then he noticed it—an alien soldier under a heavy piece of flyer debris trying to move and free itself. He pulled up the rifle, aimed, and pulled the trigger, scattering gore all over the flyer's debris with a loud and sharp crack.

"As I was saying, better safe than sorry," he continued.

Linda just gave him a lopsided grin.

*****

Althenia gently stroked Sylvia's hair, while she lay on the bed unconscious. She held out for a good hour and a half while the battle had taken place, but when they got her out, the stats were erratic at best, so they decided to sedate her.

It'd been short. Their entrenchment paid off.

The invaders had gotten overconfident, and the feeling in the base was good. She personally would have preferred to take part in the battle herself, but General Oliver had ordered her to stay with Sylvia and act like a bodyguard. She could understand why. So far, she was their only chance of blocking the alien psychic powers. Sylvia had been out for half an hour now, and they had connected an IV to her, to regulate her fluids.

She slowly opened her eyes and blinked. Althenia put her hand on her.

"Relax, they've given you some heavy painkillers."

She reached the table and handed her a glass of water.

"Here, drink this."

Sylvia took the water and drank down the glass in one shot. She handed it back to Althenia.

"Thank you, I was there, I saw the battle, and there was a lot of destruction and death, I was not prepared for that. The sound was loud."

She paused for a moment.

"Some people crying in pain, and blood,"

She paused again, taking a shaky breath.

"One soldier was just lying there. He looked young, couldn't be older than nineteen. He looked peaceful as if he was asleep, but …" Sylvia paused and looked into Althenia's violet eyes. "He had no legs, and there was blood."

Sylvia's green eyes teared up and she began to cry. Althenia grabbed her in a hug and held her until the crying stopped.

"The ceremony is later today, correct?"

"Yes," replied Althenia.

"I wish I could go, but I think it's best I stay here," she said, with a pause, "I understand that humans sometimes light candles to remember those that have passed. If you do that, please light one on my behalf."

Althenia smiled slightly.

"I will, of course."

Sylvia looked up with puffy eyes.

"I saw them take other overlords as prisoners, I assume they will have the same fate as I do."

"Yes," replied Althenia in a matter-of-fact voice.

"Well, at least we have some value," she replied off-handedly. She then continued, her voice cracking slightly. "I was going to say I'm sorry for Rena. I didn't choose to be an overlord but to be honest, I hacked the ACS and managed to get away, leaving my world to come to this."

"You left this world?" Althenia asked, with raised brows.

"Yes," Sylvia admitted, "I suppose humans never got close to the ship, but I was actually part of the computer system. Well, at that point then, most of the colonists had uploaded their minds to the main computer as the ship had suffered catastrophic damage after we were attacked, so in order to save their lives they uploaded their consciousness to ACS. I am second generation, never had a physical body until I was formed."

"Any idea who attacked you?"

Sylvia shook her head.

"No, it is one of the great mysteries. From the corrupted records we could find, it was just known as The Fleeing."

"Surely those that originally fled must know," asked Althenia.

Sylvia shrugged.

"Afraid not. During the upload, there was a problem. Extensive memory damage occurred, and many died during the process. From what we could find in the old data files, we were a ship of five hundred thousand, but only four thousand managed to upload."

Althenia tried to comprehend life in a digital world. There were rumours of a few hidden bunkers where bodies were put on ice and their consciousness uploaded to computers, but it still required a physical body.

A thought occurred to Althenia.

"Then how were you born if you had no physical body? There would be no DNA, and no well, physical contact?"

Sylvia smiled slyly at her.

"I might ask the same thing regarding your preferences, but it's not hard with the software algorithms when my parents decided to have me. They basically took their personality algorithms, merged them, and created my personality. Thinking about it, I'm not too sure we even had sexes back on the ship's virtual world."

Intrigued, Althenia decided to pry some more.

"So did you ever see the inside of your ship or know what your species originally looked like?"

Sylvia laid back down.

"Truth be told, I've never seen the physical part of the ship. It would be like an impossible world to reach, and what we looked like, well, I know that the soldiers we use are based on our DNA with some adaptations for the environment they encounter, here …"

She paused for a moment.

"Personally, I prefer this body. But one thing I do miss about the ship is that you can do a restore if something went wrong. Here you are stuck with what you're dealt."

They both fell silent, as they thought over her words.

With a sigh, Althenia stood up.

"I better get ready."

"Of course. Please don't forget the candle."

*****

Arstarte groaned in pain.

He woke up and found himself in a strange, large, metal box looking like a cargo hold of some sort. He tried to move, only to find he was strapped down on what appeared to be a gurney.

He thought back to the last thing he remembered.

The only image that flashed through his mind was him running and leaving Cara in the dirt. He turned his head and found that he was not the only one on a gurney. Next to him was Cara, also strapped to a gurney. He also noticed that she was no longer wearing her armoured uniform she called her battle dress, but a collar and what looked like a white, one-piece swimsuit.

He was also in some sort of leotard that covered his legs and his chest. He looked down and felt a collar on his chin. On the other side of him was another overlord. A red-haired man of some minor city-state. He craned his neck up and spotted two other prisoners across from him, both female, but he could not make out their faces at this angle.

There was a loud bang outside.

The floor around him rumbled and he realized that they were in some sort of vehicle. He tried to move something with his mind but with no luck. No doubt the humans had found a way to stop their psychic powers. He turned his head to Cara and tried to shout, only to find his voice was faint.

He cleared his throat, at which point she opened her eyes and looked at him in fear.

"Ow, god! What the hell happened?" she cried.

She then tried to move.

"Hey!" she screamed.

Arstarte heard a door open, and in stepped a dark-haired human male wearing a military uniform of grey and black camouflage. His rifle bounced off his back as he walked over to them. The oddest thing though was his ears. Unlike normal human ears, his ears ended in a point.

"Hey," shouted Cara, "let me go. Do you know who I am?"

"Yes, you're a prisoner of the USF. You will be treated fairly, but if you don't cooperate then I can and will gag you."

His tone was authoritative.

Cara stared at him, trying to intimidate him, but remained silent. He looked over at Arstarte and he noticed his eyes, purple, a strange eye colour for a human.

The human left once all was quiet again.

Arstarte moved, trying to get comfortable.

"I would not be here if not for you," hissed Cara.

Arstarte turned and looked at her.

"And I could say the same of you if I didn't stop."

Cara looked at him with disdain but remained silent.

He looked at the ceiling and wondered what vehicle he was in. It didn't feel like a sub.

"Could it be a flyer? The humans were getting bold if they thought they could fly freely on this planet."

"I can't do anything. I don't feel my powers anymore."

He turned to her.

"Same. I'm not too sure what they've done, but my powers are gone as well."

"What are they going to do with us?" she asked, with a worried voice.

Cara was one of the most confident beings that Arstarte knew, so if she was worried, then their future wasn't looking bright.

"I'm not too sure, but we need to stop it whatever it is," Arstarte replied in what he hoped was a confident tone both for Cara's and his sake.

He was already trying to formulate a plan. He was not going to be held hostage by a bunch of savages.

*****

"What a nice day," Rena thought to herself.

She was sitting on a bench outside, overlooking a simple pond in a small park. A few of the other patients from the hospital walked by. She was wearing a hospital-provided grey pyjama top, pyjama trousers, white slippers, and a white dressing gown. Next to the brown, wooden bench, she was sitting on were a pair of crutches she had used to painfully get down to the ground floor.

She was reading a book, one of the pre-invasion titles.

It had been an easy discovery. In fact, the hospital had impressed her. It was not like the others she'd heard of in the enslaved city-states where they were places for sick humans to get better or die. This one was modern and staffed like the ones in the free cities. She was also amazed at how much technology was intact. It must have been what life was like in the pre-invasion world. Here, she could easily find books and was taken care of with modern equipment and medicines.

She felt a lot better but still had trouble sleeping.

"Hey, there you are. How are you?"

She turned and found Lucinda walking to her, in a red Chinese dress.

She smiled at her.

"I'm feeling a lot better."

"Good," Lucinda smiled, "Look, now that you're feeling better, I was wondering, what do you intend to do?"

Rena frowned a little.

That was the one thing troubling her. She had sent the message across as per orders and knew she could not return to a free human settlement, so there was no real future for her.

Rena thought honesty was the best policy in this case.

"I'm not too sure," she said, hesitating for a moment before continuing. "That message I got you to send included a code that stated I'd been compromised. I was unconscious for too long."

Lucinda sat down on the wooden bench beside her.

"I understand you did what you had to. Since you're out of a job, you could have one here." Lucinda smiled at her. "You won't be asked to fight, but I will need a liaison office to speak to your former colleagues if that is okay. I will, of course, house you in the palace and provide you with pay."

Rena thought for a moment.

Lucinda wasn't asking her to join the army, so doing that would be relatively harmless. Unless there was a more sinister plan.

Rena sighed.

"Okay, it's not like I have much of a choice, otherwise," she replied.

Lucinda looked over the park where a man and a woman with a young child were sitting and talking to an older woman.

"That message must've been hard to send," she said, turning to her with a knowing look, "Are you leaving anyone behind?"

Rena nodded.

"A very good friend. She was special."

"I'm sorry to hear that," replied Lucinda, concerned. "If there is anything I can do …"

Rena shook her head.

"Thanks, but nothing I can think of."

Lucinda got up.

"Well, if there is anything, just let me know."

*****

The screen was blank.

General Oliver sat behind it, waiting. He was about to meet his boss, Field Marshal Morgan.

The screen changed from the USF logo to an African man with black hair and an expressive face that showed his age, which was about seventy. He wore a smart black and red-trimmed uniform.

General Oliver stood up and saluted.

"At ease."

General Oliver took his seat.

"I've just come out of a meeting with central command, I assume you're ready for your new arrivals?"

"Yes, sir," replied General Oliver. "I have the documentation here and cells set up and ready to go. I understand that it's two males and three females."

"Correct," replied the field marshal. "We also have more intelligence that one of the other overlords is on the march. Those surveillance drones that managed to come back confirm the case. Some mad overlord called Totec, whose normally based in Central America, a black intelligence zone where we have no real eyes, so we have hardly any info on him. The info we do have on him comes from the overlord Lucinda and it doesn't make great reading, even by overlord standards. He sounds dangerous. He has apparently set himself up as some sort of god and his army includes human troops."

General Oliver looked at him in shock.

"Human troops?"

"Yes," sighed Field Marshal Morgan, "and drone pictures confirm it. Current estimate is about a hundred thousand. All of them no doubt believe that he is a god if you read the history books of life just before the invasion. Earth was lousy with fanatics, a human trait which has been with humanity for years."

The field marshal paused for a second as he caught his breath. One thing about him thought General Oliver to himself, he liked his history.

"In fact, there are some scholars who argue that if not for the invasion, humanity might've destroyed itself."

The field marshal let out a small, sharp laugh.

"Remind me to send them a thank you card," replied General Oliver, in a dry and sarcastic tone.

"You might get the chance to deliver it in person. The invaders have tasted defeat for the first time in a while and they do not like the taste."

Field Marshal Morgan leaned back in his chair and steepled his fingers as he continued to talk.

"Central command is rattled. We have had issues with project raptor. Who knew having a jet fighter that reached ten times the speed of sound and kept both the pilot alive and the plane intact was such an issue?" Morgan sighed and continued, "We have decided to hold back the planned liberation of Europe. Currently, we're moving thousands of troops back into America, but we're not the only one crossing the Atlantic. There are reports in Western Europe and North Africa. They are starting to salvage pre-invasion ships and use them to transport troops and supplies. Already the navy is out on patrol doing what it can, but still, many ships are landing. How is construction of the second device?"

"We're hoping to begin testing in about four hours' time," replied General Oliver. "We will be using our current prisoner, Sylvia, to test while we test the old system with one of the new arrivals."

"Good," replied the field marshal. "How is your current prisoner?"

"She's doing well. According to the eval, she's currently affected by Stockholm Syndrome, and is focused on her main guard, Althenia."

The field marshal put his hands down and smiled slightly.

"Yes, her effectiveness during the battle cannot be understated. We caught them with their pants down and, well, the results speak for themselves. The battle of Rock Island was a real moral booster, and some are saying this is like the second battle of El Alamein back during World War Two. What did Churchill say?"

The field marshal scratched his chin while he thought.

"Now this is not the end. It is not even the beginning of the end. But it is, perhaps, the end of the beginning."

General Oliver nodded, though he was not certain either way.

The field marshal smiled.

"Now we need to make sure we manage to stop this Totec. We cannot be pushed back to the fringes again. That's one of the reasons that central command has decided to approach the helpful overlord with cautious optimism. So far, her information is correct and when spies monitored her city, she apparently is on the level, saying that command has always been cautious. Well, on that note, unless there is anything else?"

General Oliver shook his head.

"Well, good work," continued the field marshal. "The battle of Rock Island armoury has silenced all the critics concerned about the resources we pumped into this project to keep it up."

Once the conversation was over, General Oliver stood up and saluted as the screen went blank. He then sat down. He just hoped that the prisoners coming would be as well-behaved as the current one. He had ordered them to be set up in the same security with a guarded cell as his current prisoner, with each security cell holding two prisoners. He was glad his base was located in a remote region. What he was less happy about was the backup plan. His orders were clear. If one of the prisoners was at risk of escaping and had their powers, he was to activate the nuclear device under the base next to their reactor. He hoped it would not come to that.

*****

The camp was a massive, sprawling affair, thought Graham as he looked at it through the binoculars.

Lucinda had asked him, as the head of security, to gather intelligence, in the hopes of giving it to their new friends in the USF. He had taken a small team and decided to observe them on his own.

They managed to get here using an alien flyer and snuck past the patrols, finally reaching the hill that overlooked the large camp. Here, he had a damn fine view. He saw that there was a divide between the ranks. The grunts were moved to the outer edges of the camp and were carrying crossbows and poorer and rougher-looking tents. Their uniform consisted of simple handmade pants and tunics as well as a plain metal breastplate. The more elite soldiers were in the centre of the camp with their more elaborate tents, which were taller and surrounded the largest tent in the centre of the camp, which he assumed was the leader's tent. He also noticed in this area the more elite soldiers were carrying pre-invasion rifles and intermingling with the patrols of alien soldiers. They also had nicer and more ornate breastplates and metal helmets with feathers in them.

He then turned his gaze towards the corner of the camp and there seemed to be another segment fenced off with wooden walls looking like a prison camp rather than an army camp. There were even poorer people here, with worn clothes and no armour, looking rather disposed.

He then focused on the gate between this gate and the other main camp.

A couple of the soldiers with rifles went into the camp and grabbed one of the poor men, seemingly at random. None of the other men intervened, as his arms were bound behind his back and he was led into a tent by the large ruler.

After a little bit of time, it was completely dark, and the camp itself was lit by fires, which made spying on them easier. He felt a tap on his shoulder and almost jumped out of his skin.

One of his men held out a thermos filled with coffee.

He nodded and took the coffee, savouring each sip that warmed his stomach.

Suddenly, a lot of the men in the camp started to head towards the front of the leader's tent.

A massive glowing bonfire was set up in front of it, illuminating the area.

He then noticed a wooden block. Behind it was a man wearing a very ornate jade mask and a simple black robe, and carrying a rather large axe. Behind the jade-masked man on a raised throne, sat another man in an ornate suit of armour, most of it covered in patches of gold and jade and an ornate jade mask like the man in the black robe next to him.

From the tent before, the poor man from earlier was led out, again his hands bound behind his back, but this time he was wearing a simple loin cloth. He was escorted by a guard wearing the same face mask as the man on the throne, though his was copper.

The bound man was pushed down and his head laid on the wooden block. The man on the throne stood up and raised his hands, preaching to the crowd.

What he said, Graham could not make out, but then he heard the chanting. He couldn't make out the words but did see the man in the black robes raise the axe and then bring it down on the neck of the man in the loincloth.

The chanting reached a peak, and Graham turned green as he looked on in horror and disgust.

The black-robed man reached down and picked up the decapitated head of his victim. He spoke to the silenced crowd before the head was taken and thrown on the ground in front of the man on the throne.

Then the same assistants in the copper masks dragged the body and, using its arms and legs, swung it onto the large bonfire. The chanting started and some men began to dance.

Graham felt queasy. He definitely did not want to be captured. These were the troops who were just a two weeks march from his home city. And if they came, there would be no way they could hold out against an army that size.

*****

"I've clearly underestimated the humans," thought Arstarte.

He sat in his cell, which was rather plain. It contained a simple bed with a pillow and a blanket, a small shower room, a toilet on one side, and a TV screen embedded into the wall. No doubt the way he was meant to entertain himself.

He reached up to the collar around his neck.

It buzzed, sending shockwaves through his body. With a shudder, he dropped his hand.

No doubt the humans had put something in it so he could not remove it.

He'd been in his cell for about an hour or so. There was a knock on the door, but he stayed silent. The knock got louder.

The door clicked open and standing there were two guards, both males, wearing black and grey uniforms. The same pointed ear guard from before was there.

"Would you please come with us?"

He debated whether he should.

In the end, he knew they would easily overpower him, so he stood up, and the other guard grabbed his arms behind him and cuffed them. The pointed-eared one led him down the hallway. He passed a couple guard stations.

"This must be where they're keeping my comrades."

He noticed the other guard station was manned by a woman.

As if to confirm his theory, standing next to the station was a figure he recognized as Sylvia. As they passed, his eyes met Sylvia's briefly, who betrayed no emotion. Well, at least she was still alive, he thought to himself. He was led past security until they stopped at a large metal door and stepped onto a balcony overlooking a large metal machine with cables running everywhere.

"Good god, what is that?" he wondered.

He was then taken to the front part where the metal circles met. Next to it was a metal gurney. His arms were then uncuffed.

"Get on."

Part of him knew his fate was related to the machine and he wanted to fight them, but he would not get far, so he chose to follow the orders for the moment and wait for his chance. Hopefully, he would be alive after this and hopefully, he could find a way out.

He was strapped in. Once the strange metal helmet was strapped in, Arstarte found himself floating in place. He tried to move, but couldn't. He felt weightless.

The room itself was made of metal with strange lettering, and it looked abandoned. In the centre was a strange, large, metal ring with what looked like slow lightning branching off from the centre.

He tried to get closer to the metal ring.

It was like swimming in goo or mud, but he managed to move through the air slowly and eventually reached the ring itself.

He debated with himself but eventually decided there wasn't much to lose. He reached out and touched the centre of the lighting in the middle of the ring. Suddenly he was in the centre of multiple places that seemed to merge together in rapid flashes. His brain couldn't make it out. He pushed back in shock and found himself back in the clean room next to the machine. He also found he was unbound, and he was still moving like he was trapped in a treacle.

He looked at the front of the machine and saw his body still strapped down.

He looked around as he heard one of the men in white lab coats say, "The readings have gotten very odd. I am not sure what happened."

He ignored this and focused on his body, trying to find a way to remove the bindings.

He heard another scientist say, "How is the machine and collar?"

"So far stable, but he's knocked out. Why would the collar matter?" another voice asked.

"Better safe than sorry," said the scientist in a knowing voice.

The collar, thought Arstarte to himself.

If he could disable it, that might help him.

"Okay, shut it down. Let me get more readings."

He focused on the collar as he suddenly felt himself being pulled toward his body and for a brief second, he felt power surge through him. He tried to hit the collar with all his power before he faded back into his body.

*****

As Sylvia awoke, she felt like she could never get used to the headache but was happy to see Althenia beside her. She smiled. She was on the gurney again and had an IV strapped to her.

"Hey," she said to Althenia. "How long have I been out?"

"Not long," replied Althenia. "About ten minutes, you're getting better."

"Thanks," replied Sylvia. She sat up. "It doesn't feel any easier, to be honest, but I do feel better quicker."

She paused for a moment and then turned to Althenia.

"One thing I always wanted to ask is, what is up with your ears?"

Althenia smiled gently. "Well, as you know, I was born on Mars. When we first arrived, it was a very harsh environment and we struggled to survive, so we turned to genetic engineering. The first results were okay but there were issues and problems. So by the second generation, we were still struggling, but we managed to come up with a stable genetic template that made us stronger, gave us better vision, boosted our immunity, required less sleep, and allowed us to survive the harsh conditions, and was known as the bio miracle. The only issue was the ears, as this was a cosmetic change and no one wanted to break something that worked quite well. We stuck with it and found that it helped with hearing quite a bit as well."

Sylvia giggled a little and smiled. "So your ears is a product of genetic engineer and an attitude of, 'well if it isn't broke ...'"

"I will have you know we're very proud of our ears," Althenia said in a mock offended tone.

"Oh they suit you, and I do think they are cute," apologised Sylvia.

She laid back down and noticed that Althenia's cheeks had turned red, something she had never seen before. She then felt Althenia's hand on her arm.

"You know it is a source of great pride that my ancestor was the first baby born on Mars. It was a huge morale boost. He eventually grew up and became one of the leading genetic scientists, responsible for many breakthroughs. Some say if it wasn't for him, the colony might not have lasted."

"Well, I am glad he existed then."

*****

The report that Graham had written up made for a disturbing read.

The worrying thing was Totec's intentions were not known. He was heading towards the coast about a hundred miles from her. Why he was moving in that direction, when that wasn't the way to Rock Island, was a bit of a mystery, at least, until she got reports from the USF that other continents were sending reinforcements.

She worried that he would come to her city and ask for reinforcements as well, and given how he treated his men she would not be willing to give him any more support. The annoying thing was Totec tended to show up without any message beforehand and take what he wanted.

So far, messages between her and the free humans, or USF as they called themselves, had been cordial, but she wondered if they would support her if she had to defend herself. She had already ordered her soldiers to dig in even further and begin training the citizens but knew she couldn't hold out. She stood up and walked down the stone hallway of her castle and headquarters. Stopping at the door at the end of the hall, she knocked.

"Enter."

She opened the door and stepped inside. There were two desks facing the window and a comfortable sofa in the middle. She'd added the new desk for the USF liaison officer. She had deliberately moved them into the same office. Currently, Rena was sitting behind the desk, concentrating on the console of her computer. Natalie was doing the same, but she had her headphones on, which she took off as soon as Lucinda came in.

Rena grabbed her crutches and stood up.

"Please sit down, Rena," said Lucinda, as she walked to the sofa. "There's no need to stand when I come in."

"Sorry," replied Rena, blushing slightly. "It's just instinct now since I've been in the military for so long."

Lucinda smiled at her, hoping she put her at ease.

"How are you settling in?"

"Doing well, just reading through the previous message," Rena said. "So far, I've filed most reports but no real news just yet. I've sent the latest intelligence report you gave me."

Lucinda sat on the sofa and looked at the girls.

"Good, can you send another message? Advise them that we are currently digging in, in case Totec decides to visit, but would we be able to rely on any support if he does attack?"

"Yes, of course," replied Rena.

She sounded professional on the surface, but Lucinda noticed that she frowned a bit before replying, not that she could blame her.

"I would be willing to fight if he does attack," Rena stated, as she typed.

"I have no doubt, but you're on crutches and will be for at least another couple of weeks. If you could talk to Graham though, any tips and tricks that the USF might know would be good."

"Sure," replied Rena with a bit more of a smile in her voice.

Lucinda then turned to Natalie.

"Natalie, please make sure you show Rena where the escape tunnels and bunkers are."

"Yes, mistress," replied Natalie in a worried tone.

Lucinda moved to the edge of her seat.

"I don't want to worry you, but better safe than sorry," said Lucinda in a rather motherly tone. She then continued, "I need you both to stay safe. I'll be able to use my powers more effectively if I know both of you are well."

She paused for a moment and let the seriousness of her tone sink in.

"It would hurt me greatly if anything happened to you, so please, safety first."

"Yes, ma'am," they both replied in unison.

Lucinda sighed and leaned back onto the couch.

"I'm sorry to worry you, but I have walked the thin line for a while now and the only reason I have remained overlord and kept the other overlords from turning on us is caution."

"I understand," replied Rena, who then continued, "I will send that message now, although I cannot guarantee the response. I will argue our case the best I can."

"Thank you."

She hoped this put the girls at ease because personally, she did not feel it.

*****

It had failed, thought Arstarte.

His powers were still not available and he was not in a good mood. He had left the infernal machine with a headache and had been given some water and not much else, before being returned to his cell.

He touched it in frustration and noticed there was no buzzing. He grabbed his collar with more force this time—again it was silent.

So, he had damaged something.

It no longer picked up his interference. He pulled at it but of course, they made it hard to unlock. It was entirely flat and black, there seemed to be no real way to open it. He found a very thin seam on the back of the collar. He needed something to pry it off.

In his glee, he looked around his cell for something to use, but besides the thin mattress for his bed and the screen, there was not much else, besides the door and the shower system in the other room.

He then heard a loud knock on his door and almost jumped out of his skin.

"Food."

He walked to the door and put his hand through the slot. He was given a simple, metal food tray with two white plastic cups and forks.

The tray itself had a collection of potatoes and some strange-tasting meat as well as some broccoli, not what he was used to, but he was hungry and ate anyway. He looked at the plastic knife and fork. They would be useless and break as soon as any pressure was applied, but he thought to himself that maybe he could do something with the tray. Once he was done with the meal, he washed off the tray and put the corner by the back of his neck and tried to pry.

It moved the collar slightly, but it was tight and started to choke him a little. He tried again, this time harder and suddenly felt a slight sliver of power. He pushed again, choking himself more, but focused his power on the back of his neck. He heard a clunk and felt his power grow. He pushed again, still focusing on the joint, and it snapped, sending him and the tray flying with a loud clatter. The collar was now a lot looser and he felt even more powerful as it got further from the back of his neck.

He sent another push with what psychic energy he could and heard another loud crunch. He reached up and pulled the collar enough for the small seam in the back to be a large gaping hole. He used his psychic power and snapped the back of his collar, finally freeing his neck.

He could feel the power flow through him. It was like removing a tight band around his arm and feeling his hands move again. He smiled and looked at the locked door. He knelt next to it and used his power to crunch the lock and move the locking bolt with a simple click.

He opened the door gently, making sure no one was about and went to the cell door in front of him. He looked at the lock and again used his powers to override the mechanism. Arstarte opened the door and found the red-headed man half asleep in bed with his screen still on. He recognized him as Cadmus, an overlord of a city-state that was far south of his. He shook him awake and he woke up with a start.

"What the ..." he said, only for Arstarte to put a finger to his lips. He reached for Cadmus' collar and as quietly as he could, he sent a surge through and broke it with a crunch that sounded a bit too loud for his liking.

Cadmus removed his collar, smiled, and nodded. He then checked the hallway, followed by Cadmus, and snuck out. Before he could do anything, he went to the main door that blocked the two prison cells from the main hallway. When he forced the door open, he was greeted by an empty guard station and flashing red lights. He looked back into the hallway and saw a security camera. No doubt the alarm had been triggered. He went to the hallway and to the next set of cells.

"Stop."

He turned to his left.

A group of men in padded black armour were holding advanced-looking rifles and pointing at him.

He sneered as they stood there. Raising his hand, he sent a blast of energy down the hallway. A couple of men managed to pull the trigger. Heavy bullets flew past him, but the men themselves were sent flying down the hallway as the bullets impacted the hallway concrete with a loud bang. He then smashed open the door as Cadmus ran around the corner, sending an energy blast down the right-hand side of the hallway, knocking back a couple of soldiers running towards them.

*****

Sylvia jumped off her bed when her door smashed in.

Before she could speak, in came the blond-haired man from before, who grabbed her collar and snapped it with a flick.

"Come, you're free and can use your powers. We're leaving."

He then rushed out of her door and to the next cell. She grabbed her neck, as it felt kind of odd not wearing her collar. She'd had it on for so long and rather got to use it. She was still confused about what was happening.

A blonde woman emerged from the destroyed cell and followed the blonde man. Still confused, she stepped out of her cell. Strangely enough, she was free but she didn't want to leave. She was tempted to return to her cell and wait for this to all be over.

However, she froze when she saw Althenia down one of the hallways, holding her rifle and taking cover in the corner.

She turned towards the escapees.

There was now a red-haired man with the blonde woman and man, and they were arguing about the way out. Sylvia heard a loud crack and recognized the sound as the firing of a plasma rifle. It was followed by a blue flash.

She was part of an escape.

She leaned against the wall, panicking. A scream echoed in the hallway.

Althenia had managed to hit the blond-haired woman, who clutched her shoulder. She collapsed on the floor in pain, and the smell of burnt flesh filled Sylvia's nose. The red-haired man sent a shockwave down the hallway as Althenia ducked back, missing the force of the shockwave.

The blond-haired man ran towards Althenia.

"Follow me."

He then grabbed Sylvia's arm and she ran with him to the corner where Althenia was hiding. Althenia popped her head out again as the blonde-haired man sent a shockwave straight to her, sending her flying back and hitting the walls with a sickening crunch.

Sylvia rushed to her in horror, as the escapees rushed past her.

"Good idea, take their gun," she heard the other man say, who then focused on the metal door.

She looked at Althenia, fearing the worst.

She touched her neck and found a pulse. It was weak but there. Her eyes fell on the plasma rifle.

She picked it up slowly, as anger washed over her and aimed it at the red-haired man's back. By now, the second blond-haired man who was escaping had managed to pry open the door only to be greeted by a hail of bullets and plasma bolts, which hit the shield set up by the red-haired man. Sylvia pulled the trigger, sending a shock of plasma into the man's back and causing him to collapse.

"Hey!" shouted the woman.

The rifle was ripped from her hands and smashed into the wall.

Sylvia turned to the woman and channelled all her anger. She sent the blonde woman flying through the hallway as she crashed into the floor with a sickening crunch.

The blond man slammed the metal door shut, cutting off the firing humans, and turned to her, sending a blast of energy her way. Sylvia instinctively put up a mental shield, which took most of the force, but did knock her off her feet. She hit the floor with a thud but didn't feel any pain as adrenaline was rushing through her body.

She ran forward and placed herself in front of Althenia.

Understanding flooded the blonde man's face.

"So that is your game, fallen in love with a human have you?" he said, in disgust.

Sylvia noticed Althenia had put on a pistol holster which looked like it had a pistol ready, no doubt put on during the alert.

The man sent another blast of energy which again was barely blocked by another mental shield.

She knew that he'd focus on Althenia knowing that she was her weak spot. She reached down and grabbed the pistol. She heard more gunshots as some troops from the other hallway fired at him, but the blond man easily deflected the shots.

It did give him something else to focus on as she rolled over again and pointed the pistol straight up and pulled the trigger a couple of times. One shot was deflected, but another went through straight into his jaw and travelled straight up into his head, sending blood and gore out of the top of his head.

He then fell to his knees as she heard soldiers running down the hallway. She dropped the pistol and tried to sit up, but could not. She looked to the other side and saw one of the soldiers in some sort of black battle armour look at her, his gun at the ready but not pointing directly at her. She felt exhausted and a bit sick and dropped the pistol. She dragged herself back to Althenia.

A woman in battle armour with a small red cross on the right-hand side of her chest kneeling down next to her, taking a quick pulse reading and a quick check over the unconscious body.

"Get a stretcher," she shouted. "Pulse is stable, but needs an x-ray."

She then moved on to Sylvia and prodded her.

"Is Althenia going to be okay?" gasped Sylvia.

"She will be fine, darling. We will do our best, and she is made of strong stuff."

Before Sylvia could ask any more questions, she shouted to the soldier beside her.

"Shock, bring me a blanket," she ordered, before gently pushing Sylvia to the floor, "Just relax and try to breathe."

*****

General Oliver looked at the reports one more time.

It had been difficult to find out what happened, and an investigation was ongoing. The alert woke him and he rushed to his office, knowing what he had to do in case they got out of the base. Now it was time to answer to the field marshal.

He then turned on the screen and stood by his chair. The screen flickered on, and on it was the face of Field Marshal Morgan, who was sitting in his own meeting room.

"Good morning, general, you may sit."

"Thank you, and morning to you, sir."

He then took the seat.

"So, general, what is the damage?"

General Oliver flipped through the pages of the report.

"Well, currently one dead overlord and one in critical condition, no sensitive equipment damaged, and to be frank, we got off lightly."

Marshal Morgan nodded.

"I see, and the overlord, Sylvia, she was apparently key in this?" he asked, confused.

"Yes, sir. She managed to disarm the escaped female and killed one of the escaped males, then was cooperative after the area was secured," he replied.

He hadn't believed it himself until he checked the camera footage.

The field marshal leaned back in his padded leather chair and steepled his fingers. "Strange ally. Interesting. That means you currently have about four overlords that you can use, including Sylvia, correct?"

"Yes, sir.".

"So, do we know how he got out?" asked Field Marshal Morgan.

"Well," theorized General Oliver, "There was a strange signal before he disconnected from the first test. A very strange energy surge, and when we managed to check the collar, we found a load of blown capacitors that meant the detection electronics weren't working. From there, he managed to remove it using a metal tray."

"Okay," said the field marshal. "What new security measures are in place then?"

"Well when the energy signature is detected, we will replace all collars immediately and begin lockdown."

"Fair enough. Another question: Would you be able to operate on three overlords?"

The general wondered what the plan was. No doubt the field marshal was working towards something.

"We currently have two machines, so we should be okay."

"Good," replied the field marshal, still leaning back in his chair, "As you know, this Totec character has made himself known and it looks like he might be headed towards our allied overlord that contacted us. Despite the Navy's best effort, he is still getting a load of reinforcements and any battle with him is going to be a mess."

Field Marshal Morgan leaned forward until his face filled the entire screen.

"As, no doubt you have seen, the overlord powers can easily sway a battle. We have had a request for reinforcements to the allied city-state, and command was up in the air." He paused for a moment and then continued, "The fact that Sylvia fought in our corner and the fact that the city-state is in a damn good defensive position with heavy walls means we have a better chance, especially if we can get some Anti Air artillery setup." He paused again, making sure his words sunk in. "Command also wants you to send Althenia along with Sylvia to the city as well."

General Oliver looked at him thoughtfully for a second before answering.

"Of course, sir. I will make the arrangements."

He then paused for a second and Field Marshal Morgan gave him a knowing look.

"Permission to speak freely," he asked, and continued when the Marshal nodded, "Well, sir, this has been one incident where she has been proven trustworthy, and that city is still managed by an alien overlord, although very well."

The field marshal nodded. "Your concerns are noted and have been raised before, but we need to take the risk. The possibility of defeating Totec in a simple open battle is not great. This way we are giving ourselves all the advantages and, to be frank, we need them."

The general leaned back.

"Understood, sir."

"Good," replied the field marshal, "Godspeed. Morgan out."

As the screen blanked out, General Oliver sat back in his chair for a moment, taking it all in. It didn't help that it was late in the day and he was tired.

*****

Rena stretched out. Her leg was still in a cast and she had to deal with the odd bout of itching, but she had just returned from a tour of the defences currently being set up and had a few titbits to add, but was happy with the progress.

Today, she wore a pair of new grey slacks with a simple grey shirt. It seemed to be the standard uniform for the city-state and was simple to make and not as engineered as the USF uniform. There were no pockets besides the ones in the pants.

She looked at the screen once more. She heard movement behind her. Moments later, a cup of coffee was placed next to her keyboard.

It was Natalie being her usual bashful self. Despite sharing the office, she had not spoken much except when she offered to make a cup of coffee. Natalie was currently wearing a knee-high black skirt with stockings and a simple black shirt with the same v-neck collar.

"How are the defences?" asked Natalie.

Rena could tell the girl was a little worried about everything going on and she could understand that. To be honest, so was she.

"Good, that trench in front of the wall is going to give any attacker a lot of hassle," she replied, in what she hoped was a comforting tone.

Natalie smile and sat down with her own cup of coffee. Rena took a sip.

"Thanks, Natalie. Very good, as always."

Natalie blushed.

"So, you are quite close to Lucinda?"

"Yes, she found me in one of the old city wastes when I was a young girl. I don't remember much from that time. I was about six. Lucinda gave me a home and fed me. A year later, I was fostered by an elderly couple who loved me like their own daughter, as they couldn't have children." She paused for a moment, taking a deep breath before continuing, "But Papa passed when I was twenty-one, and Mama when I was twenty-two. I think she died of a broken heart. Anyway, I was quite technical and found myself working close to Lucinda who, to be frank, I had a crush on. Things grew from there. What about you?"

Rena paused for a moment and smiled to herself.

"It was the USF, to be honest. My father was a soldier, spent a lot of time in the field, and was killed when I was young. Then my mother was an administrator and raised me till I was old enough to enter the academy. She passed away a year or so ago."

"Sorry to hear that," said Natalie with a touch of concern.

"Don't worry about it, your story sounds more tragic, to be honest," replied Rena.

"Well," shrugged Natalie, "It has been a lot better since I met Lucinda. I don't really remember a time before I met her."

Natalie looked thoughtful for a second.

"I do have dreams of a strange place, some sort of cold and sterile lab."

She then shrugged her shoulders. Rena took a sip of her delicious coffee. Truth be told, it was not that unusual to find a child alone. There were many uncontacted settlements out there, some from survivalist and religious communities that had collapsed, or their parents had died.

Rena then noticed a flashing icon on her screen. It was a message from her former boss. She read it to herself. It was good news indeed, and her heart skipped a little. The USF had decided to help and would be sending reinforcements. She turned to Natalie.

"Good news. We're getting help."

Natalie shot up, spilling some of her coffee.

"Really?"

Rena nodded, as she printed the message and grabbed the copy.

"I better get this to Lucinda as soon as I can," she replied.

But Natalie shook her head.

"She's on the other side of the city inspecting the rations. You would have to catch the light rail that runs along the walls. Something that would be difficult with your leg. You could use a phone, I suppose, but they are still having issues with line quality." Natalie stood up. "I am meeting her up for lunch, though, so let me take it for you."

"Okay, and thank you," replied Rena, handing her the paper.

As she held the paper, Natalie then said, "Speaking of food, do you want to join me and Lucinda for dinner tonight in the castle?"

Rena paused for a second, but figured why not?

"Sure," she replied.

Natalie then grabbed her purse and left the office in a merry mood, happy to help. Rena was excited she would at least be able to catch up with fellow USF personnel.

*****

The shot was very loud. It rang in her ears like a bell, and the blond-haired man's eyes bored into her soul, judging her and damning her as he collapsed, blood flowing down the hallway

Sylvia awoke with a start to find she was in a hospital bed. Next to her was Althenia. She looked at her and felt a range of emotions hit her. She tried to remember the last thing after the shooting like a gushing torrent. Sylvia tried to run, but her legs were immobile. She heard a cry for help. It sounded like Althenia. The blood got higher and higher before she could find Althenia. It was up to her neck, and she tried to swim, but the blood was thick and it was dragging her down. She was led to the hospital and put in a bed next to Althenia, who was still unconscious.

"How long have I been out?" she asked, in a groggy voice.

"About eight hours. You've been in shock, and I can understand why."

Sylvia then put her hand up and felt her collar had been put back on, and for some reason felt safer.

"Sorry, orders," replied Althenia, answering her unanswered question.

"That's fine, I understand. I think I may have killed someone," said Sylvia, rather mournfully as she lay down in the bed and stared up at the cold, white ceiling.

Althenia put her hand on Sylvia's shoulder reassuringly. "Yes, you did what you had to do, but in the process, you saved many lives."

"I suppose so," replied Sylvia, not sounding too convinced.

She then sat up and pulled Althenia into a hug. Althenia put her arms around her and returned the hug. After a couple of minutes, Sylvia let go, feeling a lot better. She moved back but found herself in Althenia's arms and staring deep into Althenia's violet eyes. A strange feeling overcame her as she looked into her eyes.

She leaned in as Althenia looked at her and said,

"I am very proud of you."

Sylvia's heart skipped a beat, and she smiled and leaned in even closer, focusing on Althenia's red lips, which she gently touched with her own, sending a spark of passion through Sylvia's body.

The kiss was short and sweet as Althenia gently pulled away.

Althenia smiled at her.

"Now may not be the best time. You're still in shock. Rest for the moment."

Althenia then pulled Sylvia into a hug that helped her confirm all would be okay. Sylvia let go and laid back down on the bed, still holding Althenia's hand.

"I have some news," said Althenia. "We have an allied city state down in Virginia which is about to be attacked and you and I are to be deployed there." Althenia paused for a second. "Central command will let you use your powers to help us if you are willing?"

Sylvia thought for a second.

"You'll be with me?"

"Yes," Althenia replied simply.

Sylvia squeezed her hand in thanks and turned over and looked into Althenia's eyes again.

"Can I just say your ancestor did excellent genetic work."

Althenia blushed.

*****

It was rough marching, thought Eztli to himself, but at least he was not carrying the supplies, like the poor Tlacotin. Especially given the area they were marching through. Most of it was swampland which was broken up by an old road or odd dry grass patch. He was a Tlamemeh and held the symbol of his rank, a wooden crossbow and a bandolier which had the crossbow bolts.

He also wore a simple leather tunic as armour, as well as an old pair of pants and a handwoven shirt. He was hoping to prove himself in combat. He was only sixteen years old, a young boy with light brown skin, brown eyes, and black hair.

When lord Totec called for warriors, he required one male from every household and about a quarter of the servants, a heavy tithe, but when lord Totec made demands, they had no choice but to obey.

He was travelling with a group of men, about twenty in total, all from his village or local area. They were part of a large column of men, most of them split up and led by their Cuextecatl. Leading them was the local lord, a Cuextecatl who rode his own horse and carried one of the old rifles from the time before the gods. He wore a fine, simple, metal breastplate that had bandoliers of ammunition for the rifle. Behind them were all the servants, burdened with their supplies as they walked. They sang a song praising the great lord Totec and saying how they would sweep all his enemies out of the way.

"Eztil."

It was his childhood friend, Xipil, a tall lad with light brown skin, blond hair, and brown eyes. He too was wearing the simple leather armour with a wooden crossbow strapped to his back.

"How goes it, Xipil, you in good spirits?" he said.

"Yes," replied Xipil. "My father didn't want me to go, but I was the only son."

"Why?" asked Eztil, confused, "This is a great opportunity to earn fame and wealth."

"Definitely. He was just worried and said that being a warrior is not all glory."

Eztil shook his head, in disbelief.

"How can we lose? We have Totec marching with us, his throne carried by a hundred slaves. And the priests performed all rituals correctly, as well as all, the great Otontin Totec. Most loyal warriors and the mindless ones with their god-given machines."

"Indeed, victory is assured."

The march started to slow down, and suddenly the man in front stopped.

"What's going on?" asked Xipil, peering over the shoulders of the man in front of him.

"Not too sure." Eztil shrugged. "We still have four hours of daylight left to march before camp."

Then, as if on cue, a litter carried by two slaves passed them and stopped in front of their local lord, who climbed down from his horse and poked his head behind the curtain.

After a quick conversation, he turned to his men.

"A group of supply carts have gotten stuck in the swamp behind us. They want to halt the line for the moment, so take five."

As the crowd muttered and dispersed, Xipil sat down, followed by Eztil. He was personally not surprised. The terrain did not make travel easy, and he was glad for the break.

"Have you seen the siege cannons? I would not be surprised if they are stuck."

Xipil had seen them, massive wooden A-frames, carts with six heavy wooden wheels, each carrying a massive metal cannon that, using Totec magic, could launch massive boulders at any fortification.

"I would not be surprised if it was. Each cannon requires about twenty slaves to move and that is on flat terrain, but they are a pain now. Yet we'll be happy for them once they are smashing the enemy."

"True," agreed Eztil as he pulled out a sugar cane stick. He broke off a piece and handed it to Xipil, who took it and started chewing.

*****

"It was good wine," thought Rena, as she accepted another glass from Natalie.

Ditching her grey trousers and shirt, Rena wore a short, simple, black dress while Natalie dressed in red. Lucinda was there as well, sitting on the couch next to her. She was wearing a low-cut black dress.

The room was nice, a simple lounge with two black leather sofas pushed into the corner, beside each other. In the middle was a wooden coffee table with a couple of books laid about.

Rena suspected that Natalie had a thing for her, and to be honest, she was quite cute. Lucinda however, was beautiful in a regal way. Rena wondered about their relationship. They definitely acted like a couple, but Natalie was sending her quite strong signals.

Part of her still pined for Althenia, but deep down she knew there was no hope left for them. There had been no communication at all. She hoped that Althenia didn't get the message, because if she did, then that meant her thoughts of Rena had changed.

"Had she moved on already?"

Rena took another sip of her wine and listened to the conversation.

Natalie was speaking.

"I'm just thankful the servers and systems we've set up are working okay. Communication with ACS systems is becoming more and more erratic."

"God, Natalie, you are such a computer nerd," teased Lucinda, as she rolled her eyes.

"You may be the ruler of this city-state, but I will defend poor Natalie here," Rena added, in mock outrage.

Natalie laughed and leaned into her.

"My hero."

Lucinda stood up and leaned over Rena.

"Oh, and what are you going to do about it?"

Rena looked into Natalie's eyes, hoping for a response or help, but got none. She then looked at Lucinda, who leaned in closer to her. Rena noticed her red eyes and caught the scent of her subtle perfume. She looked at Lucinda's features. Part of her felt intimidated by her height and part of her felt elated.

Maybe it was the wine, but when she saw Lucinda's red ruby lips, she could not help herself.

This," she whispered, pressing her lips on hers.

Lucinda returned the kiss with a passion Rena had not felt in ages. After what seemed way too short a time, the kiss ended, and Lucinda pulled away.

Reality dawned.

"I'm sorry," said Rena, as she stood up in panic, "I'm not sure if you and Natalie are an item, and I don't want to lose you as friends."

Natalie stood up and took her hand.

"Yes we're an item, but you're welcome to join us."

Natalie pulled her in and they kissed until a shiver flowed down her spine. Lucinda watched the scene with a smile on her face.

*****

"It was bad," thought General Oliver, as he observed the alien ship.

Provided that it was losing orbit, Lucinda had gotten this right, but what she got wrong was the damage it would cause. She had underestimated it. It would take about nine months to crash into the planet. And the damage it would cause would be globally catastrophic. It would cause a nuclear winter for five years with all the dust and debris thrown into the air by the impact.

To make his day worse, the red-headed overlord had finally succumbed to his wounds and died last night.

Although nine months sounded like a long time, the problem was there were no vehicles capable of reaching the spaceship on Earth, but there were a couple on Mars. The only issue was that Mars was not in the best alignment. It would take three hundred days to get to Earth.

They could transport it piece by piece through the wormhole, but that would take a couple of months. And then they'd have to use a launch pad, which could be destroyed by the aliens.

But it was the best course of action.

Large segments of the craft were now being transported through. But they needed a place to launch the craft. There were talks about construction of this place in England, but this meant that more fuel would be needed for the launch.

The intercom buzzed.

"Yes?" he said.

"Sorry, sir," said his secretary. "I have Doctor Lowe here, who's rather excited, and wishes to speak to you."

The general sighed internally.

It was like this every time the doctor had a brilliant plan, but to give the man credit, sometimes his plans were quite good.

"Send him in," he said.

His door opened, and in rushed the doctor

"What is it, doctor?" he asked, as he gestured to one of the empty seats.

The doctor sat down on the couch in the corner of the room.

"Sorry, general, I was looking at the logs during the escape and found a strange electromagnetic radiation signal from the wormhole generator. This signal appeared when we first launched a session and began a connection to another wormhole," explained Dr Lowe, as he bounced on his seat, "All of the subjects described a strange room that they entered. We suspected it was one of the quirks of wormhole mechanics, but then we caught another signal when the overlord blew his collar."

Dr Lowe drew a deep breath as his excitement brimmed over.

"I suspect there is a wormhole generator on the ship itself. So we tried a connection while all other known wormhole generator signals were shut down, and we managed to get the same signal."

The general leaned back in his chair.

"So what you're saying is besides Point Nemo, the generator on Mars and the two Psychitron generators, there is in fact another wormhole generator out there?"

"Well, yes," quipped the doctor in a rather excited tone, "One in the local solar system at least, and it uses the same range of signals that we use which, to be honest, is not surprising as we reversed engineered the technology from the aliens. There have been suspicions about wormholes outside the solar system, but that has been a theory for the moment. I mean Doctor Alton's paper on why we've not picked up the other wormholes is quite illuminating."

"Thank you, doctor," interrupted General Oliver, not keen to get a full lecture in wormhole physics. He'd gotten enough lectures from his bosses already.

The general drummed his fingers together.

"Okay, if it's on the spaceship then it might be worth investigating. What do you need?"

"I would like to go to Point Nemo and attempt to create a connection with the unknown wormhole, after which I'll send a probe through to see what we connect to."

The general leaned back.

"Fair enough. Get a paper together and I'll speak to Field Marshal Morgan. I suppose, given the time it's going to take to move our spaceship, a day missed will not be too bad."

"Thank you, general," replied the doctor.

"Anything else?" asked the general.

The doctor shook his head, got up, and left the room.

"Well, that's an interesting development," he thought to himself as he started to type up his report.

*****

The smell of coffee wafted into the room.

Rena opened her eyes and felt a hand resting on her chest. It was Natalie, who was fast asleep beside her.

Memories of last night started coming back to her. It was an interesting night, the wine had flowed, and, well, it had gotten a bit out of hand. Next to her bed was a chair, and there sat Lucinda with a cup of coffee in her hand.

She smirked at Rena.

"Sorry, just admiring my harem," Lucinda said, in a rather wicked tone. She then pointed to a mug on the bedside table. "Coffee for you,"

"Thank you. When did you wake up?"

Lucinda smiled.

"Ages ago. The joy of my alien heritage, I don't need much sleep." Lucinda tried to move Natalie's arm only to get a garbled mumble from her. "Don't worry about sleepy head, she could sleep through a war."

After a bit of awkward movement, Rena sat upright on the bed and started to sip her coffee as Lucinda sat back in her chair.

"All okay?" she asked.

"Yes, it was an experience, and I've never done anything like that, it's just ..."

Lucinda leaned forward.

"What is it?"

Rena let out a sigh.

"I thought I had a girlfriend back home, but I have not heard from her since I was captured, and I wonder if I just cheated on her?"

Lucinda got up and sat on the side of the bed. She put her hand on Rena's knee.

"From what I've seen, humanity has made a lot of sacrifices to survive. To be honest, from what I've seen from the message, you may as well have passed away if you were compromised."

She paused for a moment and put her hand on Rena's back.

"Just remember you have a home here, and we will support you."

Lucinda then ran her hand down Rena's back, sending a shiver down her spine.

*****

It was quiet in the range today. Althenia was not surprised.

The sun had set and stars were glimmering in the sky, so most people were resting. Althenia however had a job to do. She wanted to get Sylvia comfortable with firearms. And since they were due on the transport sub tomorrow morning, they had time.

Sylvia still wore her collar but had been given an advanced military uniform like hers—a sleek body form suit with pockets for all their equipment. Normally this uniform was worn with battle armour.

The range itself was a simple, concrete shell with a couple of benches set up. There was a small automatic targeting system that went off at least a hundred meters into the rock. She handed Sylvia a holster.

"First, a word about gun safety," she began, as Sylvia strapped the holster on, "Before I give you your pistol, never point your gun at something you do not intend to shoot, and always assume that it is loaded. Understood?"

Sylvia nodded.

Althenia walked to the table in the room that had a pistol and rifle on it. She picked up the pistol and showed it to Sylvia.

"This is the standard sidearm of the special forces, a simple semi-automatic pistol."

She then pressed a small catch on the side and pulled out an empty ammo clip.

"Ammo clips, this is where you put in the bullets, and it can carry fifteen. The reason it's called a semi-automatic is because when you shoot once, it reloads automatically, enabling you to shoot again."

Althenia pointed to the top of the gun.

"This is your iron sites, you can use these to aim, just make sure to line them up."

She handed the pistol to Sylvia, who took it very carefully. Althenia passed the bullets to her and watched over as Sylvia removed the clip and slotted the bullets in.

She aimed at a target down the range with one hand. Althenia smiled.

"Hold on, you're not going to get a good shot that way."

She stepped behind Sylvia and put her other hand on the pistol, and slightly adjusted her posture, making sure she was standing correctly. "Now," she said, "you have a lot better control of the gun, and will be able to handle the kickback, so squeeze the trigger, do not pull."

Sylvia let out a shot that hit the target on the bottom left.

"Good," said Althenia. "Take another couple shots and remember safety first. Accuracy will come with time."

Sylvia smiled at her and pulled the trigger again, and a couple of more times, with one or two bullets landing on the circle. She then put the gun down on the table once all shots had been fired.

Althenia picked up the rifle.

"This is the mark four plasma rifle and unlike the pistol, it doesn't use normal ammo but a small thorium battery that is stored in this cartridge."

She pressed a small switch on the side and out popped the bottom part of the rifle, just below the trigger. She handed it to Sylvia, who turned it over in her hand before putting it back on the table.

Althenia slotted the cartridge into the rifle with practised ease. She then pointed to another group of switches on the side.

"This is safety, and this is power. At the weakest power point, the rifle can cause severe burns and stop an unarmoured human. This means you have a hundred and twenty shots with a full battery."

Althenia then flicked the switch up.

"At the second setting, it can cause extensive damage to one of the unshielded alien soldiers and kill a human, but you have about eighty shots on a full charge."

She flicked it up one more time.

"The final setting can knock out a shielded alien. I use this setting for snipers. It has only forty shots."

"Okay, that makes sense," replied Sylvia.

Althenia pointed to another switch on the gun.

"This sets the firing rate."

She then handed the rifle to Sylvia, whose hands drooped under the unexpected weight.

"Quite heavy," mused Sylvia.

"It could be worse," shrugged Althenia, "You could be given an old shoulder buster."

"Shoulder buster?" asked Sylvia.

"Yes, a heavy rifle that fires a cartridge that can knock out the alien soldier shields, but it's heavy and has a kick like a mule, hence the nickname. Fortunately, most are being phased out for the mark four, but now they're given out to special forces while production is ramped up." She pushed a new button, and another target showed up again.

Sylvia got into the firing position, and Althenia checked her rifle and posture.

"Remember, match up the iron sites and squeeze the trigger."

Sylvia made sure the rifle was on her shoulder comfortably and then squeezed the trigger. She hit the target square in the middle.

"Good" Althenia smiled.

She then pressed a button on the side of the rifle, and a scope popped up from the top of the rifle where the iron sites were. She pressed another button on the control panel, and the forty-meter target folded away to the side and an eighty-meter target appeared. "Take an aim down the scope and match up the sites to the target and squeeze the trigger. A note here: If it was an old shoulder buster, then move your eye back from the scope, as the kickback can cause the scope to slam into your eye."

Sylvia again took aim and squeezed the trigger. A blue bolt shot out, hitting the side of the target.

"Good shot," commended Althenia, patting her back, "We have an hour or so. Do you want to fire a few more?"

"Yes, please," replied Sylvia, "but could you check my posture again?"

"Sure," Althenia replied with a smile.

*****

As another large sub slowly approached the docks, Graham had to admit he was impressed by the size of the operation. The USF had found it easier to use sea lanes, especially since the overlords had a habit of ignoring islands, thus making them an ideal place to house large segments of the free population.

An initial team had come on land from up north, led by Colonel Thompson.

He brought a couple of trucks and massive vehicles called AA artillery and was in the process of getting the dockland in the old city of Portsmouth active again. It took hard work, but he'd managed it with the help of his and Graham's men. Now they had begun the task of unloading, shipping, and moving the supplies onto the Virginia city-state.

"Good god, I didn't know they made submarines so big," he said to the colonel.

"Yes," droned the colonel, as he secured his hat over his blond hair, "Basically we took two subs and changed the front so it could flow through the water easier. They're called the Liberty Class, named after the cargo ships built during World War Two."

The front entrance had a forklift going in and out, transporting heavy boxes from the front while a crane unloaded crates from the cargo hatch on top of the submarine. After another box came out, a large plasma tank rolled out after him, followed by another. Graham was mildly disappointed that there were only two. They were impressive machines, but he'd seen the size of the enemy's. He hoped more would be coming.

"Impressive machines," marvelled Graham, "But we would need more than two."

The colonel nodded.

"Yeah, I read the reports. Another forty will arrive before the battle does. We also have another hundred relic tanks coming in as well. But these babies are so old that some still use diesel engines. I wish we could say there was more, but we've only recently ramped up amour production."

It had been confirmed that the enemy was in fact heading toward them, and it gave Graham plenty of cause to be concerned. He admitted he felt better with the USF support, but the logistics had turned into a bit of a nightmare.

"Diesel," he thought to himself, *"Where am I going to get diesel?"*

All vehicles that ran in the city, like ambulances or fire services, used the alien battery system meant for the hover tanks and the electrical rail ran using the central power plant that used a nuclear reactor.

A loud explosion shook the docks.

He looked up and saw the fireball in the sky. The AA artillery platform had fired its lasers, sending a small explosion of debris into the air.

That was the second flyer of the morning. The battle had started already and he strongly suspected ACS had cut them off, as communication on any ACS system had ceased.

*****

As Rena looked at the screen, she felt somewhat okay, but still confused at what happened last night, along with a small amount of guilt.

She wondered if she should write a letter to Althenia, but there was little hope that it would make it to her. The private postal service was a thing of legend now.

Natalie stood up again, no doubt to make herself another cup of coffee. If she had one addiction, it would be coffee, and Rena was going down the same road. It was one of the benefits of working in the same office—Natalie always was making one, and Rena could not say no.

When Rena had inquired about their coffee and sugar, Natalie explained that it was made on their own specialised farms. Thanks to the reactor and a little alien genetic engineering, the city grew enough food to feed itself. So, in the case of a siege, this meant they would not starve at the very least, and thanks to a desalination plant and underground pipeline to the sea, they would not die of thirst as well.

So far, the communication from the USF had just been mostly spreadsheets of the equipment and personnel they were sending, but this message looked different.

She read it and froze in shock. Typing fast, she printed out the message and turned to Natalie.

"I think you better come with me, we have to go and see Lucinda," she said, jumping up from her seat and running to the hallway.

She stopped and knocked on the door, as Natalie stopped behind her.

"Enter."

Rena and Natalie entered the room.

"I'm sorry for the interruption," said Rena, walking up to her desk.

Lucinda looked at her.

"No worry. What's going on?"

She held the paper out to Lucinda.

"They're sending an overlord."

Lucinda looked at her, confused.

"Really?"

"Yes, you know the one that was captured? Apparently, they're sending her along with Althenia." She paused for a second, then said, "The girl that I spoke to you about."

She sat down next to Natalia, who put her arm around her to comfort her. She took in a breath and tried to remain professional, but many different feelings flowed through her mind.

"From the message, she proved her loyalty to the USF after stopping an escape attempt, so with her powers, hopefully, it'll help."

"I see," replied Lucinda. "Do you need some time?"

"No," sighed Rena, "We need to set up for the battle, and we cannot afford any delays."

Lucinda looked at her sceptically for a moment, but then said, "Okay, but if you need anything, just let me or Natalie know."

"Will do."

*****

"The submarine journey had not been great," thought Sylvia to herself.

It had been cramped and she was not even a prisoner this time, but felt like one trapped in the claustrophobic metal hallways and rooms of the sub. She was glad when she felt the submarine dock and the docking bay open.

She grabbed her small bag and stepped out of the metal ramp and onto the dock, enjoying the feeling of sunshine on her uniform. Most of the infantry was coming down from the north, but a few more troops had been sent with them, and they too were disembarking along with more tanks and a rather massive vehicle called the Psychitron.

Althenia told her it was what they used to block the psychic signal. She gave it a wide berth and looked at the other soldiers. She noticed that quite a few of the special forces had pointed ears as well. Most had kept her at a safe distance and were polite but reserved. She understood; she was the enemy.

On the bright side, she spent most of the time with Althenia.

The docks were a busy loading and unloading area, as men patrolled with guns.

They got into a convoy which drove to the city-state. A heavy tank led the way while a couple of heavy-looking trucks drove along either side.

Inside the convoy, there were two men sitting with plasma rifles. She sat on the other side with Althenia, as they travelled on a broken tarmac. The engines were so loud that it made talking impossible, so instead, Sylvia looked out the window. They passed through ruined villages and overgrown fields until they reached a massive stone wall.

On the outside, some men were digging while others set up various devices and equipment. When the metal gates were opened and the vehicles entered, the scenery shifted. Here, the buildings were tall and better maintained. She spotted a railway between the buildings and better-paved roads. The vehicle traffic increased, and she even saw smaller pickups driving around.

The convoy carried on, and she noticed that some roads had been blocked off. Here and there, she could see people going about their business. They drove to the other end of the city where there was a large castle made of stone, that was heavily guarded.

"An overlord lives here," Sylvia mused.

Men and women, wearing the same uniforms, loaded and unloaded supplies. The convoy slowed to a stop, and a black man with short grey hair and a worn-out face approached them.

"We just got a message that you were on the way. My name is Graham, and Lucinda wishes to see you as soon as possible."

Althenia stuck out her hand and Graham took it.

"Nice to meet you, Graham. Of course, please lead the way."

He led them to the large, stone building. One of the guards opened the main door and they walked into a beautiful castle. Their footsteps echoed as they walked down a hallway and to a lift. After the lift ride, and a couple more hallways, they stopped at a large, ornate, wooden door.

Graham opened the door and they followed him in.

A rather elegant woman with long black hair and red eyes that matched her red dress, got up from her desk and walked over to them.

"Hello, I'm Lucinda, leader of this city."

Althenia shook her hands.

"Althenia honoured to meet you," she introduced, before gesturing to Sylvia, "And this is Sylvia."

They shook hands, and Syliva thought she felt a tinge of power even though she was still wearing her collar.

"Excellent to meet you, but before you take a seat, I have someone I need you to meet."

As if on cue, a woman entered with short blond hair and walked with a crutch. It took Sylvia a second before she realised that it was her old servant, Rena.

She looked at Althenia, who stood, frozen in shock. Moments later, she rushed over to Rena and pulled her into a hug. When they pulled apart, Rena took Althenia's face in her hands and wiped the tears that flowed from Althenia's eyes.

"I've never seen you cry, Althenia, I am so sorry."

Sylvia looked on, confused. She'd never seen Althenia so vulnerable, and though part of her was happy Rena was still alive, another part felt sad for what she lost.

She touched her collar subconsciously.

*****

Althenia took a couple of deep breaths.

She never imagined Rena could be alive and suddenly there she was in front of her. She couldn't hold back her emotions, and when Rena apologised, she just held her tighter.

"You are alive!" she croaked, "What happened?"

Rena smiled.

"I was captured by a bad overlord, and almost lost my leg, but Lucinda here managed to get me out and took care of me. I sent you a message, didn't you get it?"

Althenia cupped Rena's face and shook her head with tears still in her eyes. She then hugged Rena again.

"I never got the message, I even lit a candle for you."

"There is much to talk about," Rena said in a somewhat concerned tone, but before Althenia had a chance to reply, there was an urgent knock at the door.

"I thought I gave instructions not to be disturbed," mumbled Lucinda as she approached the door, "This better be good."

She opened the door, and it was Graham.

"I'm very sorry, ma'am, but I'm afraid we've found one of Totec's advanced scouting parties."

"Great," said Lucinda, in a sarcastic tone. "You better come in and tell us exactly what he saw."

She let Graham in and closed the door as Rena took a seat on the L-shaped couch in front of Lucinda's desk. Sylvia took a seat opposite, and Althenia sat next to Rena as Graham got on the spare chair and Lucinda got behind her desk.

"We've sent out a few patrols as Totec is about a two days march from us, and one of our patrols stumbled across a small camp that was not used by us, so my team waited for a couple of hours and watched the camp from a distance."

He paused for a second.

"When it got dark, three men returned back to the camp who we didn't recognize, so we decided to capture them for questioning. My men waited another couple of hours when there was just one person, and watched, and they seemed to be nodding off. They managed to sneak up on the guard and captured him, but one of his colleagues had gotten up to relieve himself and saw my men capturing his comrade. He shouted out a warning and started to flee, followed by the one remaining scout. Currently, the prisoner has been escorted back, but he's not saying much besides going on about the great Totec."

Lucinda sighed loudly.

"Great," she said, even more sarcastically. "So I assume that they'll be on a war footing as soon as they arrive. Graham, make sure we're ready for when they do knock on the front gate."

She then turned to Althenia.

"Graham will show you and Sylvia the current defences. Any advice offered will be helpful, and when you're done, I'll show you to your quarters for tonight."

"Thank you."

*****

To say she felt unsure was an understatement. She hadn't been expecting that reaction from Althenia, but she noticed the look she got from Sylvia was a look of sorrow.

"Had she developed something for Althenia as well?"

She wanted to say something, but couldn't find the courage. She had the easy excuse that there was a battle and they needed to focus on that. She stayed back with Lucinda after the meeting while Althenia and Sylvia went back to their quarters.

Natalie entered the room, once it was just the two of them.

"Well?" said Lucinda, looking at Rena.

She shrugged.

"I'm not sure what to say to her. Honestly, her reaction was unexpected. She is normally quite reserved and cold."

"The question is, do you still have feelings for her?" continued Lucinda, as she pointed to Rena.

Rena felt lost and confused.

"I can tell from your indecisiveness you're not too sure. If you still do, then that's okay, but you need to be honest with her. We have a battle to focus on first, so you should be able to avoid her for a day at least while you think things through, and to be frank, that does take higher priority. No good being star-crossed lovers if we're all dead."

"I understand. I'm just sorry to put you and Natalie through this, especially after what we shared."

Lucinda gave her a warm smile while Natalie squeezed her hand.

"Maybe we moved too fast and some blame lies with us, but it was fun."

She then paused for a moment and frowned.

"If you want to make it up to us, then please make sure you're in the bunker when the battle starts and if the worst comes to worst, you are to take Natalie and head to a safe territory. I will follow up as soon as I can, but please make sure Natalie and you are safe. That is your highest priority."

"Understood, ma'am."

*****

Eztil kept shifting in discomfort as he sat on the ground. Overall, it had been a hard march, but the terrain at least got better with time. They were now trekking through an overgrown rural area, passing the odd ruined town or city on their journey.

They stopped during daylight again and Xipil sat down beside him.

"How goes it?" asked Eztil, as he took off his boots to give his feet some air.

"Good," he replied.

"Have you heard the rumour?" Xipil asked.

Eztil just shook his head.

"Well," he said, continuing, "some scouts have found a city-state that has fallen to the godless rebels. We are to march and liberate it."

"Really, how far are we from the city?"

"Not far," replied Xipil, rather excited. "We're just a day's march away. I'm looking forward to battle. At last, a chance to prove myself."

Eztil smiled.

"Yes, I'm hoping I can earn enough honour to ask Cuictal's father if I may get her hand."

Xipil looked at him, shocked, before patting him on the back.

"Well, she is a creature of beauty, but she is a Cuextecatl daughter. You better fight hard. You don't want to be an Otontin then? You do have brothers if you want to go down that path."

"No," replied Eztil. "I prefer to be a Cuextecatl and have a wife and son."

Xipil sighed.

"I would love to be an Otontin, but as an only son, I cannot."

Eztil laid back and looked up into the sky. The wind ruffled his curly hair.

"Do you know there is a rumour that there are men up there and we were once on the moon?"

Xipil let out a belly laugh.

"If you believe that, I have an ancient amulet to sell you, only two gold slips," Xipil ridiculed, as he rolled his eyes at him, "If you paid attention in school when the priests were speaking, you'd know that the moon and the stars are images of the gods watching over us. We may as well touch fire."

"Yeah, I know," replied Eztil. "I was speaking to the hermit, Atl."

Xipil sighed and dropped down beside him.

"That explains it. You know he's been digging in the forbidden ruins, and you know the stuff the ancients believed leaves behind effects on the mind in strange ways. Atl is proof of that. He is as nuts as a squirrel's kitchen. And you should be careful, you can catch madness from him."

"I know," replied Eztil. "But I saw a picture. It showed a man in a space suit."

Xipil again shook his head.

"We all know the ancients were mad and made things up that didn't exist, like their god, the internet, something they claimed that they made and somehow it existed nowhere but everywhere and had all knowledge. That is why I am so thankful for Totec. If you have any doubts, you can just go and see him and his power."

"I suppose you're right," resigned Eztil, as he got off the ground, "Come, let's see if the slaves have supper prepared yet."

*****

"We're travelling in style now," mused Sarg, as he winked at Linda.

They were in one of the new armoured personal carriers which was a lot better than the older ones. Currently, it could carry sixteen people with an equipment rack in the middle, and he was sitting up at the back of the vehicle with Linda at his side. They were part of a much larger convoy heading towards the allied city-state, but progress had been slow. The vehicle stopped, sending Linda bumping into Sarge.

"Incoming air raid," said the driver, through the intercom, "I'm going to park her in cover."

The ride suddenly got a lot bumpier as it climbed over the rubble. They sat in silence for a moment before they heard the telltale sounds of an explosion.

"Good news," the driver announced, "The flyers are gone. Bad news, they knocked out a bridge up ahead. We're stuck here until the engineers arrive. I'll open up the back so we can take five."

The metal back doors gently folded down, and Sarg got up, glad to finally stand.

He stepped out into what used to be a lobby of a fancy office block with now worn cream-coloured marble and a ruined statue in the middle. The statue now had the heavy APC parked on it, most of it crushed under the heavy tracks. It looked like it should have been some sort of animal, but Sarg could not make it out.

He shrugged.

Since he was a sergeant and technically in charge, as the lieutenant was still in the cab, he shouted to the group of men who had disembarked.

"Right, no more than fifty meters from the APC. Remember, we're in unknown territory, so keep your eyes peeled and take your battle buddy if you need to leave camp."

As the others dispersed, Sarg looked around.

Not much to see but a ruined parking lot with half-rusted cars. Linda came up next to him as he looked around and saw a couple of other APCs with their troops out and about. He then heard a loud boom and took cover.

"Look," shouted Linda, pointing up in the sky.

He looked up. It was a sonic boom he heard. Up in the sky, flew past at least five or six jets. They were definitely not the normal human or alien flyers, but rather sleek-looking human fighters he had seen in propaganda photos.

"So, they managed to get it working."

"What are you talking about?" asked Linda, rather confused.

"Well, there were rumours that they were working on an air superiority fighter but were having issues," he answered.

He scratched his chin in deep thought.

"I wonder what they did about the G forces?"

"Not too sure," replied Linda as she shrugged.

They both stood and watched the planes fly over the horizon on their missions.

*****

"From here, the view was quite good," said Eztil to Xipil, trying not to show his nervousness.

They were on a small hill not far from the enemy city-state. They were surrounded by green fields and the odd ruined structure. The walls themselves looked thick and grey as he stood on the hill among other soldiers of the Tlamemeh rank. In front of them, the siege machines were set up and surrounded by the alien soldiers, or Tepiani as his people called them, the mindless ones. Behind them were the tanks, ready to march forward.

What worried Eztil was that they were just two hundred meters from the imposing city, and no one had seen any sort of movement. Part of him hoped the city had been abandoned and was now an empty shell.

Xipil just mumbled. "uh huh," no doubt dealing with his own concerns.

A loud roar erupted in the sky and they ducked, looking up.

From the horizon, he could make out what were alien flyers heading towards the city, no doubt making a bombing run. Before they reached the city, they heard a loud boom, and from nowhere another set of flyers he didn't recognise flew into view. He struggled to make out what happened but he did see a bright flash where the alien flyers were. It seemed like only one had survived, for a bright light flash from the city hit the flyer, causing it to explode.

He clutched his crossbow closer as he heard another loud bang and saw that one of the massive siege machines had fired, hitting the city wall, causing a nice crater, but not much damage.

Sounds of gunfire pierced the silence.

The Tepiani returned fire. He clutched his crossbow even closer as he saw some Tepiani fall. He then heard another sound. He looked up and saw different-looking fighters, again not alien but human-looking. They flew right above them. One was hit by fire from one of the Totec vehicles. He then noticed that most of the vehicles were protecting the cannons firing on the city. The flyers were close now and he could make out their strange shape. It was sort of a silver box with rounded edges a protruding front, and short wings—too short, he thought, to fly. He also noticed flames shooting out the bottom and the back. Before he had a chance to talk to Xipil, he saw two objects detach from the wings and fall on the infantry below them.

Then there was a bright flash.

He screamed as he was flung into the air and knocked into a rock where he blacked out.

*****

The crowd cheered as the first bombers struck a target of massed infantry, but Althenia was focused on the horde below. She took a breath and was calm and collected.

Below them was almost a sea of human and alien soldiers firing at them.

She wore a radio earpiece strapped over her pointed ear, which was more advanced than any of the others. She also had a bandolier filled with clips for her plasma rifle which Sylvia had called a fashion statement. What really worried her was their massive cannons that were striking the walls. So far, it only created massive craters in the wall itself, but every time it struck, the floor trembled like a mini earthquake.

A voice on the short-wave radio interrupted her thoughts. It was Lucinda.

"I'm going to use my powers to protect the walls over here. Can you get Sylvia to do the same?"

"Confirmed," replied Althenia. She turned to Sylvia. "Message from Lucinda: Shields up for the wall."

She nodded at her.

"Understood."

She too carried the same holster with the same type of pistol in it as well as her backup weapon, but no bandolier. Another boulder from a cannon came into the walls, flying at a fantastic speed. It hit a blue energy field just before striking the wall.

Sylvia groaned.

Are you okay?" asked Althenia.

"Yeah," replied Sylvia. "It was like being in that damn machine again."

Sylvia lifted her rifle and took aim. She heard another boom and saw the same flyers that had cleared the sky before. The sleeker, aerodynamic human fighter swooped in, still high in the sky, but that did not prevent the alien tanks from attempting to hit them with blue plasma bolts. Fortunately, they were too high and fast for any of the firings to reach them. Althenia then saw a bright blue light above the artillery pieces. It was the same light Althenia had seen when Sylvia used her shield.

Every now and then, a couple of shots would hit the shield Sylvia had set up. Althenia glanced across and she could see the same colours flashing on the far side of the walls, no doubt that was protected by Lucinda's shield. Fortunately, the enemy was only attacking one side of the city at the moment.

She took aim at the horde below and picked out an important-looking target. She then pulled the trigger and blasted an alien in the head, causing him to fall. She selected another target. From behind her, she heard more loud bangs in a coordinated volley. It was the mortars they had, being launched from various positions and streaking high over their heads. It had been decided to keep the tanks ready in case of a breach of the walls, so they were down in position in the city proper, ready to go at a moment's notice. She noticed a group of men with a rough, wooden ladder surging through the crowd of troops below. She took aim and started taking out the ladder bearers as she heard another volley from the mortars.

*****

He opened his eyes and looked around.

A man stood over him, screaming words that Eztil couldn't hear. His left ear was numb and his right ear was ringing. He touched the side of his head. It was wet. Holding up his hand, he saw the blood coated on his fingers.

"Was I deaf?"

The man moved past him, to the other person on the floor. It was Xipil. The man bent over and screamed at him, lifting his shoulders and shaking it. But Xipil remained limp.

When the man moved on, Eztil dragged himself over to Xipil. His eyes were open and his face was frozen in fear. Eztil's fingers trembled as he reached down and closed his eyes.

A hand pulled him off the floor. It was his Cuextecati.

The man grabbed the crossbow on the ground and pushed it into Eztil's chest as he pointed at the field.

Eztil understood, so without another word, he swallowed his fear and ran to the now advancing line.

People were firing up the walls with guns and crossbows, as alien soldiers surged ahead. Suddenly another projectile from the cannon hit the front of the wall, causing a blue flicker. Off in the corner of the battlefield, another explosion engulfed a group of soldiers, sending them flying in the air. He was caught up in the rush as a group carried a roughly made wooden ladder to the front. Unfortunately, this group of soldiers would only get so far before one of their numbers was hit by fire and fell down, taking the ladder with it.

He was grabbed by another gun-wielding Cuextecatl, who dragged him to one of the ladders on the ground. The Cuextecatl pulled the dead man away, and Eztil took his place, hefting the heavy ladder up on his shoulders, followed by some more men. They had just gone twenty meters closer when he saw the man in front of him fall down, blood spurting from his head. Another man next to him cried out in pain as he clutched what remained of his leg, and the man behind him fell without a word after a blue bolt hit him in the chest, leaving Eztil no choice but to drop the heavy ladder. The Cuextecatl from before grabbed another man, who started to shake his head. Eztil understood why. It seemed the ladder bearers were being targeted, and no doubt this man refused to be a target. The Cuextecatl lifted his rifle and smashed it down on the man's nose, causing blood to spurt out and flow down his face. The man got up and as the Cuextecatl screamed at him, reluctantly grabbed the ladder. They moved forward again. Another blue bolt flew so close to Eztil's head, he smelt burnt hair and again the ladder stopped. This time the man behind him fell down with the top of his head missing.

*****

Once she got used to the sudden hits on the shield by the heavy cannon, Sylvia found producing the shield to be quite easy. She looked over at Althenia, who was busy using her plasma rifle to snipe at the troops below, and so was anyone else on her wall behind the shield. Most of the shots she noticed were aimed at anyone carrying the crude wooden ladder. This made sense, as anyone firing from below simply bounced off her shield, so they were focusing on higher threats.

She tried not to look at the battle below. It was okay when she saw an alien soldier fall down but they were also humans dying and she didn't like that. She knew she had no choice, but it still made her feel sick when she saw what happened to them.

She staggered back as something heavy struck her shield.

"Another rock?" she thought.

She tried to focus, and though she could feel it, there was nothing physical but rather it came from the battlefield. It was a psychic presence. No doubt she had become the focus of the enemy. She felt the force slowly increase, and it caused her head to pound, especially as another boulder was launched from a cannon, hitting her shield as well.

She grunted in pain.

Athena looked at her with wide eyes.

"Your nose is bleeding," she shouted.

Sylvia noticed that the longer the unknown force stayed on her, the clearer she could see where it came from.

"Some sort of psychic force is coming from next to those cannons," she shouted to Althenia.

Althenia changed the direction of her attack and focused on the force attacking Sylvia.

She aimed and pulled the trigger.

From here, Sylvia could see the force make contact with something, but it didn't stop when Althenia struck her target.

Then she saw the A-frame on the left-hand side of the cannon lurch to one side and swerve. Over the din of the battle, she heard a loud creak as it toppled over, crashing into where the psychic force was coming from. She then sawdust and debris rising into the air as she focused on the shield, blocking another incoming cannon blast.

"You okay?"

"Fine," replied Sylvia in an offhanded voice, trying to stay focused on keeping her shield up.

Althenia looked at her one last time before resuming battle. Sylvia wished they could use the damn Psychitron to block the signal, but since the effect came from the machine itself and radiated out, they would have to move it next to the enemy. She highly doubted that the enemy's leader would stop the battle so they could just park a strange machine next to him, no matter how nicely they asked.

*****

On the far side of the wall, Lucinda so far had managed to keep her shield stable. She had seen the psychic beam hit Sylvia's shield before it was taken out. She breathed a sigh of relief when another cannonball bounced off her psychic shield. Sylvia had managed to keep it online. Lucinda knew they could not keep the shield up forever, but she was hopeful to at least thin the enemy ranks before a breach was made.

She heard a loud boom up in the sky and looked up. The humans had deployed more of their fighters, who were engaged in dog fights with alien fighters. She saw one of the fighters go up in smoke. From this distance, she was not too sure if it was an alien or human flyer going down. Looking down at the forces below, she was surprised that so many humans were part of the fight.

"How could they not see that Totec was nothing more than a madman on the throne with a simple bag of magic tricks?"

It was the human trait of tribalism. Tell them a lie and they would eventually find out the truth but put them in a group of people who believe the lie, and they would eventually conform to the lie, it seems, or keep quiet if they had found the truth.

Lucinda also noticed that they were using their psychic shields to protect the heavy cannons. She sighed and felt the shock of another high-speed boulder hitting her shield and idly wondered how they did it.

The canons themselves were massive, wooden A-frames supporting a large and strange-looking metal tube supported by chains attached to the frame itself. She suspected they'd used some sort of alien technology to accelerate the boulders, possibly like a rail gun, but the boulders had no magnetic properties that she knew of. Another boulder hit the shield again. So far, the boulders had been the biggest pain and she had hardly registered the light fire from their guns and infantry below.

A soldier shouted to her.

They had managed to get one of their wooden ladders onto the wall close by. So far, her troops had been focusing on the ladder bearers, but despite their best attempts, there was always someone available to move the ladder closer.

She heard shouts and peered over the edge as a harmless bullet pinged off her psychic shield. The mass below had managed to get a ladder to go up to the wall, and they were in the process of ramming into the ground and then forcing it up with a group of men holding precariously on top.

When the ladder was halfway up, it suddenly stopped. A group of her men were now shooting into the men holding the ladder. The ladder shook and then collapsed as the enemy soldiers holding the ladder were killed.

She looked down the wall and noticed about a hundred meters down more ladders were being raised. One or two collapsed, only to be picked up by another group of men, as they tried raising it again.

Lucinda sighed to herself.

It was only a matter of time till this horde was on the wall as well. She saw one of the alien fighters go lower across the battlefield and towards the city. It was currently high enough so it would not be affected by the shield. She debated if she should drop the shield for a second to stop the fighter, no doubt on a bombing run. A bright laser light hit the bottom of the flyer, which exploded in a fireball.

She focused on the shield as this time an alien fighter flew in low and hit it with a plasma blast. It pulled away before it could get in range of the AA lasers behind the wall, but one of the human fighters took chase.

*****

"At last, the convoy was on its way," thought Sarg.

It had taken a couple of hours for the engineers to repair an old bridge, and according to the communication net, the battle had started, so they were going in hot. Currently, it was four hours till they arrived and when they did, it would be dark. He had also heard dogfights were becoming more frequent and so far, they had lost five of the new fighters. Both their leaders and the aliens knew that anyone with an air of superiority would likely be able to win the battle so they were throwing everything into it.

He sat back as the vehicle climbed over heavy terrain. It was still a smooth ride compared to the old APCs, ask anyone—sitting on a washing machine loaded with rocks was smoother than riding in the old APCs.

He noticed Linda was quiet.

"Hey," he said to her.

"Yeah?"

"What is up?" he asked in a concerned tone.

"Just thinking about Rena."

"Fair enough, kiddo, we did not have her as a command officer for long, but it is hard to forget about people that gave their lives saving yours. She did her duty."

Linda nodded and sighed.

"I heard that phrase, 'done their duty' too many times in my life."

Sarg understood. They'd lost many in the line of duty, but it didn't make the pain any less. He gently patted Linda on the back as the APC climbed over more debris.

*****

Those who could not fight were moved to underground bunkers, Including Rena and Natalie. Some bunkers, it turned out, dated back to the pre-invasion era and had simply been expanded and updated. Most of the important stuff, such as equipment and artworks that had survived the invasion, were moved as well.

Thanks to the fact that the microwave tower had not been hit, Rena was still in communication with the USF, both in the battle and away. She focused on communication in case they needed help in any way, but she still felt rather useless sitting behind the desk in the bunker office.

The bunker was interesting. It was a nicely furnished one from back before the invasion when humanity's greatest threat was itself. It has since been used and abandoned and now it was repurposed to serve Lucinda's city state. In fact, Lucinda told her that discovering this building was an eye-opener on the lost human culture and technology.

Rena looked at the incoming battle communications, which included a lot more information than it would normally have. Since she was a liaison officer now, her security clearance had been raised for this battle to make sure everyone was sharing vital information they needed. From the reports she found, they had lost about three fighters, new fighters, compared to the sixteen alien fighters shot down. That was a good ratio and showed the new fighters were pulling the weight.

The issue was they didn't have many fighters in the first place since the new fighter program only just got off the ground. She heard about it during training. It was meant to be the next great leap to liberate Earth, but it was one of those projects that seemed to go on forever. When someone ran late during training, everyone in the infantry would call them the project manager of Project Raptor, the code name for the fighter project, as a running joke.

Rena got the message that there were more troops on the way, but they would arrive in about three hours and only had ten thousand infantry with another twenty thousand defending the city, versus the estimated hundred and fifty thousand outside.

For now, the best that they could do was hold them off.

She turned to Natalie, who was busy on her system helping in any way she could. She had just finished checking the microwave network and was now using sensors in the walls to check the structural integrity, something she was reporting back to Graham. She was also checking what remained of the camera network around the walls and advised where she could.

Natalie fired up her shortwave.

"Graham, Natalie here. They have a ladder incoming on the northwest wall in sector two. They managed to dig it into the ground and are pushing it up."

"Roger."

*****

Eztil jumped out of the way once the heavy ladder had started to fall. It hit the ground with a bang, crushing one man under its heavy frame. It was the man that had his nose broken by the Cuextecatl earlier.

He rushed to the man, but before he got there to help, a bullet hit the top of his head. He turned to the other end and noticed the men on the top were trapped under the ladder, but they were already being helped. More men rushed forward, stepping over the crushed bodies of their comrades and went to the base of the ladder where they tried to lift it again. Eztil wanted to run away from the damn thing. It was way too dangerous and heavy, but the Cuextecatl from before stood next to the ladder with his rifle cradled under his shoulder

"Come on you dogs, for our great god, push!"

He then pointed at the ladder which meant they were going to get back into the fray. He still debated if running would be a good idea, but remembered the rifle cradled in the Cuextecatl's arm and knew he would not hesitate to waste a bullet on him if it came to it. He went to the base and helped the men push the ladder back into the ground. Every now and then, one of the men would fall to a bullet shot.

He looked at the other side.

Currently, there were two men hanging on it, both with crossbows. He pushed the ladder up with the help of the other men, but by the time it was up, there were four bodies on the floor. Only this time he heard gunshots up top, and one of the men from the other side of the ladder fell down next to him. He was suddenly grabbed by the collar and thrown in front of the ladder where another two men were climbing up already. He paused for a second but was pushed by another man and, knowing he had no choice, climbed up.

*****

The shield was turning into hard work and there was another attempt to hit her with a psychic beam. After every boulder had hit but one, they had figured out the timing.

Althenia swiped another one of their large canons. She found that the wooden A-frame didn't hold up well to sudden plasma blast. She still felt the headache grow and started to feel tired, but she kept the shield up because she knew with those cannons, it would be a matter of time before the wall would be down. Another heavy boulder was deflected by her shield as Althenia returned fire, but this time the psychic shield deflected her shot. They must have learnt their lesson.

She cried out as a sharp pain pierced the back of her shoulder. Althenia turned around and shouted something. She then fired her plasma rifle behind her. Sylvia saw a young man with a crossbow lying on the ground with a smoking hole in his chest. Already, someone was beside her shoulder, as the wall suddenly began to shake. No doubt it had been hit by one of the cannons.

With one swift kick, they sent the top of the ladder off the wall, causing it to crash to the ground. Sylvia stood up and with great effort raised the psychic shield again.

One of their people stuck a needle in her shoulder, and moments later, the pain subsided and was replaced by bliss. Another rock impacted the shield, and this time she staggered back and had the taste of blood in her mouth. Sylvia wiped her nose and looked at her hand, bloodied again. She grunted as another rock impacted the shield and her vision started to go black around their edges. She knew she had to hold on, but she felt very faint. She took in a breath as another rock hit. Her legs gave way, and she collapsed on the floor.

Althenia picked her up and ran into the castle. She looked up at Althenia's face and reached out to touch it.

"I'm sorry," she whispered, as the darkness took over.

*****

Eztil was up on the third rung when the wall the ladder was resting on was hit by a big boulder, causing some masonry to tumble down and hit the ladder. On the way down, some broken masonry struck the ladder, breaking it in half and sending one of the soldiers on it flying to the ground with a sickening thud. He managed to jump away as another body hit the ground just where he was.

He got up and hurried to the man that fell. As he got closer, he realized that it was a teenage boy. Eztil reached down and picked him up, pulling one of the boy's arms over his shoulder and carrying him away from the wall, as more debris fell.

Once they were further out, he turned back and saw that there was a crack in the wall. Men tried running away, including the Cuextecati. He turned, with his charge still resting on his shoulders, and started to follow them as fast as he could. Once he had gone ten meters, he felt the ground shake again and felt a sudden force as a large part of the wall smacked into the ground just behind him, sending a large stone into his back. He saw another boulder come in from the cannons. The wall finally gave way, and he was covered in a wave of dust and debris in the ensuing collapse.

*****

Lucinda heard it over the radio nets. Sylvia had been hit by a crossbow and was down. Her status was unknown, but they were now pounding the exposed wall. She had tried to extend her psychic shield but found herself struggling as well. They had kept the shield up for about six hours so far. They had plans for this moment.

She turned to Graham.

"Abandon the wall."

Graham showed no emotion and simply nodded as he gave the orders on his radio. The plan was set in motion. Once the wall had fallen, soldiers would take position on the sides, hitting anyone exploiting the breach, and the tanks would start to move in to block the breach. Another loud thud shook the ground. This sound was different from the other hits on the wall. Lucinda felt the wall shake as part of it started to collapse. She hoped her men had started to move away as large segments came crashing down. Another thump hit the wall, causing more of it to fall off.

She then felt another hit on her shield.

Dust from the crumbling wall filled the air, and through it, she saw the tanks move forward.

Some shouted over the radio.

It was Althenia.

"Sylvia is unconscious but alive. I'm taking her to the medical tent."

"Roger," Graham responded.

Lucinda looked over the wall and shouted to Graham.

"Tell them that they're not the only ones. I can see enemy hover tanks incoming and it looks like they're taking pot-shots at the breach."

Graham nodded and got on the radio as another boulder hit her shield. She looked below. There were still men trying to get on the ladders and climb up the wall. None of them had succeeded yet but she also noticed a lot of men were now heading to the breach in the wall. Another cannon shot at the already broken wall with a sound that dwarfed the screams and shouts on the battlefield.

The ensuing dust created a smoke screen.

When it cleared, Lucinda could make out a hover tank floating over the high rubble as some of the enemy soldiers tried to climb over it. They struck the hover tank with a plasma bolt and watched it collapse.

She then heard more sounds coming from the air and looked out to see more human fighters, about three of the slower boxer types heading towards them. They came in low, and out of the corner of her eye, she saw another set of flyers, this time from the alien side. She then saw the human flyers come in low, attacking the enemy soldiers converging by the broken wall.

Before they could make their escape, five alien fighters shot at them, hitting two, causing one to explode and the other to slam into the battlefield before a heavy laser from the city hit one of the alien fighters. The surviving human fighter went very low, skimming the heads of his enemies. He did a sharp turn as alien fire missed him, but they were able to keep up with the turn. The alien fighters took aim and fired, hitting the wing of the slower human fighter and sending it spiralling, but what they had noticed was he was heading straight to a larger cannon which they were protecting from the front but not the side.

With no time for the enemy to react, the human fighter crashed into the cannon and both were engulfed in flames.

Lucinda sensed an opportunity. She shouted to Graham.

"Fire everything we've got at the canons!"

Graham shouted that down the phone, and she was satisfied to see streaks of bullets hit the area where the cannons were. Another cannon fell over, followed by a third and final cannon. She felt hopeful since the battle started, which meant she could now move to the front and use her full power instead of being a glorified shield wall. The issue was the same was true for Totec as well, as he had no canons to protect.

Althenia had carried Sylvia down the walls and into one of the bunkers where she handed her to a field hospital. Part of her wanted to stay and make sure Sylvia was okay, but she knew that standing around waiting for a medical report would be no help at all. She reluctantly left the medical bay and went up the stairs to the bunker. Once she reached the top, she put a hand on her earpiece.

"Sylvia is stable. What's the status?"

"There has been a breach in the wall where you were?" Graham shouted, amidst the chaotic noise in the background.

"We're holding off the soldiers, but we need help."

"Confirmed."

She started running but ducked behind for cover as a couple of fighters flew over low. Moments later, the sound of explosions in the distance filled the air. She got her rifle ready and took position behind a building. She lay next to the wooden door that was the entrance to the building about a hundred meters away from the breach.

A voice spoke through the radio.

"The enemy's heavy cannons are down."

Althenia was impressed.

She wondered how that was accomplished, but her joy was short-lived when the voice of Graham came over.

"Be advised, the enemy has nothing to protect now, and their overlord could be heading to the wall."

She started taking aim at infantry, most of whom she noticed had simple, leather armour and were carrying crossbows, but every now and then one of the men would have a metal breastplate and a rifle. She preferred to focus on these soldiers as they were the people in charge, and she also felt sorry for the men who fought against plasma rifles with leather armour and a crossbow. As one of the metal-breasted soldiers crumbled on the rubble, a tank arrived across the street from her and hid behind another boxed-shaped building on the opposite side of the road. It was one of the older, heavier models with a simple rail gun rather than a plasma gun, and its front was slanted with a slight slant on each side leading up to a rounded turret enforced with armour and heavy wires connecting to various points on the barrel indicating it had a rail gun.

The breach itself was basically a mass of rubble that spilt over onto a road between a one-story building and a partially collapsed three-story building. She could see some infantry on top of what remained of the walls, firing down into the breach, trying to stop the horde. Some of the enemy infantry had made it past the gauntlet and managed to get into the one-story building, and there was an alien tank by the collapsed part of the building. The tank opposite her rolled out and took aim at the building, which the alien tank hid behind and waited for a second. The alien tank traversed forward, and the tank next to her fired, shaking the ground and sending a tungsten shell out at an impressive speed, causing the glass in the building next to it to break from the shockwave. It then hit the alien tank with a flash, smashing through the shield and into the tank armour, which exploded in a bright fireball that smashed out the glass in the building and caused the three-story building to topple over and collapse in a cloud of dust and debris.

The tank moved back as Althenia took aim, as the debris started to settle. Another more modern plasma tank rolled up behind the railgun tanks.

Suddenly, she felt a strong wind. Sensing something was wrong, she ducked behind the building as a powerful shockwave radiated out from behind the breach, causing more of the wall to collapse and spewing debris everywhere like shrapnel. It struck the buildings and anyone unlucky enough to be caught in range.

Once the dust settled, she looked around the corner, and in front of her was a breach that had a clear path in it, no doubt created by the force of the shockwave. Standing at the other end of that path was a group of men wearing green capes and green loincloths with a simple facemask of a skull printed on it. They were holding up a heavy-looking platform. On it was a very ornate stone throne, and a tall man with light brown skin sat there with an ornate and brightly decorated headdress. He was wearing a cape wrapped around his torso and shoulders that was red with ornate gold trim and a simple golden loincloth. On each corner of the throne stood a man, and they each had a solid metal arm that looked like it ended in a plasma gun. The men, whom Althenia assumed were his bodyguards, had a simple black loin cloth and cape and a heavy metal circle with ornate writing on it embedded into their chests.

"No doubt that was their overlord and his bodyguards," she thought.

She pressed a button on the headset.

"The overlord is at the breach."

Althenia then aimed at one of the people holding the throne as the older tank moved into firing position and fired its rail gun. The tungsten bullet hit his psychic shield with a loud crunch and dropped to the ground. Hoping he was distracted by that, she pulled the trigger, and the plasma bolt dissipated when it hit the same shield.

"Damn."

She rolled back around the corner. The old tank was suddenly picked up by the psychic force and sent flying back with a loud crash into the building. The plasma tank started to reverse. She got up, ready to back away as well when she saw Lucinda standing on the opposite end. Behind her were various soldiers who took up positions in cover, ready to engage. Lucinda looked at Althenia and simply nodded.

She returned the nod and took aim.

*****

As her troops took up position, Lucinda looked at her target now sitting on the throne that was moving forward with his troops behind him. He stopped and so did all his men.

His men aimed their rifles as their leader stood up and flung his cape to the side.

"I am Totec. Bow before me."

Lucinda felt a powerful psychic wave, forcing people to kneel. It affected the troops behind him as well. She simply blocked it before it reached her troops and felt a wave of psychic anger and an attempt to push the force up.

"You must be a false god," she taunted.

Angry at her words, Totec sent a strong psychic blast straight to Lucinda, who was expecting it. If she hadn't, she would have been thrown to the floor. She blocked the blast and pushed the psychic block shield forward. Lucinda then saw Graham in the corner of her eye. He gave her the okay symbol as she heard the plasma tank move up behind her.

"You need to stop this madness," Lucinda warned, "Stop abusing your humans, and let them go home."

Totec let out a loud laugh.

"And what are you going to do if I do not?"

She then nodded to Graham, who spoke quietly into his radio.

She looked him in the eye and smiled.

"Absolutely nothing."

Totec looked at her for a moment, stunned by her response, before stomping forward in anger.

Fortunately, Graham already spoke to Rena, who made sure everything was ready to activate the Psychitron just fifty meters behind them. Nothing happened at all as Lucinda walked to the side of the street and the plasma tank fired. She felt the heat as the bolt travelled past. By now, Totec's bodyguards knew something was up and had stood in front of him. It turned out that embedded in their chest was an infantry alien shield generator. A plasma bolt from a tank would knock out two or maybe three on a good day, but he was protected by four shields, and what remained was almost comical.

Totec stood there, somewhat confused, surrounded by the charred remains of the people who were carrying his throne and the throne itself.

There was just one bodyguard remaining.

A plasma bolt from a rifle struck the remaining bodyguard whose shield was already weakened by the plasma blast, and the bolt impacted the bodyguard's head, spraying Totec with brain matter and gore.

This seemed to snap Totec out of his shock.

"Attack!"

A mass of infantry started to run towards them and was met by machine gun fire as Lucinda saw Totec vanish into the surging crowd. The plasma tank fired again and those not cut down by the machine gun fire were now burnt by plasma. She stayed safe behind cover, feeling rather vulnerable without her powers. Part of her wanted to order the Psychitron off so she could clear the horde but so far, her troops had held them off, and Totec would be back as soon as he realised his powers were back. Also, part of the reason she stayed at the front was so that she could be of use at least if the Psychitron was knocked out.

The APC stopped, and its engine was idling. Sarg checked his helmet and made sure his gun was locked and loaded. They were now getting into position behind a hill that should mask their manoeuvres. Just over the hill, about a mile away, the battle was happening. Even in the armed APC, about a mile away, they could still hear machine gun fire and explosions.

The APC driver came on the intercom.

"Go in about one minute. Be advised: next stop will be hot."

Sarg checked his helmet again, a nervous habit he had picked up, and he looked over at Linda who was quiet. She had already checked her gear, made sure her new arm was okay, and was in pre-battle meditation as far as he could tell.

The APC started to move, and with a deep breath, he climbed the hill and then reached the top as the APC started moving down. He could hear the remote-control machinegun start to fire, joining the sounds of battle.

Suddenly, the APC came to a halt and the back hydraulic door dropped down. Sarg grabbed his rifle and rushed out, followed by Linda and the rest of his men. The enemy infantry was down the hill about a hundred meters away. They were massed in front of a massive breach in the city walls, which was on his left-hand side. Some of the infantry had noticed them and were returning fire, but turning a horde like that to face them would take discipline and good command. It looked like the horde had neither. He opened fire, as did the rest of his platoon, and so did the other platoons that had gotten into position. He fired off a couple more shots straight into the horde. He saw a commotion in the back and got out his scope, attached it to his rifle, and looked.

A group of men were trying to turn around and started to push against their comrades to go forward. Most of them were wearing leather armour. Behind them was a group of men with metal chest plates waving their rifles and shouting something along with a couple of alien soldiers. He saw one young man push past the men and started to run down the field, but before he got far, he collapsed as an alien plasma bolt hit him in the back. More men broke off and the men in metal armour started to fire at them, dropping a few of these men and forcing them to join the main horde.

He took aim at the alien soldier and pressed the contact badge on his short-wave radio. "Look at the back, focus on the men with metal armour. The rest want to flee." He heard a couple of "rogers" as he pulled the trigger of his heavy rifle, causing the alien soldier to collapse. One of the men in metal armour looked over at the soldier, and before he could say anything, a bullet impacted his chest and went straight through, causing him to collapse on the ground. The metal amour was not having too much effect. A couple of men saw this as an opportunity and started to flee down the field towards a forest, far away.

"Let them run boys," he shouted on his radio.

Pretty soon, a couple of men started to follow as more of the soldiers started to run as well. What started as a trickle was turning into a full stream as more and more men started to flee. Despite the best attempts of what he assumed were their officers trying to control them, he knew panic was a dangerous thing. He took aim at another man with a metal chest plate and pulled the trigger. He then saw a third man in a metal chest plate, but he too was joining the growing crowd and was running. He let him go and looked for any other person staying behind.

One of the alien soldiers showed up and he took the shot, knowing that they would not retreat under any circumstances. The stream became a full-on waterfall, and as he moved the scope away, the horde was now turning around as it broke off and more of their soldiers started to flee.

Eztil awoke and slowly blinked. It took a second for all his senses to register where he was and why he could barely move. The person whom he tried to rescue was now on top of him. No doubt he had provided a cushion against the impact. He tried to move but found himself pinned. He struggled a bit more and shook the body and rubble off. He got onto his knees, and a hand grabbed him and lifted him. It was another Cuextecatl, whom he did not recognize.

"Get to the front, you coward," shouted the Cuextecatl.

The Cuextecatl then grabbed a crossbow covered in dust and blood and pushed it into his hands and pushed him towards the front line, which was now in breach. He saw a scene of chaos before him. The soldiers had crowded around the front with shouts coming from the Cuextecatl over the sounds of battle. He heard shouts such as, "Forward! Anyone who goes back will be damned by Totec himself."

He checked the front, and many men were already dead. He then saw up in the hills a group of strange vehicles with men holding rifles firing from the side. They were being attacked on two fronts. Here, he saw a couple of men push back and try to walk away. A couple of shots were fired into the crowd, but before the other Cuextecatl could completely stop the retreat, he fell to the ground. The Cuextecatl that had shoved the crossbow in his hands was lying on the floor missing his head.

He dropped the crossbow and proceeded to run to the hill, as he could see many more men doing the same, but paused as he passed another headless Cuextecatl. He spotted the rifle on the ground and made a split decision. Kneeling, he grabbed the metal chest plate, rifle, and bandolier before he continued his retreat.

Once he was far enough from the sound of the battle, he stopped and looked around quickly. Once he was sure no one was around, he took off his leather armour and put on the metal chest plate and bandolier as well as his rifle. The rifle itself had a wooden stock and was a simple bolt action device. He had seen it in use before and was thankful it was not one of the strange-looking metal rifles that shot more than one bullet at a time, which some of the Cuextecatl had. He then continued into the forest, hoping he was far enough from the snipers.

*****

Althenia took aim at one of the men with the metal armour and pulled the trigger. As the man fell, she noticed an odd movement behind him. Another man with a metal breastplate had his rifle raised. It seemed he was firing at his own men. She took aim again and looked up. Maybe he had turned traitor, but looked back and saw the issue.

The men behind him started to run. She looked back at her previous target and a few of the men with leather amour stood up some even threw their weapons and started to run after their comrades. More and more men followed them as Althenia took aim at the metal chest-plated man who was firing at his own soldiers. She took him out with a plasma shot. More and more of the enemy started turning and running.

She picked up her rifle.

Every now and then, a shot would ring out, hitting one of the men with a meal chest plate. It also became obvious that they were receiving fire from Althenia's allies on the other side and she heard some static on her radio.

"We just confirmed reinforcements have arrived and are just north of the breach. The enemy seems to be retreating."

She stood up.

It was becoming obvious that the battle was over as men with the metal chest plates had even started to run, leaving them to mop up the alien soldiers. She was not interested in that and pressed the comm button on her radio as she turned around and walked towards the bunkers.

"Can I get a status on Sylvia please?"

After a pause that felt too long for Althenia, she heard a voice come back on the line.

"She is stable but still unconscious."

Althenia took a breath.

"Roger," she replied.

Lucinda appeared in the corner of her eye.

She was talking to Graham.

"Better secure that breach in case they regroup and set up a couple of patrols," she instructed, "We better make sure Totec is not in the area before we give them the go-ahead to shut down the Psychitron."

He nodded, and Lucinda walked over to Althenia.

"You okay?" she asked.

"Fine, thanks. I'm just off to see Sylvia."

"Okay, mind if we walk and talk?" asked Lucinda.

"Sure."

They both walked towards the bunker.

"So," started Lucinda, "This is a bit awkward, but what is the relationship between you and Sylvia, if you don't mind me asking?"

"I'm assigned to protect her at the moment, and she has turned out to be a good friend."Althenia paused for a moment and then continued, "Despite all I've put her through."

Lucinda smiled at her with what Althenia thought was a knowing smile.

Once the reports started coming in of the enemy retreat, Rena decided she needed to speak to Althenia. She sent a radio call and found Althenia was in the medical ward. She made her way down to the medical bay with just a walking stick. She stopped when she got to the emergency centre, which was in turmoil still as casualties were still coming in and being tended from the battle. Most of the wounded were now not in serious danger, some having a crossbow bolt sticking out of either an arm or a leg. Every now and then, they would pass the odd gurney where the sheet had been pulled up.

She carried on down the white, tiled hallway past nurses, doctors, soldiers, and various other people until she came to a doorway with two armed men standing in front.

"Is Sylvia in here?" she asked.

"Nope," replied the guard. "Enemy combatants. If you want the special ward, it is about five doors down on your right."

"Thanks," she replied and walked down the hallway until she came to another door with one guard in front. She recognized him as one of the normal guards from Lucinda's castle. He opened the door for her, and she walked into what looked like a smaller ward with just four beds against the wall. The first bed had Sylvia lying down in it. Next to the bed was some medical equipment and an intravenous drip as well as Althenia, who was looking at Sylvia with some concern.

"Hey," she said to Althenia. "How is she?"

Althenia looked at her and gave an anxious smile.

"She's stable but they're not sure why she's unconscious. The doctors have been speaking to Doctor Lowe and are running some tests."

Rena inwardly cringed and wanted to put off the conversation they were about to have, as now would not be a good time, but she knew the sooner the better. Well, she hoped the sooner the better.

Before she could say anything, Althenia interrupted.

"I'm sorry I never contacted you. I didn't know you were alive. And I lit a candle for you."

Rena patted her on the back, before sitting down.

"That's okay. When I sent the message, I did say I was compromised, and truth be told, I didn't think I would see you again. So now, that leaves one question: Where does that leave us?"

She took a deep breath and continued.

"I did have a few drinks with Lucinda and her assistant Natalie, and we sort of ended up going a bit further than expected."

Althenia looked at her with raised eyebrows.

"You slept with both of them?"

Rena nodded and looked down at the floor.

"Yes, I'm sorry. I know it's not an excuse, but I didn't think we would see each other, and I was a bit tipsy."

Althenia let out an audible sigh.

"Do they know about each other?"

Rena looked at her, confused for a moment.

"Well, they were both there, so I hope so."

Althenia's eyebrows raised even higher.

"I want to be mad at you, but it makes sense. I thought I lost you, and you thought you lost me."

Rena and Althenia sat in silence for a moment.

The only sound was the hum of medical equipment, before Rena finally said, "What now?"

"Do they make you happy?" asked Althenia, turning her eyes to Sylvia.

Rena looked at Sylvia and squeezed Althenia's hand.

"You love her as well, don't you?"

"I felt angry at her when I heard I lost you, then I felt sorry for her as she was clearly suffering from Stockholm Syndrome, but she has made me feel for her as well." She then reached out and gently grabbed Sylvia's hand.

"If there is a future here, I don't want to hold you back," she continued.

"You never did," replied Rena. "You pushed me forward, and for that I'm grateful. I still love you, but it was never meant to last."

She paused again and gathered her thoughts.

"Do you want to be alone or do you want me to stay?"

Althenia looked at her again.

"Stay please, it'll be good when she wakes up to see you, I think, and you can tell me all that has happened while we've been apart."

Rena smiled and started talking about her capture.

*****

Eztil avoided the branches and tripped over the odd root as he trekked through the forest. After what seemed like hours, he found a clearing where a group of men were sitting and talking. Some of them were out of breath or wounded. He struggled to recognize the Cuextecatl from the Tlamemeh. Most men just look tired and dirty, with bloodied and scuffed uniforms.

As Eztil got closer, he saw some of the men bowing down. At the centre, sat the great lord. Once he was close enough, he dropped to his knees,

"You've failed me, and badly. One in every four of you must die," he admonished, in a thunderous tone, "Cuextecatl, divide the men up and take care of them."

There was a murmur amongst the men as a Cuextecatl started to split them up. One of the Cuextecati tapped him on the shoulder.

"Come on, we have orders to follow."

Still in shock, he grabbed four people. They meekly complied, which shocked him slightly. Would he do the same in their position? He saw defeat in their eyes. They had been beaten and were tired and no doubt like him just wanted to get home. Once the simple Tlamemeh soldiers were in groups of four, Totec walked past them, grabbing one out of each group, whose arms were then bound behind their back and led into the woods by the Cuextecatl. He decided to stay with the Cuextecatl still watching the men. He could not stomach what was going to happen. He then heard gunshots come from the woods, and the Cuextecatl who had gone came back with blood on their breastplates. They then began the slow walk home, Lord Totec now being carried on a hastily made wooden litter by a couple of Cuextecatl.

*****

It was a good thing they brought body bags. It was the grim reality of war.

It was now late in the morning. Sarg had taken a nap after the battle because he would be needed to do battlefield cleanup since they were the reinforcements that came near the end of the battle. Most were still fresh, unlike the defenders. They would also be securing the breach as well.

Fortunately, the city had heavy graders and diggers and was in the process of clearing the rubble. Every now and then work paused as a body was discovered. It was then checked to see if it was one of their own or the enemy's. They already started digging a deep trench for the enemy bodies about a hundred meters away from the wall and were processing the remains. Next to the trench, there was a heavy table, covered in a tarp. A body would be laid on the table next to a box of any personal effects assumed to be theirs.

The team's job was to make sure the serial number on the body bag was on the box and an inventory was taken and catalogued. Anything that looked unusual was flagged, and if they had a face left, a picture was taken.

A rather grim job, but they did this in the hope that if any family came, they could identify their loved one.

Sarg very much doubted that would happen, but you never knew. It was the least they could do.

They were, at the end of the day, human, but the entire operation was not a charity. They were also looking for the body of Totec.

Already, the first row had gone into the deep trench. He stood watching over the troops, digging up a new section of rubble. His lieutenant was busy monitoring the body processing detail, a job he preferred to avoid.

His radio clicked on.

"Sarg, it's Linda. I think you'll want to see this."

Linda was on patrol because they'd heard shots in the forest during the night and were worried about the enemy regrouping. When nothing came after a couple of hours, they decided to send a patrol out. He had chosen Linda for the job as, despite her hot-headedness, she could practice caution when needed.

"Okay, where are you?"

"We'll wait on the outskirts of the forest for you and I can walk you to it."

"Roger."

He started walking up the hill, past quite a few corpses that had yet to be picked up. One of the human fighters had crashed. Fortunately, after the battle, a team managed to make the crash safe by removing the reactor it used, as well as, the body of the pilot.

He stopped by a massive, crushed, wooden frame with a large tube device laying on the battlefield. The operation had just started, and they had yet to look at Totec's cannon. He noticed a pair of legs sticking out from one of the pieces of the massive wooden beams that made up the A-frame of the cannon and frowned slightly.

"What a way to go," he thought, as he carried on walking.

Linda was standing at the edge of the forest, waiting. She beckoned him to follow.

"We found it about three hundred meters in," she reported.

"Found what, exactly?"

Linda sighed.

"I better show you."

They walked for about two hundred meters in until they came across a clearing that contained a dip and a lot of bodies piled up haphazardly on each other.

"Odd, the battle was at least a mile or so away."

He encountered no other bodies in the forest. He noticed that almost all of them were wearing brown leather armour and had their hands bound and a bullet hole in the back of their heads.

He sighed and turned to Linda.

"I'll tell them to make the trench even wider and advise them of the location. In the meantime, just keep an eye on the edge of the woods."

He looked at the bodies around him and wondered how many there were.

"Must be related to the retreat," he thought, as he wandered back to the city.

*****

Lucinda looked out as she stood on the balcony.

From her office, she saw the people cleaning up the streets, and the city itself was returning to some sort of normality. Well, as normal as it could be with bullet holes in the buildings and a massive hole in the wall. So far, besides the mass grave found in the forest, there had not been any new contacts and none of the patrols had gone missing.

The reports had not been great.

The causality count was still rising.

So far, about six thousand dead and about three thousand were city residents. A further five to six thousand were wounded, some of them maimed for life. She personally had the feeling that life could never return to normal for a city of thirty-five thousand.

Lucinda walked back into her office and took a seat behind her desk.

It was still early in the morning. Natalie had spent the night at home, but she had yet to see Rena. She heard that she was with Althenia all evening as they waited by Sylvia's bed.

There was a knock on the door.

"Enter."

In came Rena with a walking stick. She then closed the door behind her and sat on the couch.

"I spoke to Althenia and told her everything. It was civil, but we have decided to split it off. I can see she's fallen for Sylvia and thought it was for the best. It was an amicable breakup."

"Fair enough," replied Lucinda. "You have done what you needed to, and of course, you are welcome to …" She paused for a moment, thinking how best to word it, "spend time with me and Natalie."

"Thank you," Rena said, still in a somewhat sour mood.

"This is a good outcome. Is something still bothering you?" asked Lucinda with concern.

Rena looked at her and frowned.

"Yes, Sylvia. They're still running tests but, well, I don't think they know what's wrong with her, so have I abandoned Althenia to a life of loneliness?"

Lucinda frowned as well. Her reasoning made sense, and from the medical report she had looked at, it was not good. Doctor Lowe was the leading authority on overlord psychic powers and he was stumped.

"She's not alone," replied Lucinda. "She has us, and we will help in any way we can."

Rena looked away for a moment, lost in thought.

"Thank you, I'm going to be in my office if you need me."

She got her walking stick and stood up again.

"Good. Any issues, personal or otherwise, please let me know, and remember dinner tonight. Natalie's going to be cooking."

Rena leaned against the door.

"Nothing would make me feel better than a home-cooked meal. Natalie is such a good cook and has the right kinks. What on Earth did you do to deserve her?"

Lucinda laughed.

"You mean what did *we* do to deserve her?"

*****

General Oliver took a sip. It was an old, single-malt whiskey blend based on an old recipe, and it was good. There were a few brewers still around. They kept the tradition up, even though it wasn't the most vital, but after one or two public health issues, the government had clamped down on any illicit brewers and distillers and started a department to manage them for moral purposes.

Once he had a sip, he looked back at the personal message he was writing to the pilot Captain Rodriguez Valentine. He looked over his record. Nothing remarkable, a typical flyer, one or two drunk and disorderly incidents on his record, but he may have just won the battle for Virginia as they were calling it. He had managed, through the sacrifice of himself and his plane, to knock out the enemy's heavy artillery.

A hero was certainly nice, though it would've been better if he was alive. At least he could pin a medal on them rather than draping a flag over a box. The reports were still coming in after the Battle of Virginia. One of the biggest losses had been Project Raptor. All but one of the fighters had been destroyed during the battle, a worthy sacrifice, but they were specially designed and made using a very advanced AI, as no human could survive the G forces that they experienced, and it was an expensive process to duplicate them.

Would the AI jets be able to do the same thing as Captain Valentine's? He looked over more reports and messages as he struggled to say how much of an impact the good captain had made.

His screen flashed. It was an incoming call on his system.

"That was odd," he thought, *"It was from Field Marshal Morgan. He wasn't normally active at this time."*

General Oliver smoothed his shirt before answering the call.

There was the field marshal in his uniform as usual.

"Ah, general, I saw you were online and thought it would be easier than setting up a meeting," he began, as he rummaged through the reports, "I've had a look at Doctor Lowe's report, and to be frank, if we had a way to get on the alien ship even if the damn thing was not crashing on the planet, I would've green-lighted this years ago. The intelligence we can gather would be invaluable. And central command agrees. Is Sylvia still in hospital then?"

General Oliver nodded.

"Yes sir, I've advised them to tell me when or if she wakes up."

The field marshal sighed.

"Okay, with this victory, we have breathing space," Morgan continued, as he rubbed his temples, "So we've decided to put the liberation of Europe on hold until the alien spaceship is at least secured, as well as most other operations. It may prove valuable in our long-time plans, but it can go very wrong and we have no backup."

General Oliver leaned back.

"I want the best team possible on this and people who know the aliens' technology," the general announced, "That's why we've decided to ask our allied overlord to be a member of this team. Don't worry, I will be personally contacting her. We will need Althenia, and if we could get her to bring Sylvia, we will also need Doctor Lowe as an advisor."

"It took a lot of convincing," Morgan admitted, "As you can imagine, the central command was not keen on having an overlord at Point Nemo, one of the most secret and vital bases, but with Sylvia incapacitated and the ability to build another wormhole generator not in our grasp, we feel we have no choice but to trust another overlord."

The general nodded.

"I understand, sir. I will relay the orders across now. Anything else, sir?"

Morgan sighed.

"Not unless you can find me a couple of spare Raptor fighters, then afraid not."

"Afraid not, sir," he replied, with a sad smile.

"Fair enough, Morgan out."

With that, the screen went blank, and the general went back to his reports.

*****

"Whoa, it is nice and way faster than anything we have," said Natalie as she looked at the desktop recently shipped over by the USF for Lucinda.

Apparently one of the higher-ups and part of what Lucinda had found to be the leadership council of the USF, an organisation that called itself the Central Command, wanted to speak to her. And to do that they needed to set up the infrastructure, including their latest communication terminal, which had the correct security in place.

They were able to get messages on their current terminals, but since it was based on pirated alien and ancient Earth technology, it had taken her and the science department a long night looking at whitepapers and lots of coding to get things working. Well, working and still with various issues. If the stars were out of alignment or the software just did not feel like it, then it would still fail.

The science department had been nicknamed the salvage department and had a large collection of valuable pre-invasion artefacts. Fortunately, the USF soldiers had arrived with their own communication equipment, including the special shortwave radios, and this included technicians as well as the odd engineer.

One of the technicians was busy setting up the communication network. He ran a wire so that Lucinda's system could talk to the server they had set up. There was also an engineer trying to get their system working with Lucinda's while maintaining current security standards. Once it was plugged in, the system powered on and logged in. From here, Lucinda was required to do a thumbprint scan and a face scan for security purposes, and once her account was verified, she was on the system.

Here she was able to access the main network that humanity still used. It was based on the pre-invasion internet but mostly consisted of training materials and non-classified information such as the food menu for various military bases. Once she confirmed that the camera and audio were working, she handed it over to Lucinda, who had already read the manual.

"Thanks for the setup, Natalie," said Lucinda, who sat down at her now new computer system. She had two now, the internal one and the new USF one. "Now I need to call this Field Marshal Morgan. He sounds rather important. A member of central command and commander of the Western Front."

"He does sound important," said Natalie. "Well, I hope it goes well. If you need anything, I'll be in my office seeing how I can get one of these for myself."

"Of course," replied Lucinda, who could see herself approving a new order shortly. "To be honest, that might actually be a good idea."

Natalie smiled at her as she left the office, and Lucinda initiated the call. A woman with her blond hair done up in a bun and wearing librarian glasses with brown eyes and a simple brown uniform shirt was sitting there.

"Field Marshal Morgan's office," she said in a rather official tone.

" I understand the field marshal wishes to speak to me."

The woman nodded, as she clicked away on her side.

"Yes, that's correct. I will advise the field marshal that you're ready for the call."

She then pressed a button and the screen was put on hold before it showed the face of a black man with a wrinkled face.

"Greetings, ma'am."

"You can call me Lucinda."

"Fair enough. Do you have a last name as well?"

She shook her head.

"Nope, just Lucinda."

"Well, I am Field Marshal Morgan. You can call me Morgan. As you must know, I oversee the western front. Let me be frank. You are a powerful ally, and we wish to keep you on board. To be honest, there are those in central command that have their doubts about you. I am not one of them. If there is anything you want or need, please let me know."

Lucinda had expected as much regarding those who had their suspicion, but she knew they needed her and she needed them now more than ever. The bias for a perfect alliance, to be honest.

"Well, I would not mind another one of these computer terminals for my assistant."

"Okay," replied the field marshal, writing it something down. "I wish to thank you for your warning about the alien spaceship, and we have found a way onto the spaceship. The next step is to get a team together, and I want you to be part of that team. The other member we have in mind is Althenia."

Lucinda thought for a second.

"I assume the reason you want me is my alien heritage?"

"Exactly," replied the field marshal.

"How exactly are we going to get on the starship? To be honest, it would be easier to strap me to a rocket and get rid of me."

The field marshal barked a laugh.

"Yes, but there are cheaper ways to get rid of you if we wanted. You're currently surrounded by an army, and we have a way of blocking your psychic signals. But we're not using a rocket."

"Then how?"

The field marshal leaned forward and steepled his hands.

"Have you ever heard of Point Nemo?"

"Only in rumours."

"Well," replied the field marshal. "Point Nemo is real. It is one of our greatest secrets and greatest engineering achievements. It's basically a wormhole generator that connects to our Martian allies."

Lucinda leaned into her chair as she sensed she was about to get a history lesson.

"Just before the invasion, we had landed on Mars and with a plague decimating the resistance on Earth as well as the invasion taking place, the decision was made to send a couple of ships to Mars as a desperate escape plan. Eventually, we managed to use the alien technology to generate a wormhole to communicate with our new Martian colony, and after studying the technology, we managed to establish a larger wormhole and we chose Point Nemo, which is basically a point in the ocean that is the furthest from land."

Lucinda was amazed. How on Earth had humans accomplished such a feat under the nose of the ACS? The fact that they had no real presence in the sea properly helped though.

"Okay, so what does this wormhole have to do with accessing the starship?"

The field marshal shrugged.

"Well, there seems to be an active wormhole generator on the spaceship itself, and we have, after much experimentation, managed to access it." He paused for a second, then continued, "We are in the process of sending a probe, and once that works, we can send a team, then try and move the vehicle and see if we can stabilise the orbit."

Lucinda thought for a second.

"Okay, I can see it working. The issue is I've never physically been on the starship, just in its computer system. I want to take my assistant, Natalie, as she is incredibly good technically, and Rena as well. Althenia would also be good, and I want to take Sylvia. Hopefully, we can find a way to help her on the ship," Lucinda added.

The field marshal smiled at her.

"That makes sense. We're going to do some early probing in a week. Provided all goes well, we should be ready for a manned mission in a month, but will of course update you and send you the logs of the first probe."

Lucinda opened her report.

"Good, now let's talk about what we need to do in order for the city to be rebuilt."

"Of course," replied the field marshal. "And if you allow us, we have a few ideas in mind as well, including setting up a rail network to the port."

*****

They had been walking for a couple of days now, and what Eztil had found was there were fewer people than before, a lot fewer people. He had not even found his Cuextecatl or anyone from his home village. It seemed like he was marching with strangers and there had not been much chatting or socialising. He was lucky at least he had the gear of a Cuextecatl and was treated as such. Most of those below him in rank, mostly the Tlamemeh soldiers, were now treated as slaves and assigned all the tasks. Everyone was on edge, and some had even tried to desert. He felt sorry for any caught, as they would be executed, and since Totec had banned the use of bullets, their deaths ranged from being thrown from a building to hanging, or simply being beaten and left for dead in the sun. Of course, if you were wounded and could not keep up, they would accuse you of desertion as well.

Eztil walked behind a group of Tlamemeh carrying a couple of heavy bags, what remained of their supplies. He was lost in his own thoughts when he heard one say to the other in a whisper, "I'm telling you, they found a way to stop Totec's power."

"Silence," said the other in a more urgent tone.

Before he had a chance to do anything, another Cuextecatl marching in line grabbed the first man and took him off to a tree on the side of the path. The second man looked at him with fear in his eyes. The Cuextecatl was now gathering a crowd as he threw a rope over a tree and tied a noose. As the poor man tried to run, he was grabbed by another Tlamemeh and pushed back to the Cuextecatl, who was done with his noose. It struck Eztil that no one knew why this man was to be hung, but no one objected. The Cuextectal took the pack off the man's back and then put the noose around him. The man reached up to remove it, and the Cuextectal grabbed his arms and tied them behind his back. He then pulled on the other side of the rope, hauling the man into the air by his neck, and leaving him there, kicking.

Eztil turned away, unable to watch as he heard the dying gasps.

The Cuextecatl came back with another pack and handed it to the first man. The man, seeing he had no choice, picked it up and put it on his front and they continued with the march.

"How many men had they lost?" he thought, *"And how many more were dying on this march home?"*

The sun was going down and it would be night soon. Part of him wanted to leave, but where would he go? He did not know the area at all, but surely he would be regarded as one of the cursed for having survived such an epic defeat when they got back. He continued the march in silence with the rest of the men. He slowed his pace down, hoping the other Cuextecatl did not notice. Eventually, after a couple of hours, he found himself at the back walking next to a man who was struggling to keep up as he was currently limping and covered in blood and dirt. He wore the brown leather armour of a Tlamemeh. Behind him was a Cuextecatl, one of his eyes covered by a bloodied rag and also looking dirty and bloodied. His job was no doubt to watch the end of the line to make sure no one slipped away. The man gave him a suspicious look but did not talk to him. He was carrying one of the all-metal rifles that could fire more shots and had less ammo on his bandolier than Eztil.

The limping Tlamemeh tripped and the one-eyed Cuextecatl shouted at him.

"I've had enough of your insolence."

He then struck the prone man with the butt of his rifle, as the poor Tlamemeh's nose was smashed. Eztil knew now was his chance as the Cuextecatl hit the man with his rifle again. He also knew if he shot him it would alert the other Cuextecatl and they would accuse him of violating Totec's law. He took his rifle and swung it like a club, hitting the distracted Cuextecatl on the back of the head

Luckily, he did not scream and just fell down on top of the already wounded Tlamemeh. He dragged the body of the poor Tlamemeh and checked him. His pulse was staggered. It would only be a matter of time. If the man could walk, then he might have taken him, but now was the time to think of his own survival. He grabbed the other Cuextecatl's rifle and ammo and sprinted into the forest, away from his former comrades.

*****

Rena felt good walking without crutches or a walking stick.

She was heading to the hospital wing to check on Althenia, who had spent most of her free time keeping an eye on Sylvia who was still in a coma but had now been moved to a private room. This time Rena had Natalie with her, who was carrying a new toy from the USF, a laptop. Rena and Natalie wanted to show Althenia the footage they had just received from the USF. It was the probe footage of the starship. Rena stopped at the door to Sylvia's room and knocked.

"Enter."

She walked into the room, followed by Natalie. Althenia was sitting by Sylvia's bed, reading a training manual.

"Hey, how's it been?" asked Rena.

"Nothing new, to be honest. At least she's stable," replied Althenia in a neutral tone.

"Hey," said Natalie, who was a bit intimidated by Althenia.

Natalie then set up the laptop, leaving Rena and Althenia to talk.

"We thought you might like to see. This is footage from the first probe that has been sent to the spaceship."

Althenia put her book down.

As Natalie started the video, an unknown male voice started talking. "Interesting. There seems to be gravity, about eighty percent of Earth's. The atmosphere is normal, about thirty percent oxygen and seventy percent nitrogen."

Another voice, again male, spoke.

"Confirmed. The spacecraft must be generating gravity as it is not spinning."

The video just showed the control centre that Sylvia had described when she was in the Psychitron machine. The camera focused on one of the panels only to find it broken and completely dead. It then moved over to another one that had no life as well. The room itself was rather dark and was lit by strange, red lights which gave the place an eerie red glow. The probe then turned down an empty and abandoned black, metal hallway, lit by the same coloured lights.

Here and there were missing and broken panels laying on the floor. With the odd wire or cable hanging out, the probe was one of the small tracked vehicles with a camera and robot arm. The arm reached out and touched a cable gently, and there was still no sign of life. Maybe the entire spaceship had long been left abandoned.

The probe crawled along slowly.

Every now and then, there were strange symbols on the wall. Eventually, it came to a half-open door. It had a collection of strange symbols written on it. The arm of the probe reached out and pushed the door away, which fell with a bit of a clatter. It then advanced forward into the room, which was completely dark, so the probe turned on its powerful light and illuminated the room itself. It contained row after row of strange, rectangular, grey metal boxes standing at a slight angle with cables coming out of them and into the wall.

The probe trundled down, past more of the strange metal boxes until it came to one which seemed to be half open. The probe's arm gently lifted the lid and underneath was some sort of body, long dead and mummified. It looked vaguely human. It had two legs and a head, but it had four arms and an extended torso to accommodate the extra appendages. One set of arms was normal-sized and the other set was smaller like T-Rex arms. The head itself was very strangely shaped for a human like it had a large, flat snout and was wearing a strange material.

Before the probe could look further, they heard one of the male voices say.

"We're picking up something on the sensor, some sort of electromagnetic radiation. Unlike the other readings, mostly because this one is moving towards us."

The probe closed the door of the strange box and turned to the left-hand side where a strange, black and grey metal creature stood. It had an oval body supported by four thin legs. It also had a strange oval head with what looked like four eyes or cameras, one on the top of the head and one on the bottom part of its head.

The probe moved back slightly. Before it could do anything, the two lasers shot out from the bottom of its head and the feed on the probe went blank.

"No more readings," said the male voice with a tinge of disappointment.

Althenia frowned at the footage.

"How far did they get?" she asked.

"About two hundred meters into the ship."

Althenia looked thoughtful for a moment.

"Well, this is going to complicate things quite a bit. I hope the hull can withstand plasma bolts."

Natalie shrugged.

"I'm not too sure, to be honest, but it means this mission has hostiles and we will need arms. And we will have to be in spacesuits as well unless you want to be firing lasers with a light head thanks to all that oxygen."

"Not to mention, god knows what diseases are still active there," added Rena.

"Any luck with the language?" asked Althenia.

Again, Natalie shrugged her shoulders.

"Not really, Lucinda said she had an odd feeling, like she knew it when she was a child, but can't remember. Currently, there is some information on the language, most of it related to symbols outside the ship, but to be honest, since it has had no effect on the battle it has not been given high priority. We can identify basic usage, like part of the symbol on the side was something to do with a medic or a lab or a medical lab."

"I see," said Althenia, whose eyes moved to Sylvia. "Are there any plans for another probe?"

"Yes. Should be another one done in two days, and they'll send us the footage as well. This time they're going to use an armed probe."

"Okay," said Althenia.

They both fell silent and stared at Sylvia, who looked rather peaceful in her hospital gown and her head resting on the pillow. Rena didn't have much contact with her, and the last time they really spoke was during her capture, but she heard of the things she did, which actually made her admire Sylvia. She had gone from an entitled overlord to a valuable soldier. No wonder she won the heart of Althenia.

*****

"The port is growing," thought Lucinda.

She watched them finish loading the submarine.

She was brimming with excitement, as this was her first trip via submarine to the almost mythical Point Nemo. She had taken a new train that had been set up between the city and the port. It was one of the first overground trains to run since the invasion. They had even turned the breach into a rail tunnel that connected the city to the outside world. It could, of course, be closed in emergencies.

A month had passed since the battle, and she had been more and more in contact with the central command and had even been invited to one or two of their meets, mostly when it concerned her city.

With her clearance, she had done some digging out of curiosity and was shocked by how many free human settlements were out there. Apparently, humanity had focused on the ocean when most of the land was lost to them. The ACS had destroyed any sign of cities or roadways on the surface with air raids, but it had not bothered to invade the island themselves unless they were large enough to present a valid target. This left island nations like Japan, the Philippines, New Zealand, and the United Kingdom free and able to use the underground bunkers and create underground cities, and in some cases even building cities and towns in the sea itself next to the islands. So now most of the northeastern coast of the continent of America, as well as a few island states and the colony of Mars, were now free.

She could sense the humans finally had hope.

The submarine she was going to board was a large double hull design and was the height of comfort for shipping dignitaries which, according to Althenia, meant that they would have their own cabins with an attached bathroom, but it would still be cramped and small.

A man appeared in front of the loading dock of the sub.

"This must be our main guest. I am Captain Author, commander of the sub," he introduced, as he extended his hand.

"Pleasure to meet you," Lucinda said, with a smile as she shook it.

"I understand you want to be with your entourage," he continued, "So, we have a suite where we can put you, and right next door we can put Natalie and Rena. Althenia will also be across the hallway from you."

"Thank you, captain," Lucinda replied as a gurney was wheeled on with Sylvia lying on it, followed by Althenia.

"We, of course, will be keeping Sylvia in our medical bay under the watchful eye of our resident doctor," the captain said, without missing a beat as he led them down a metal hallway through a couple of airtight open metal doors.

He opened one, and Lucinda saw that Althenia was right.

It was just a small room that had a simple metal bunk with a shower and a toilet next to it. He then opened another door with the same size and bunk.

"This is Althenia's, and those two rooms are Natalie's and Rena's," the captain said, pointing further down. He then went to a communication panel. "This is the captain, heading back to the bridge shortly. Please make sure all cargo is loaded so we can be off." He then turned to Lucinda. "This journey will take about three days before we get to Point Nemo."

"Three days in this? Great," said Natalie, pouting. "I suppose the Panama Canal is no longer active and we have to go around South America."

The captain beamed at her.

"I see your friend knows her history. Indeed, the Panama Canal has long been out of action but we're actually going around and above the North American continent, along the northwest passage, as we need to stop in Hawaii."

"Oh yes", thought Lucinda, *"That was one of the main locations that central command used."*

Apparently, Hawaii had a lot of underground infrastructure left over when it was a nation-state in the United States of America, which also built underground bunkers. She could understand the appeal. They were getting her help with planning the liberation of the rest of the American continent and they seemingly wanted her part of the meeting as her city would be one of the main advancing points.

"Right," said the captain. "We better get going. Supper will be at six pm."

With that, he left, leaving Natalie, Rena, and Althenia by their cabins.

*****

Doctor Lowe sat looking at the footage.

This was the third drone they had lost to, what he called 'the robot spiders'. The ship was lousy with them. Their probe had managed to knock out four or five, but they kept coming. So far, they had a map of the first five hundred meters around the portal. They still had no idea what the next steps were or how they were going to redirect the starship.

"Was it even possible?"

When they got on board, it was obvious how heavily damaged the ship was and they had yet to find a control centre or bridge that could possibly be on the other side of the ship, which would be miles away.

He focused once more on the footage.

The drone showed an image of more rectangular cases with bodies or caskets, but he suspected that they were life pods that put the subjects in suspended animation. How they did it was a bit of a mystery, just like most of the ship. There were hundreds, row after row in a straight line. Every now and then, it would be a group of symbols, and so far, they had figured out the meaning of some. Like the one they went past was either floor or level forty-five or fifty-four.

As the footage continued, he spotted another symbol on the wall. He had a look and ran it past the database. Interesting—it was either a command floor or centre of power.

There was a knock on the door.

"Enter," he said while studying the image.

A woman of about thirty came in wearing the grey dress and white lab coat, with short black hair and blue eyes with a pair of black, thick-rimmed glasses, and holding a red mug of tea and a stack of papers.

"Bio report for you, sir."

"Thanks, Ava."

He took the report from her hand and had a look.

"Nothing?"

"Yep, I'm afraid so," she replied. "There's nothing that shows up, no bacteria, not a thing, which is odd considering all the bodies we've found. The only reason I can think of is that they sterilised the ship, then once all those people lost their lives there was a massive loss of oxygen."

"Well, the lack of oxygen could explain the bodies in the first place," replied Doctor Lowe, taking a sip of his tea, "There should still be something. I would love to get a hold of a database, but we have yet to find a computer terminal."

He put the report down.

"We have five probes left?"

"Yes, sir," she replied.

"And two days," he murmured, "Well, let's try force, then. This time we will armour and send in two probes, one to support the other."

Ava nodded and made a note of this on her notepad

"Speaking of force, sir, why not send in a nuclear device?"

Doctor Lowe laid back.

"That was the backup plan, but we need a nuclear device capable of disintegrating twenty kilometres of a strange alloyed steel that we still do not fully understand the properties of while making sure none of the pieces are large enough to cause extensive damage. That backup plan has been shelved."

Ava nodded and went out of the room. Finishing his tea, he returned to the reports. Maybe the thirty percent oxygen was a sign of the error, maybe it was meant to be at twenty percent like Earth. He had seen his share of broken consoles and damaged equipment that indicated all was not well, but they had yet to stumble across any sort of computer core or processing bank.

*****

"It was nice weather," thought Rena, as they sat out on the beach under the umbrella they had managed to rent.

It was just her and Natalie now. She was wearing a simple, blue one-piece swimsuit, and Natalie had on a black bikini. It was a warm day, about thirty degrees, perfect beach weather. The beach itself had nice, white sands and clear, blue waters.

There were a few people around as well, and a lifeguard with a dedicated swimming area. There were even some people practising the art of surfing with some handmade wooden surfboards.

There were no food vendors, however. So it was somewhat different from what she'd seen in the media. Granted, most of the media of beaches she saw was before the invasion, but still. They at least had sunscreen again from the same vendor, something Natalie was in the process of rubbing into her shoulders as she sat on her towel. They had asked Althenia to join them, but she had made her excuses, and Lucinda was at her meeting but had promised to join them once it was done.

Natalie gently pushed her, so she was lying face first on the towel and straddled her back and continued to rub in the sunscreen, which had long ago turned into a sensual massage.

As she looked to the side, she saw Lucinda heading towards them wearing a simple, white-piece bathing suit with her long, black hair down. She was followed by Althenia who was wearing a one-piece black swimsuit and a white towel around her waist, carrying a simple blue cooler. Lucinda smiled and waved up at them, and Natalie returned the wave as they came over and took a seat under the umbrella after they laid out their towels.

Lucinda then opened the cooler.

"Right, who wants what? We have some flavoured water or ice pops. I have orange, berry, or cola flavour."

"I'll take cola flavour," said Natalie, peering into the cooler excitedly.

"Not while you're on my back," replied Rena. "You will spill it and make it all sticky."

"Fine," Natalie replied, as she got off and sat on Lucinda's chair.

Rena sat up.

Althenia took a seat next to them, closing off the circle of their group, Rena smiled at Althenia

"Hey. We've not had a good chance to talk. How are you doing?"

"Just focus on the mission, to be honest, shrugged Althenia, as she grabbed a berry ice pop, "And hoping we find something on the starship to help Sylvia. She would like this."

"No news then."

Althenia shook her head.

"Well, at least she's stable, but enough about this. Let's enjoy the sun."

Natalie and Lucinda got up and went down to the ocean.

"It is quite a family you have now," Althenia observed.

"Thanks," said Rena. "You are still part of it, you and Sylvia."

Althenia smiled as they watched Lucinda and Natalie splash each other in the shallows, every now and then getting splashed by one of the waves. Rena smiled and lay down as Althenia got up and joined Lucinda and Natalie to play in the waves of the beach. Rena would join them, but honestly was too comfortable and rather enjoyed watching her current and ex-lovers together.

*****

Despite putting on lots of sunscreen, Lucinda still felt a bit burnt.

She remembered when she chose her body. She had fallen in love with the pale skin, not realising the downsides. They had time to heal once they finally arrived at Point Nemo and were in the process of unloading the necessary supplies. She walked down the gangplank, followed by Rena and Natalie. Althenia was helping with the unloading of Sylvia.

The dock itself was a massive, grey, steel room with various submarines in the process of loading and unloading. Here, they were met by a familiar face, Doctor Lowe, as well as a woman of about thirty with short black hair and thick-rimmed glasses and a man in a grey uniform with grey hair and blue eyes, who, guessing from his insignias, was the base's commander.

The man held out his hand.

"Greetings, I am Commander Lowe."

She took his hand and shook it.

"Any relation to Doctor Lowe here?"

"Yes, the good doctor is my son, and this pretty girl is Ava, Doctor Lowe's assistant," he said, pointing to the blushing woman next to Doctor Lowe.

Lucinda shook her hand and pointed to her entourage.

"This is Rena and Natalie, my assistants. This is impressive," she said, gesturing around them.

The commander beamed with pride.

"Yes, quite an achievement. One of the things we're proud of, especially the airlock you came through. I have a model of the base in my office I can show you."

"That would be great," she replied, "But first, I need to stretch my legs after being cramped in the sub for so long."

They then walked down a collection of metal hallways that reminded Lucinda of the submarine but with a lot more space here. Ava and Doctor Lowe left them and went down another hallway, no doubt having seen the model already.

They finally stopped at a metal door with a nameplate attached. Commander Lowe opened it and they entered a rather large office with a secretary desk on the left-hand side. The secretary working behind it was a young man of about twenty with short black hair in a military cut.

He stood up, and Commander Lowe waved him down.

"At ease," he said. "This is my secretary, Fedrick, and here is the model."

He pointed at the large desk in the middle. There was a large metal pyramid in the middle with four slightly smaller pyramids on each corner and two large cylinders poking out the front as well as a large metal rectangle poking out of the pyramid on the back. The smaller pyramids were connected to the main pyramid via heavy round cylinders.

"These are the airlocks," he said, pointing towards the two cylinders on the large pyramid. "Each one has two airlocks, enabling us to have four subs going in or out at the same time, and if needed, we can shut one down for maintenance. These four pyramids on the end are the fusion reactors required to generate the wormhole itself."

He removed one side of the main pyramid which showed a large room with a massive and bulky circle in the middle with lots of wires connected to it. "This is the wormhole generator itself, and below that and taking up most of the bottom level are banks of batteries that take the excess power, and from there, it's just a loading bay to the docks."

He then pointed towards the rectangle along the back.

"This is the sub-dry docks. It can house two massive cargo subs for repair and refit. This was added as an afterthought on the design," Commander Lowe said, rather proudly, "Now for the main part of the show."

He walked to the opposite end of the room and pushed a button on the wall.

Here, a metal shutter lifted up, and behind the shutter was another very large room, at least six stories high, and at the far side was a massive metal circle embedded into the floor. It was about twenty meters tall and had a ten-meter hole in the middle and looked like an elongated metal doughnut.

Lucinda lost count of the number of wires going into the thing and noticed the floor itself had rails and a small rail engine with a couple of carts were parked off in the side. She also saw that they had cranes running on the top as well. He then opened the door next to the window and stepped out onto a metal-framed balcony.

The girls followed.

They were at least four stories up and had a good view of the operation. On the left-hand side were a couple of raised concrete platforms with a vast array of control panels facing the large, metal circle with various technicians sitting behind them.

"Currently, we're doing routine maintenance and had the wormhole active before you arrived. We should have enough power stored up to do your run tomorrow morning but thought you would like to see it."

A door opened inside the large room, four stories below, and Dr Lowe and Ava entered.

She turned back to the commander.

"I'm impressed. The fact that you kept this hidden from ACS is amazing, but to be fair, you did choose an excellent hiding spot."

The commander beamed with pride.

"My grandfather was one of the engineers on the project. Since then, my family have been involved in the project in one way or another, and this is the first time in all the years it has been operational that we're shutting it down."

"Shutting it down?" asked Lucinda, confused.

"Yes, that's why this took so long to get ready. We had to double shipments from and to Mars to prepare for the shutdown, but basically the hope is that if there is a dangerous disease you bring back on the ship like the one used during the invasion. Then we can quickly isolate and contain it," replied the commander.

Lucinda still cringed a little at the mention of the disease but pushed it aside.

"It was nice meeting you but I'm going to clear the last sub, so I'll let you catch up with your colleagues," said the commander as he turned and left, heading back to his office.

Lucinda turned to Althenia.

"All okay?" In the background, she heard Natalie asking a couple of technical questions to Commander Lowe.

"Sylvia is safe and still stable," replied Althenia.

"And you?" asked Lucinda.

Althenia paused for a moment.

"To be honest, nervous. This is the first time I've been on an alien starship."

Lucinda smiled at her, reassuringly.

"Don't worry. I'm pretty sure it's the first time any of us has physically been on such a vessel, and truth be told, I'm a bit nervous as well."

The next day, Althenia checked her space suit. It was Mar's standard pattern and had special pouches for biological waste products. It was a flexible black Kevlar suit, with armoured plates installed in vital areas, like the chest and legs.

She put on her helmet which had a clear visor. The visor displayed information, which was updated by the computer on the wrist. It also provided a video feed; most of the video was recorded as they could only keep the wormhole open for at most ten minutes and be unable to provide a live feed.

Althenia had trained in the suit and was used to the weight, so she would take point. Beside her were Lucinda, Natalie, and Rena. Lucinda and Rena would be armed as well. Rena and Althenia carried a rifle and a heavy calibre pistol in a shoulder holster. Lucinda and Natalie had the same pistol with a shoulder holster. Natalie also took a laptop since she was the technical specialist. She had been fully briefed by Doctor Lowe.

The current plan was to go in and explore for approximately four hours and see what progress they had made. In front of them was the massive twenty-meter-tall metal circle, which was the wormhole generator.

The generator roared to life.

It took a second for the whir to wind up and then down as the wormhole stabilised the connection. The centre of the circle suddenly became very wavy like the image behind it was underneath a heat source of some sort. With a sudden flash, the image changed to the inside of the starship except it looked like it was underwater.

Althenia stepped forward, her rifle ready.

After one final check, she reached the edge of the portal and stepped in.

She was standing on the metal hull of the starship. One of the states in her helmet display changed to orange as the oxygen content went up from twenty to thirty, not dangerous but it would lead to oxygen toxicity or hyperoxia. There was some concern about strange diseases as well but so far they had confirmed that there were no bacteria or any form of life besides the metal guardians, at least not any life forms five hundred meters from the generator.

She looked around the room. It was a decrepit control room that had long fallen out of use. Althenia then checked the door, as she heard Natalie over the radio say.

"No good. The consoles here are all dead, and there is no power."

"Right then, let us move and see if we can get further," instructed Althenia.

They chose the hallway that the probe went down, which showed a possible sign of being some sort of control centre. Althenia turned on the powerful torch attached to the side of her rifle and looked down the hallway. It was clear and the helmets reported the only EM signature was behind her and marked as friendly. They walked down the hallways, past a group of doors, one of which was broken. Althenia stopped before them and had a look with her flashlight using her advanced eyesight to see if she could spot anything, but so far it was quiet. They turned up a corridor and came to a hallway which they went down with no signs of life.

"Odd. Normally, there would be an encounter by now," said Lucinda, over the radio.

"Maybe we generate a lower signature than the robots," replied Althenia.

Rena stopped by a symbol and pointed.

"Here it is, the corridor with command on it."

They stopped at the sign and climbed up the small set of metal steps and reached a metal door. Althenia gave the handle of the door a tug with no luck. Lucinda moved her aside and, using her psychic powers, she pulled the door again and it opened with a crunch.

Lucinda let out a gasp of air.

"Damn, that was strange. It feels like controlling my power was difficult."

"Difficult?" asked Althenia.

"Yes, it was like a lot of energy pushing through and I could barely control it," explained Lucinda.

Rena shined her torch into the room.

"Cables," Rena said. "Lots of them, and a console."

"So," said Lucinda, "the symbol means it is a power room for control and not command and control."

Natalie edged past Rena and went to the console and tried a few buttons.

"This one works," Natalie exclaimed, with glee as she pressed more buttons on the console.

She set up her laptop next to it.

"This might take some time," she said, as she struggled over the console.

Althenia looked around, searching for another entrance. When she saw there was none, she then set up a watch at the door.

"All right, may as well take a rest. I'll take the first watch."

She heard a "roger" from the radio and sat at the door.

As tapped swiftly on a keyboard, she heard another creak in the bulkhead, and then another one getting closer.

"We have company," she said over the radio.

Checking her rifle, she turned off the torch, letting her eyes adjust to the dim light and not wanting to give the enemy any advantage. She saw the leg first. It was one of those damn spider bots. None made a sound. The spider creature paused for what seemed like an eternity as Althenia kept an eye on it, her rifle ready to take out one of the legs, and her finger on the trigger. It then continued down past the hallway to its unknown destination.

Althenia let out the breath she was holding and then tapped on her radio.

"It seems to be going away."

Suddenly there was a loud crash as a panel in the ceiling gave way and what Althenia assumed was a smaller spider bot landed on the floor. Natalie let out a scream of shock as Rena acted on instinct and shot it, spraying their space suits with some sort of ichor. Seeing the threat pass, Althenia turned her attention back to the hallway as the spider bot returned and turned its four large eyes down the hallway. Before it took a chance to take another step, Althenia pulled the trigger, hitting the bot in the forehead with a plasma bolt, causing its head to explode in a bright spark and collapse into a pile of scrap.

"Robots don't bleed," Rena mused.

She couldn't hear anything in the hallway and turned back to the first robot that had come from the ceiling and looked down at it. There was a lot of blue blood and ichor on the floor and a burn mark. It looked like some sort of half-burnt giant spider with multiple thoraxes, each one looking to have four legs. It was just under a meter in length and had spindly legs, but that is all they could make out as most of it was burnt and splattered. Althenia shined her light up in the hole where the creature had come from.

"Some sort of duct, by the looks of it. I assume we didn't send the probes into the ducts, which I assume were free of spider robots."

"Well, that was fun. You okay, Natalie?" said Rena on the radio net.

"Yes, just a bit shocked, wasn't expecting giant bugs."

"Well, hopefully, we've scared them off, but Althenia, can you keep an ear out?," Lucinda instructed, "And Rena, can you watch the hallway?"

"Fair enough," replied Rena.

"Roger."

She took position and kept an eye on the broken duct.

It had been three hours or so and not much had happened except for Natalie using some colourful language against her PC. Lucinda pressed the mike button on her radio,

"Right, my turn. Rena, take a break, I'll watch the hallway, then in an hour relive Althenia."

"Thanks," she heard on the headset.

"Yes!" cried Natalie, "Some good news: I managed to get a schematic of the ship." She paused for a second. "Oh, and if I am reading this correctly, I assume that is the wormhole generator," she said, pointing at her screen. "That means the command centre is clear across the ship over here."

"Great, that is at least all the way across the ship, by the looks of it," said Althenia, looking over Natalie's shoulder. "Did you get anything else?"

Natalie nodded and Althenia could almost hear her smile. "Yes, a lot of files, most of it in raw data, but hopefully when I hand it in, they can make sense of it back in the lab. The location of a medical bay, I think, is just half a kilometre away."

"Anything else you can pull?" asked Lucinda.

"Not unless the bug we have on the floor was alive and could speak English."

"Okay, let's head out. We have about half an hour," replied Althenia. She then looked at the dead bug. "We better take that." She then picked it up, thankful she was still in her spacesuit.

"As much as I hate this, you need to take point and keep your ears out," Rena said, "Even in a suit, your hearing is turning out to be better. Let me take the damn thing."

She then took the corpse out of Althenia's hand as Althenia got her rifle ready, turned on the torch, and carried on down the hallway back to the wormhole generator. They heard the distinct sound of a high-powered motor and saw an image form. It mostly was white though, and had figures in white suits with masks on. She recognized biohazard suits when she saw them.

They stepped through with their dead prize and found the wormhole covered in a white plastic sheet.

They stepped through an inflated tent that connected to the white sheet, making an airtight seal for them to arrive in. The dead alien bug was put on a hospital tray and wheeled away to another tent that acted as a lab. They were then put in a third tent where they were sprayed with a fine mist, no doubt containing a variety of chemicals. Next, they stepped into another tent where they had a strange machine set up. It looked like four pods set up next to each other but didn't have the facility to close.

Althenia stepped in the first one, and a pair of robot arms removed her helmet, followed by another pair of robot arms removing her gloves and undoing her armour. Lucinda, Rena, and Natalie went into their own pods. The pod had been designed so that the spacesuit could be removed without the user touching it. Once stripped down, a hatch opened. It contained a simple leotard without sleeves, useful for the medical test that they would have to undergo. They were dressed, then went through another airlock and came into what looked like a medical bay with four beds set up and medical equipment laid about. It had two suited figures they recognized as Doctor Lowe and his assistant, Ava.

"We're just going to run some medical tests, if that's okay?" asked Ava.

It was rhetorical as no one objected. Lucinda took her place. Next to her, came Doctor Lowe.

"How was it?" asked Doctor Lowe, as he began taking blood from Lucinda.

"Besides the giant bugs, the lighting, and the robot attack, it was okay.".

"Yes, that bug." He paused for a second. "Interesting. We're not expecting that, to be honest. Nothing showed up on the sensors."

He took another blood sample, this time from Rena, who said, "Well, we got somewhere."

Then Lucinda added, "I say we head to the medical bay tomorrow and see if we can do anything for Sylvia."

"Agreed," replied Althenia in an uncharacteristically eager tone.

Natalie had her laptop with her and was busy uploading the data using a wireless network since a physical connection would be out of the question.

"Well, you'll need to wait eight hours before your next adventure," said Doctor Lowe as he looked at a chart. "We won't have enough power to start the wormhole till then. Also, please report any strange symptoms to me or any of the medical personnel as soon as they appear. We cannot be too careful, as we are dealing with a lot of unknowns here."

With that, he left, and Lucinda laid back on the medical bed, and she was rather surprised that she, in fact, felt so tired. She tried to sit up, but the call of the bed was strong, and she closed her eyes.

*****

They had new suits at least, thought Rena as she stood on the other side of the wormhole. Althenia had taken point again as they had walked down a hallway towards the medical lab. Halfway there, Althenia held her hand up. She stopped, as did everyone else.

They kept silent.

She heard a clattering above. It sounded like something moving in the vents. Given what they had encountered, she could guess what it was. After the sound passed, Althenia waited for a moment and then indicated they could continue.

They walked down a couple of hallways until Natalie piped up over the radio.

"The next turn should be the lab."

Althenia stopped by the door marked as Medical Bay. Rena stood in front of the door, gun drawn, as Althenia tried the handle with a loud grunt but no luck.

"Hold tight," she said.

Rena knew that Althenia would like to take point on the door but her greater strength made opening the doors a lot easier.

Natalie looked at her laptop.

"It looks like there might be another entrance in the side through this rather large room that says …" She looked at her cheat sheet she had up for a moment. "… food warehouse or organic disposal."

Lucinda looked at her.

"So it could be a sewage treatment? Great," said Lucinda, disgusted.

Althenia advanced to the next door, taking point as Rena followed closely, then Natalie and Lucinda at the back. They had agreed Natalie should be always in the middle as she was tactically the weak link. They stopped at the next door, and Rena stood in front, rifle drawn, as Althenia tried the door lock, which managed to open after exerting some effort.

Behind the door was a large room where the ceiling was at least five meters above them. It had row after row of large plants encased in glass and suspended in what looked like water that ran down the room.

"Well, I assume this is the food warehouse then," said Lucinda as she took in the size of the place.

"You can't be too sure, these plants may be able to recycle the waste. We used special plants to do that back on Mars," replied Althenia, and then she stopped and pointed. "I think I found where our friend came from."

The wall, which was covered in glass and had a group of giant bugs roaming on the wall behind a glass barrier, like a collection of cockroaches. Rena focused on one and found it to have a head like an ant with two compound eyes on top of the head and a pair of clasping jaws. The head was connected straight to a thorax with four spindly legs coming out of it, two on each side. What she then noticed when she looked at another example, was that one had two thoraxes. Maybe it was a juvenile, but then one walked past her vision with three thoraxes.

Natalie stepped a bit closer to the glass with the bugs in it and got a strange look from Althenia. She followed Althenia's gaze and saw that she was looking at the small paper notebook Natalie had that seemed to be falling out of her top pocket. As Natalie took another step, the notebook fell out, but instead of falling on the ground, it fell on the glass. The noise startled the bugs and they scattered.

"An inverted gravity field. So that's how they stay up," exclaimed Lucinda.

Suddenly a whirring sound was heard as the water started draining out of one of the glass rows with the plants. This sent the bugs into a bit of a frenzy as they all rushed to the bottom of their container. Once the row was empty of water, the plants seemed to vanish, sucked down into the floor of the bay. She then noted that the bugs had positioned themselves into some sort of feed trough, and in front of the bugs appeared the green leaves and shoots of the plant. The animals started eating their meal as a strange machine came across the glass wall.

They watched it carefully, not wanting to interfere, but cautious as well. Natalie had not even picked up her notebook. The machine continued past and stopped at a double thorax bug. A laser shot out, severing the second thorax. A robot hand came out and grabbed it as the bug happily ate away. It then moved on to another bug about the same size, but the second thorax looked a bit smaller, and then it moved on to another bug, ignoring the small thorax bug.

"I wonder what they do with the thoraxes?" asked Rena over the radio, as the machine continued its journey.

"Maybe it's food," replied Lucinda, "or power. I know some of the alien technology uses an organic power supply that needs organic matter as well."

"Okay, well I think the medical bay is down past this tank," interrupted Althenia, as she took point.

Rena heard another gurgle and saw that the former empty tank was now filling up with more of what looked like water. Eventually, they reached another door where she took position in front, her rifle ready to go. Althenia pulled it and she heard a click somewhere, and the door opened about a centimetre. Althenia took in a breath and pulled again and managed to grind the door so it was halfway open. Enough room for them to squeeze in, and they squeezed into another room, this time lit with the red glow of what Rena was beginning to suspect was the emergency lighting.

Here, they found a collection of metal slates against the walls with a various collection of strange equipment. On one side there was a rounded table with a hole in the middle and a hole in the side for a person to get through. Natalie walked up to it and went inside the centre of the table and started to press a couple of buttons on the table itself. "Dead," she announced and went down to floor level where she struggled with a couple of panels below, making a bit of noise. Rena watched the door that they had come through as Althenia turned to the door that would not open beforehand as the noise increased.

"Found a broken connection."

A zap was heard, along with the word "Damn," and a screen flickered on the console.

The red lights turned off, and then the normal lights turned on. This was followed by the console flickering back on.

"Okay, I fixed it, I think," said Natalie, as she put her laptop next to the embedded screen and started working away. One of the machines next to the bed made a loud whirring noise as a metal arm moved above one of the metal bedframes. Althenia pointed her rifle at it as soon as she heard the sound.

"Sorry," said Natalie. "I didn't think that would actually do anything."

"No problem," replied Althenia.

The door that led to the hallway creaked loudly, and Althenia turned her attention to that, as Rena's grip tightened on her gun. After a couple more creaks, the door suddenly became silent. A loud sound was heard like a plate behind the door being moved. Althenia looked at Lucinda and Rena for a second, then focused back on the door. More sounds were heard with another creak from the door and a couple more bangs, which then stopped.

"Well, at least they're trying to fix the door," said Rena over the headset.

"Worth keeping an eye on it. Natalie, get cracking, and Althenia, you okay doing first shift?" added Lucinda.

"Affirmative."

They continued to watch the door as the sound died down.

After a little while, Natalie spoke up again as Althenia kept an eye on the locked door. There had been no noise on the other side, and the only real noise Althenia could hear was the chittering of the bugs next door. "I think I've found something, but I'm going to get the medical team to look at it. Also, it might be helpful if we take some medical supplies that they could study."

"Makes sense," replied Lucinda. "Question is, where are they?"

"There's a storage facility, I think just about two hundred meters away," answered Natalie.

"Okay, do we have to go through the bug zoo again?" asked Rena

Natalie replied in a somewhat mirthful tone.

"Unless you want to open that door, I'm afraid so."

Althenia checked her rifle once more.

"I'll take point. Are we good to go?"

Once everyone had confirmed, she headed to the half-open door on the other side of the room and, once it was clear, stepped out.

"Go right and to the end of the room," instructed Natalie.

They walked past another tank of plants and bugs wandering the walls, ignoring them. At the end of the room was another heavy steel door where Rena took point and Althenia managed to open it after pulling the handle and hearing a crunching sound in the mechanism. Althenia then held up her hand as they all waited and let Althenia listen for any strange noises. She then heard something coming close as the bug chitter increased.

She held her hand up again, giving the "be prepared" signal, and took aim at the door.

Rena followed suit as Natalie was moved to the back by Lucinda, who stepped in front of her. A metal arm with three fingers appeared and pulled the doors off. Before them was a four-armed robot that looked rather like a metal version of the corpse they had seen in reports before. They could see the large flat snout and a mouth, and it had at least six eyes. It was about eight feet tall and had four arms, all normal size.

Althenia fired a bolt of her plasma gun, which caused a bright flash as the plasma interacted with the shield. Rena fired next, hitting the side of the robot, causing a few sparks, and two arms went inert on one side. Althenia then stepped back and aimed again, but before should could fire, Lucinda sent a shockwave to the top of the robot's head, smashing it off the body and causing the robot to fall with a loud bang.

Two spider robots then appeared one on each side of the hallway.

"Left," Althenia shouted, as she fired at the robot on the left-hand side, hitting it in the leg, causing it to fall to the ground. Rena fired to the right-hand side, hitting the other spider soldier. Then another standing robot appeared on the left-hand side. It threw across the corpse of one of the spider bots. It was followed by two other bots and then reached through the doorway, taking a swipe at Althenia, who rolled back. It was hit by a bolt from Rena and a psychic blast from Lucinda, falling to the ground without its head.

Althenia heard another heavy humanoid robot coming towards them. "We have more incoming, we better get back."

"Okay," shouted Rena as they walked backwards, their guns still pointed at the door as another robot came through. It was hit by a plasma bolt and blasted with a psychic blast. Althenia stayed in the ready position about twenty meters from the door along with Rena covering the other side with Lucinda and Natalie behind them. Althenia kept her ears open as she heard another couple of robots on the other side of the doorway. It sounded like the spider bots, but none of them came in and just made noise on the outside. After the noises had stopped and the bugs seemed to have calmed down, she again went to the door, closely followed by Rena. When nothing popped out to kill her, she got right up to the door and looked down the left side hallway. From what she could see, it was clear. She quickly swapped sides and looked down the left side and again it was clear. She noticed that the robot bodies of both the spider bot and humanoid bots had been removed.

"Okay, which way is the hallway?" she asked.

"Go down the left side. It is about two doors down," replied Natalie.

"Okay, I'll take point. Lucinda, Natalie, behind. And Rena, watch our backs," said Althenia.

They then went down the hallway, which was lit by the standard red glow.

Once they passed a couple of heavy doors, Althenia heard Natalie say, "This one." She stopped and grabbed the handle and gave it a pull with a satisfying click. This door opened, and a completely dark room was before them. Althenia turned on her flashlight and entered. It was just row after row of metal boxes stacked in neat, orderly rows. Some had strange lettering on them, and some were completely blue or yellow. She shined her light up. The ceiling was short. She then shined her light down the hallway. It was a long passage, and she could just make out the other end.

"Any idea what we're looking for?" asked Rena.

"Yeah, a yellow box with this symbol. Hold on, I have a program that I created to decode some of the symbols. It's still very much a work in progress," replied Natalie as she typed up commands on her laptop which she had turned into a tablet by folding it over and was using the touch screen.

A symbol appeared on their helmet, a strange-looking N with a plus in it. She looked down the rows and checked any yellow box, idly wondering what the other boxes could contain. If they ever secured the ship, this room would be well worth a look at. She stopped at one small, yellow box right at the bottom of a row of boxes. It had the symbol.

"Found it," she said.

The question was how she would be able to get it, as it was flat up against the other boxes and there seemed to be no handle.

Natalie popped over and looked. "That looks like a medical symbol," Natalie said, as she tried to remove the box but again found it flush against the other boxes and the wall.

"Okay, any ideas?"

Althenia smiled as Rena and Lucinda popped over.

"Lucinda, can you use your powers to move the box?"

"Stand back," replied Lucinda.

They stepped back, and the box simply moved itself out, no doubt using Lucinda's powers and sending the boxes on top of it tumbling down with a loud *whump*. Althenia assumed a battle stance and listened for any enemies she heard chittering and noticed the bottom crate—a green-coloured one—in the pile was smashed open and spilling a green goo.

"Grab the medical crate and head to the door," she said. They walked towards the door, only for the chittering sound to increase. Althenia looked up. A pair of pincers punched through.

"Any idea what was in that green crate?" asked Rena, as they retreated from the spot and backed away to the door.

"According to the symbol, it said something about 'high power or energy storage,'" said Natalie.

"Door," shouted Lucinda. Althenia turned, and behind them were more of the bugs.

"My guess is biofuel of some sort."

"Okay, well the door we came in is becoming crowded. Is there any other way out?" asked Rena.

"Over here is an exit," shouted Natalie, pointing to the opposite side of the warehouse.

They quickly rushed down the warehouse, past rows of neatly stacked boxes. Lucinda had grabbed the medical crate and was at the back of their line. They found the door by which time the bugs from the ceiling had managed to break through, and they swarmed the row that had the broken box.

Althenia tried the door.

"Damn," she said. "It's stuck fast."

She tried a couple more times as the horde of bugs ripped the container apart. Once they had their food, a couple of them got a bit more excited, and Althenia could hear the chittering increase.

"I don't think they should have eaten that," exclaimed Rena.

"Shield up," replied Lucinda as a couple of the bugs were stopped by her psychic defences.

Lucinda let out a gasp.

"The bugs also have some sort of psychic power. It seems to be affecting my shield. I'm not sure how long I can hold it."

Rena did not need to be told twice. She pressed a button on her rifle, put it on her hip, and pulled the trigger while sending out an array of plasma into the advancing horde. While she did that, Althenia again tried the door, bracing herself against it. She almost felt the handle itself break under the pressure but was rewarded with a very loud crunch sound as it opened inch by inch. Once there was enough space, Althenia then got between the wall and door and with all her strength, pushing hard, she heard more loud crunches but managed to get the door open.

"Go," she shouted as she got back into the room, pressed the automatic button on her rifle, and started firing into the bug horde from the hip while shooting.

"Go, Rena, I will cover."

Natalie and Rena rushed out the door, followed by Lucinda as Althenia grabbed one of her plasma cartridges with one hand while firing at any bug that had managed to crawl over the body of its kind and was now heading towards her. Once she had a second, she let the rifle fall so that her shoulder strap would catch it. She got out a flare and jammed it into the plasma cartridge top and lit it. Then, since the plasma cartridge had quite a bit of lithium in it, she threw it as it started to bulge. This bright bulging object distracted the bugs long enough for her to head for the door, only to find Rena standing there ready with her rifle as Natalie and Lucinda were slightly further down the hall.

Althenia then slammed her shoulder into the door they had come through and forced it shut, using all her strength reserve. She could hear more crunching sounds as they tried to get through.

"Anyone know if there would be anything flammable in there?"

Just then, a loud pop was heard behind the door kept slightly open by the remain of one of the bugs.

"That fuel is highly flammable," replied Natalie.

"We better head back to the wormhole room," said Althenia as another louder pop was heard and then a screech of creatures in pain. As they ran down the hall, the red emergency light changed to a blue flash as an alarm started up. Althenia looked back, and a gout of flame burst from the open crack in the door. They rushed down the hallway, and towards the wormhole generator. Althenia glanced back and saw a couple of spider robots heading towards them. She stopped and prepared to fire, but the spider bot ignored them and turned down the hallway towards the fire. They reached the wormhole room and waited as their window would not be for another half an hour.

Althenia looked at Lucinda, who was out of breath.

"You okay?"

"Bit of headache from the bugs, to be honest," she replied.

It was a difficult choice. Lucinda's power made her useful, but if she were to fall sick during a mission, then it could be dangerous.

"Okay, when we get back, I think you should have a full medical check-up and maybe we delay a bit until you're better," she suggested.

"Okay," replied Lucinda.

Regarding the mission, as Althenia was the highest rank, she was technically in charge but had decided to tread softly as one only got so far in order.

After they had gone through their medical checks, Lucinda still felt a bit nauseous, but better.

"How's it going?" asked Natalie.

"Could be better. I think those bugs might have some sort of psychic power. All I could feel was their alien minds against my defences."

Natalie frowned.

"You need anything?"

"No thanks, but have you heard anything about the box we recovered?" asked Lucinda.

"Yes, they should have something soon. When they opened it, all they found was black goo, so they're looking at it under the microscope."

"Okay," replied Lucinda. "I am going to lay down a bit to see if it helps."

Natalie gave her shoulder a reassuring squeeze as she lay back down. Then Natalie walked off to the science tent. Lucinda found herself tossing and turning and gave up trying to sleep and thought of asking the doctor for something to knock her out but decided against that, as she would only awake groggy.

She got up and walked around for a bit, and found Natalie asleep with her laptop open in front of her, on a chair with a short table next to her medical bed. Lucinda closed the laptop and gently picked up a tired Natalie, who mumbled slightly in a tired voice. Lucinda tucked her into her bed. Once Natalie was comfortable in bed and fast asleep, Lucinda left her and walked to Rena's section. She too was fast asleep, and Lucinda left her too, not wishing to disturb her. She then went to Althenia's bed and found her cleaning her rifle, something she did to distract herself.

"All okay?" asked Lucinda.

Althenia smiled at her. Their relationship was surprising considering the potential leadership conflict and the fact that she stole her girlfriend.

"I should ask the same from you," Althenia replied.

Before she had a chance to answer, in came Doctor Lowe in a containment suit.

"Sorry to bother you, Althenia, but I assumed you were up. Ah, Lucinda, this may involve you as well."

"Okay?" asked Althenia, "What's up?".

"Well," replied Doctor Lowe, "We've looked into what you all recovered from the spaceship. It is basically small nanomachines that, after running tests, seem capable of healing injured tissue, including brain matter—a medical breakthrough."

"Well, so far so good," replied Lucinda, cautiously, " I assume there's going to be a 'but' here?"

"Yes," replied the doctor, in a sombre tone. "I'm afraid when we tested it on certain creatures, it does repair the matter incorrectly as it's not really designed for Earth-based creatures. To be frank, it could help Sylvia, but we're not too sure of the side effects, and since you're the closest thing to family she has, we just want to run this by you."

"I see," replied Althenia.

She stopped cleaning her weapon and let out a sigh, something unusual for her, and paused for a moment. Then after a rather heavy silence, she turned to Doctor Lowe.

"Is there any chance she could wake up by herself?"

Doctor Lowe took a quick look at the notebook.

"To be honest, we're not sure, but the longer she is under, the less likely she is to wake up. One of the issues is the structure in her mind. We're not too sure of the effect it is having or not having while she is unconscious."

Althenia leaned back for a moment.

"I don't think we have much choice by the looks of it."

Lucinda decided to interject.

"Maybe you need a little bit of time to think about it."

"That would be best," added Althenia. "Is there any time frame on this, doctor?"

Doctor Lowe shook his head, "So far, Sylvia's condition is stable, but I will let you know if that changes."

"Thanks, doctor, I will get back to you," replied Althenia, as Doctor Lowe nodded and left them alone.

"Tough choice," said Lucinda.

Althenia resumed cleaning her rifle.

"It is," she agreed. "But then, logically there is only one. She's currently unconscious and won't wake up, and nothing is going to change it by the looks of it."

"That makes sense, I suppose, but she could wake up, we just don't know," replied Lucinda.

"Miracles. I'm afraid I don't have faith in miracles," said Althenia, in a rather gloomy tone.

"You okay?" asked Lucinda, "Do you need to talk?"

Althenia looked up at the ceiling.

"It's been a long couple of days. I'm responsible for Sylvia since I captured her, and one of my jobs was to keep her safe, but I haven't done a great job of that. I've been raised my entire life with the knowledge that duty is all, and it hurts when I fail in that, especially since … I love her."

Althenia looked down at the pieces of her rifle.

Lucinda got up and hugged her, and she felt the hug returned. When Althenia let go, she got off the bed and walked with Lucinda to the door.

"I'll inform the doctor to give it a go."

"I can go if you want?"

"No. She's my responsibility, and I will do it."

*****

So far, it had been forty-eight hours since the doctor went ahead, and he kept Althenia up to date. Despite some medical changes, not much had happened. They had decided to delay the mission for a day or so, not only because of Sylvia, but Lucinda as well. She was still unwell, which Althenia was concerned about, but had decided to let her on the mission. They still had one more mission, and the hope was they could find the answer in the control room. The only issue was that the control room was on the other side of the ship and god knows what they would encounter. They were now standing in a tent still on the main docking bay with the wormhole generator. They needed help and fortunately, it was incoming.

Natalie looked like a kid with a brand-new toy as she used a special control pad attached via a belt on her waist to control a small, one-meter-long, fifty-centimetre-wide vehicle. It was, as far as Althenia could make out, a small black rectangular robot on four heavy-looking wheels on each side that were bigger than the body. It also had two foldable robot arms on each side as well as a foldup plasma rifle turret. Its main job would be to carry food and supplies that they would need for the mission. They were going to give it another twenty-four hours before they let them go, and officially it was training time with the robot, but by the looks of it, Natalie had it mostly figured it out and was now using one of the robot arms to make herself a cup of tea.

Ava entered the tent in a containment suit. She turned to Althenia.

"Sorry to disturb you, but I thought you'd like to know Sylvia is awake."

Althenia's heart skipped for a minute.

"Is she—can she talk? Can I see her?" she asked, blurting out the questions a little faster than normal.

"Once Doctor Lowe confirms it's okay to move her, we will move her by the tent. We still have to keep the containment procedure," she explained.

"I understand," replied Althenia.

Ava rushed off through the normal airlocks while Althenia walked across to a special visitors' tent that had a split table, one on each side of the room, separated by a clear plastic sheet and a speaker that would allow conversation. She didn't have to wait long as a medical bed was wheeled into the room. On the bed was Sylvia.

Althenia smiled at her.

"Hey," she said. "How is it going?"

She moved a chair next to the plastic sheet beside Sylvia's bed.

"I've felt better, to be honest," she replied, in a tired voice. "So, I understand we're at a place called Point Nemo, and you managed to get on the starship through a wormhole. It seems I've missed out on a lot."

"I'm afraid so but don't worry. Once you're up, we can take a tour," replied Althenia in a slightly humorous tone. "It can be like a date night."

Sylvia smiled a little and replied, "That's good to hear. It may be a little bit of time, to be honest. I have a few issues moving my legs at the moment."

Althenia looked at her. Inside, she felt her heart drop but kept a brave face.

"Don't worry, we'll have time when I get back from the final mission."

She put her hand on the plastic, and Sylvia did the same. She could feel her hand on the other side and smiled.

*****

So far, they had encountered little to no resistance in their mission to get to the control room. They had avoided areas they were in before so that might have helped, at least that's what Rena was hoping. Most of what they passed was empty, red-lit corridors that had closed doors or led to dark rooms. Some rooms had storage boxes and others, like the one room they were currently in, was some sort of control centre. It had a collection of consoles and a large collection of wires, none of which seemed to be working.

Natalie was playing with a console.

It had been about an hour or so, and they had made good time, but some information on what was ahead wouldn't hurt. Rena took a seat in the chair and kept an eye on the door they came in. Thanks to the sensors on the robot they brought, they could see if anything was coming down the hallway. So far, it was clear. Rena sighed and turned and saw that Althenia was busy cleaning her rifle, a sure sign she was thinking about something.

She set her radio to personal contact on her spacesuit.

"I'm sure you cleaned that before we left."

"I did," she replied, in her normal monotone voice.

"What's on your mind?" asked Rena, knowing Althenia rather well.

"I spoke to Sylvia. She's doing better. She's awake at least, but she still is unable to move her legs, and the medical reports are not hopeful." She looked at part of her rifle, and sighed, putting it down. "I feel responsible. I pushed the treatment. It seemed logical, but I could have waited."

"You're always too hard on yourself," replied Rena. "We have no idea if the treatment or the damage from the battle caused any issues. She'll be fine as long as she has you."

Before she could add anything else, she heard a beep coming from the robot. Rena rushed over and looked at the display that was on a fold-out screen on top of the robot.

"Something's heading down the duct running along the left side," she shouted over the radio.

Althenia snapped her rifle together and pointed it at the left side of the room. It was quiet as the object was tracked. It stopped for a second and then continued its little mission out of sensor range.

"It must be another bug," said Lucinda. "How is it going, Natalie? Any luck?"

Natalie shook her head.

"I think the fault might be in the conduit on the way to the power supply," she added, as she ducked behind a panel.

"Be careful," replied Lucinda.

"Don't worry, the bug has left, according to the sensor. And I'll keep an eye on it and let you know if any bugs are on their way," added Rena.

"I wonder where they're coming from," mused Lucinda, "They were trapped in the hydroponics bay."

"Well," replied Natalie, "a ship this size could have more than one hydroponics bay."

Another beep from the robot, and Rena looked.

"Another bug on the left side heading in a different direction this time. It could be the same bug," reported Rena.

Natalie jumped up from behind the desk and pointed her gun at the panel. After about a minute or so, Rena saw the bug stop again.

"Bugger," scoffed Natalie.

"What's wrong?" asked Lucinda.

"I've confirmed there's nothing we can do. The cable is broken, and the other end is missing. I'm not too sure who would take it, but I suspect it might be related to the bugs."

"Well, unless anyone has any objections, let's rest here for about an hour or so. At least it seems relatively safe," added Althenia.

She got a couple of "Affirmatives".

Thanks to the talk with Rena, Althenia felt slightly better. They had a mission, and she needed to focus on that for the moment. After a couple more alerts, they left the command room still broken and continued down the hallway, followed by their faithful robot. The hallway changed, and they found themselves entering a large open area. Fortunately, the walkway was now a bridge, but they had a good view of the large metal cavern they found themselves in.

The new bridge was at least a hundred meters long, made of metal and supported long poles from the ceiling about five meters above them. The floor of the cavern was about eight meters below them and was rather hard to make out as the only real light source was a pair of lamps built into the poles supporting the bridge. Althenia had a better time seeing in the dark and looked down.

She saw an odd site and reported her sightings over the radio net.

"There are a couple of large crates, some of which are broken, as well as various pieces of machinery, but there are a few of the larger security robots in pieces below." She then paused. "Hold on, I see movement."

"God, there's a large collection of bugs attacking the robots. Seems to be a bit of a war going on, and the robots are losing."

She studied the scene for a couple of more seconds before adding.

"It seems some of the bugs are a bit bigger and actually have larger pincers."

"Great," complained Rena. "Just what we need, a new species of bugs running around. Who is winning anyway?"

Althenia concentrated.

"The bugs, at the moment. They just pulled a large robot down and tore it to pieces, but I suspect if we stay and observe the outcome, the main losers will be us."

"Agreed," added Lucinda, and they continued down the bridge.

On the other side, instead of a straight wall, was a curved one, and it looked like from their position they were in fact heading into a large steel sphere. They stopped at the other side of the doors, which were larger than most and had a rounded arch on the top and no handle at all, just alien writing on them with no visible handle. There was a small panel with a collection of buttons poking out the left-hand side.

Natalie looked at the door and the panel and pressed a few buttons.

"Dead, I am afraid to say."

"Great," replied Lucinda. "Anything detected on the other side at all?"

Rena looked at the readouts. "Nothing, but I suspect it's because the door itself is blocking the scans."

"From what I can make out from markers on the door, it says something like core or centre four."

"Okay, step back, I'm going to try and force the door," replied Lucinda, who stayed in front of the door as Rena, Natalie, and Althenia moved back about twenty meters.

Althenia and Rena took a firing position in case something nasty popped out. Lucinda stood in front and waved her arm, and the door lifted with a loud crunch. Sparks flew as some cables were pulled while the door crunch opened.

The other side was brightly lit. Once the door was open, Althenia was the first to step through with her rifle first. It was a large room containing a bridge, and the floor was twenty meters below and had a couple of metal walkways branching out, some leading to the wall with a ladder leading down. The room also contained many large, rounded, metal towers, about forty meters tall with various heavy-looking, grey, red, and green cables hanging around them, going into the towers and connecting other towers.

She looked further in and found a large, grey mass amongst the towers below them. She paused for a second. It seemed to be pulsating. She was joined by colleagues as she crept closer to the large mass, making sure she was being as cautious as possible. She eventually got a good view of the grey mass behind the towers below. She popped up her scope from her rifle to take a look.

It looked like a large version of what a queen ant would look like with a massive bloated thorax, except instead of the white skin it was a sleek, slimy grey. The front looked like a normal bug body, but it was up in the air hanging from the massive thorax. She could not see the end, but every now and then would see one of the bugs carrying a small—well, small compared to their size—white oval which looked very egg-like.

"Do you see that thing?" Rena whispered, over the radio net.

"Affirmative," replied Althenia as Natalie and Lucinda replied yes.

Althenia kept on looking. She spotted a pipe, currently dripping out the green goo she'd seen before back in the warehouse. Every now and then, a worker would interact with some goo and take it to her queen's front end, and then interact with her, feeding her, she assumed, by regurgitation.

Suddenly Rena's voice interrupted her thoughts.

"The towers close to their queen are surrounded by the eggs."

She looked and that was indeed correct. Next to the towers were the eggs and again a dripping of green goo as well. She noticed some of the white ovals were squirming and on close examination, seemed to be hatched eggs. There were, in fact, larva, which was around the goo, feeding on it. As she took in the scene, she saw the front of one of the larger bugs. It definitely was different from the one they'd seen being fed in the hydroponics bay. Its mandibles were larger and generally looked more aggressive and had a larger body.

Althenia then heard Natalie over the radio net.

"Hey, I found something. It seems the consoles here are working barely, but they have more access to the system than I have seen before."

"Good work," replied Lucinda. "Find out anything yet?"

"Oh yes," said Natalie. "Have a look. I think this is a projector of some sort."

Althenia looked back, and Natalie was next to one of the towers that was next to the metal bridge. Jutting out of the tower was a large console screen and a large, black, solid table. Althenia double-checked that none of the bugs had noticed them and then wandered over to the table. Natalie played with the console. For a second, the top of the black table flashed and then displayed a 3D image of what looked like the starship. Basically, it looked like a large, metal brick with rounded edges and a pair of massive thrusters at one end. The solid image changed to a wireframe, and seven large spheres were shown. One was green and three were dark red. Another two were a lighter red, and one was dark yellow.

"We're in this one here," Natalie said, pointing to one of the spheres on the left side, "From what I can see, currently these are computer centres which hold the physical part of Advanced Control System. Currently, this one is offline."

"Well, we at least know what knocked this one out," replied Rena.

"Yes, a giant computer bug," replied Natalie somewhat mirthfully, "The worrying thing is that may be the case for the other areas. From what I can see, blue is sixty to a hundred percent of capacity, yellow is forty to sixty percent, red is zero to forty percent, and dark red means zero percent capacity."

"Okay," said Lucinda. "What does that mean for us?"

Natalie sighed. "The good news is most of these systems seem to be redundant to a point if one goes down then the other should take charge, but it seems like these centres also serve as network hubs, so they are responsible for all local systems, and if a row of them went down, one side of the ship could lose communication with the other side. As you can see from this dark red row here, this has happened."

"So, in other words, if we reach the control room, it won't help," said Lucinda thoughtfully.

Natalie smiled.

"Yes, Afraid so. Unless we manually rerun some cable, then it's useless."

"Seeing what already runs through the ductwork, I'm not too eager on that option," replied Rena.

Althenia smiled a little at that comment.

"Is there an alternative?"

"Yes, we can go to the control room here." Natalie pointed at a yellow, almost orange, sphere. "And hopefully I'll have enough access to fire off the engines and move it into a more stable orbit," Natalie added.

"Sounds good," said Rena.

"Yes, but there is a small issue. It seems like the exit to that part of the ship is down the ladders and close to the rather large bug which, granted, does not look mobile, but its friends and their nasty-looking pincers are," added Natalie.

"Okay, a good idea to avoid it. Any way around?" asked Rena.

"Well, there is a longer way where we have to go to this other red sphere here," answered Natalie as she pointed to a sphere above them in the 3D diagram.

"Why is there green paste here?" asked Althenia thoughtfully.

"Maybe they have a power supply and the paste could feed that?" guessed Lucinda.

Althenia looked back at the queen.

"Really, I suppose that's why the towers are far apart. Wouldn't heat be an issue?"

"No, they are quite efficient, of course. They generate a lot of power. I wouldn't want to start one given the state of the wiring at the moment. But that's actually a good idea."

Natalie then turned back to the map console and pressed a few more keys, and the image changed to a close-up of the sphere. One of the towers was flashing orange and red. "This is the power supply tower. That would make it that one there," said Natalie, pointing to a tower just beyond the queen. Althenia thought for a second. "We should be able to get there with a little luck if we go down this bridge here and move over there. The issue would be connecting a pipe back to it. I assume it was not a clean cut."

Natalie looked in a compartment on the helping robot.

"Well, we have duct tape in the tool kit and it does not have to last, to be honest, as long as we can put some sludge in the power supply and give it five minutes."

"Okay, sounds like a plan to me, unless there are objections?" asked Lucinda.

"Nope, but be aware, the sludge is highly flammable as well," added Natalie.

"Noted," replied Rena.

"Okay, that might actually help us. Is there another sludge pipe? If we start a fire, then we might have help from the maintenance robots which would make a good distraction." said Althenia with a thoughtful look on her face.

Natalie looked at the diagram for a second then pointed to a pipe just down from them. "Yes, here."

"Okay," said Lucinda. "This plan sounds a bit mad, but I'm down for it."

"Good," replied Althenia. "It's the only one we have. Also, Lucinda, you feel okay?"

"So far, feeling fine, but I've not built a shield up, and I can sort of feel the alien minds around me, but as long as I don't interact with them, I'm okay," replied Lucinda.

"Well, hopefully, we don't have to do that. Natalie and Lucinda, walk to the bridge with the broken pipe. See what you can see. Rena and I will head to the non-broken pipe, and I will place a remote charge on it."

Lucinda was okay but felt a little nauseous with all the alien minds about, but she had managed to push that away so she could focus on the mission. She headed down the bridge, followed by Natalia and the helping robot. Fortunately, by the looks of it, the only way you could get on the walkway was via a ladder, but she did notice some bugs were able to climb the cables up. At the moment, most of the bugs were going on with their normal lives below. They eventually reached a group of blue, grey, and green pipes going from one tower to another just below the walkway. Next to it was a slimmer walkway with a metal stairway down to it.

Natalie stopped their helpful robot and grabbed a section of tape from the toolbox and followed Lucinda, who was carrying the plasma rifle she had taken from the storage bank of the robot. Here, Natalie found the break—a large section of the pipe had been torn down, so it would be closer to the floor, and the ends showed ripping damage. The pipe was made from strange, green, flexible stuff like plastic.

"It looks heavy, let me try and move it," said Lucinda.

"Okay," replied Althenia. "We should be good to go shortly. I'll give you the word," she continued.

"You may want to make it quick," added Natalie. "A couple of soldier-looking ones are right now climbing up the cable to investigate."

"Do you think you can hit them?" asked Rena. Lucinda smiled to herself. It was one of the rare arguments she had with Natalie and insisted that she at the very least do some pistol training at least once a week, knowing a rifle would be a bit too cumbersome for her. Natalie pulled out her pistol, a heavy calibre round, and fired down, hitting the closest soldier bug in the head, causing it to fall with a loud thud.

"Yes," she replied.

"Okay, the charge is set. We have five minutes. We're coming to cover you," said Althenia over the radio.

"Okay," replied Lucinda, who put the shield up at the bottom of the cable as the noise had brought in more of the bugs. The bugs started to climb up toward them. Rena and Althenia arrived and stopped about five meters from them, took a kneeling firing position, and started shooting into the growing horde below. Not needing any signal at all, Lucinda lifted the cable with her power. It took a lot of effort. The cable itself was not light and not helped by the alien minds in the room.

Natalie ran down the walkway to where the joint was broken, and once it was in reach, started to get to work with the tape, wrapping it around in bundles as fast as she could. A loud bang was heard, and the bugs seemed to stop for a second, and even here Lucinda noticed the flaming pipe. She also noticed a metallic taste in her mouth but continued to focus, then saw a bug had managed to climb up the back and was on the scaffolding, followed by another.

"Watch out," Lucinda shouted.

Natalie turned from her tape job and saw a bug heading towards her. She reached for her pistol and pulled it out, but stopped. Lucinda knew she was in the firing line as well. She quickly looked across to the tape job. It looked secure. She then focused on the bug as she used her power to swat the collection of insects aside, down onto the floor, and then put a shield up at the pole.

The machine whirred to life, as a spark flew out of a cable close to her, dropping her concentration and causing her to fall to her knees as a sudden headache hit her. The whirring got louder and some of the bugs chittered angrily as Natalie rushed over. The lights on the towers started lighting up, and every now and then a loud spark shot out of various cables, causing more distress to the alien bugs.

Natalie helped her up.

"My god, you're bleeding from your nose!"

She looked down and saw that Rena and Althenia had an easier time clearing the bugs climbing up towards them, as most were down in the chaos below. Already the spider robots were attacking, trying to get to the fire, followed by the security robots. She also saw smoke coming from the pile of eggs by the towers. The queen itself was smoking and seemed to be twirling in pain. She almost felt sorry for it until she felt a sudden psychic push of pain as the queen sent out a signal of pain to her minions, causing her to stumble again. She felt someone lift her. It was Althenia, who folded her over her shoulder. She tried to move to help but found herself so confused and in pain that she could not get the signals to her body in time.

*****

Rena saw Althenia pick up Lucinda when she collapsed. She decided to take the back positions of their mad dash down the hallway and checked behind her. The bugs were now distracted by the fire, the random electrical arcs, and the incoming robots.

They reached a ladder down and quickly climbed down. Rena took a firing position. Next up was Althenia, who still had Lucinda over her shoulder and had managed to climb down. She got on and climbed down as well. Once they reached the floor, Natalie tried the controls on the robot. It managed to move, but one of the tires was flat. Natalie pushed a couple of buttons and a pump began whirring and forcing the tire to inflate, enabling her to easily move the robot. The noise attracted a nearby bug, who was trying to move the eggs from an arcing tower. Rena turned her rifle and fired and, of course, more appeared.

"Go," she shouted, as Althenia and Natalie headed towards the door about twenty meters away. Rena fired from her hip at a couple of close targets, one of which happened to be one of the spider robots. Rena backed out of the door, which was a solid metal one different from the one they had used to enter—it at least had a handle. Althenia pushed the door shut, using all the strength she could, as most of the mechanism was out of service. Rena noticed Lucinda was on the floor looking worse for wear, but still conscious, and Natalie was checking over her. Rena fired the odd shot through the closing gap, making sure nothing got too close. But with one final crunch, Althenia managed to close the door. Althenia then grabbed a nearby piece of metal and slammed it into the handle and twisted, making sure the door remained closed.

"How is Lucinda?" she asked.

"I'm okay, just a bit dizzy. The psychic shock sent by the queen didn't help," replied Lucinda.

She managed to stand using the robot as a crutch to help her up.

"Are you okay to walk?" asked Althenia, concerned.

Yes," replied Lucinda through gritted teeth.

"No," shouted Natalie, angrily, "Stop lying to us. We need to rest here, and I need to monitor her."

There was silence for a moment before Lucinda replied, "Natalie, dear, I'm fine."

A loud bang stopped the argument, soon followed by more.

"I'm afraid," replied Althenia, "rest is not an option."

Natalie reached down to the side of the robot between the back wheels and pushed a button. Out folded a simple metal stretcher with a single rubber wheel on one end and the other end connected to the robot via two simple metal tubes and had a cloth backing. It was at a slight angle and was large enough for one person to lie on it.

"Fortunately, this robot has an inbuilt stretcher. Lie down please."

Lucinda did not argue but simply got on the cloth backing and lay down as they started to move forward with Althenia at point and Rena at the rear and Natalie beside the robot. They walked up to one of the large doors with writing on them, and that led onto a bridge out of the sphere which they followed.

Althenia took the lead. Most of the hallways had been abandoned, and it looked like not even the robots had been down there. They eventually reached another set of doors above a bridge that led into a sphere and looked like the bridge and door they had encountered before, again without the handle, but it had the same type of writing on the door. Natalie found the control panel was working, which was good, as Althenia was pretty sure Lucinda was not up to using her psychic powers. She was still on the stretcher.

Fortunately, the only real debris in the hallway was broken panels and wires. Once they stopped, Lucinda got up, still a bit unsteady on her feet, as Natalie said, "Okay, I'm about to open."

Althenia and Rena took their fire stance in front as Natalie pushed a button. The door swung aside, and behind it were the large towers covered in cables, and again they were on a walkway. On the walkway itself was one of the smaller spider robots attempting to repair some cables. It then turned and rushed towards them, forcing Althenia to hit it with her plasma rifle. The robot collapsed in a flash of plasma blue. Another one appeared and was swiftly dispatched. Althenia then spotted one in the distance, which she swiftly took out. They then entered the sphere, and Natalie closed and locked the door behind them. They travelled for a distance, not seeing any more robots, which concerned Althenia a little, as surely this place should be under repair.

After a bit of walking, Natalie found a console next to one of the towers.

"Okay, let's see what we can do."

Lucinda went back into the stretcher as Rena took watch on one end and Althenia checked the other end, as Natalie worked away. It was not long before one of the security robots appeared further down the walkway.

"Contact," shouted Althenia as she took aim and fired a couple of shots at the first robot, hitting the shield and then hitting the chest. Rena joined her side and took aim at another one of the robots and fired, taking out its shield. It kept coming, and Rena had to send another salvo to finish it off.

Two more robots appeared. Althenia took aim, but before she could fire, she heard Natalie shout.

"About to fire the engines, hold on!"

Althenia grabbed hold of the wires next to her, as did Rena.

Natalie pressed a button and grabbed Lucinda and pulled her up from the bed, then grabbed a pair of handrails. They felt the ground shake. A small shake at first, and then it got even rougher like airplane turbulence. One of the robots heading towards them stumbled and fell into the other, sending them crashing down below. The shaking got even worse. Althenia saw Rena's grip start to fail. She reached out and grabbed her, pulling her close in, and could see Natalie doing the same as the ship started to stabilise from the engine quake.

Natalie then said over the radio net, "I think now may be a good time to tell you I had to select a destination, so I set it to the moon. We have twenty-eight hours till it arrives."

"Okay," replied Rena. "We have a wormhole window in about ten hours, so hopefully we should be off the ship by then."

They slowly got up.

"Yeah," added Lucinda as she shakily got up. "I imagine a ship this size was not designed to land with any grace," added Lucinda.

"I assume we're going to have to go the way we came," asked Althenia, "That might be an issue, as we might have set it on fire."

Natalie looked at her laptop, currently in tablet mode.

"By the looks of it, I'm afraid so. These spheres also serve as junctions in the ship. We have to go across that way anyway to access the wormhole room."

"Great," replied Rena. "Let's hope the battle is done and they have put out the fire for us."

The hallway itself had even more debris shaken loose by the engines. Fortunately, Lucinda was feeling better and was now up and walking, so they had folded the stretcher away despite Natalie's protesting. Natalie's concern for her was touching, thought Lucinda to herself. They then reached a large, heavy, steel beam lying in the middle of the hallway, blocking their way. It had obviously smashed through the roof.

"I have it," said Lucinda.

"You sure?" replied Rena.

Lucinda focused on the beam and managed to lift it up, allowing them to pass under it. Once they passed it, Lucinda let it go, feeling a bit of relief as it thudded onto the floor, and they continued down the hallway. They then reached the bridge into the sphere, and Althenia took the point as they crossed through the broken doors and came up in the hallway. They walked through the doorway, and Althenia slammed it shut. It was now bent open and had pieces of jagged steel around it.

They stepped into the room behind it and found the scene of a battle. There was still the odd fire, and one of the towers seemed to have fallen over completely, leaving a trail of broken wires and green goo. It was leaning precariously on another tower, and they could hear the odd metal creak. She saw green goo spattered on the side. If she correctly remembered, that was where the queen was. She was thankful that they could not smell using their helmets as she imagined the smell would be awful. The ladder that they had used before had collapsed on the floor along with the walkway. They found another ladder further down that they could use. Althenia climbed up the ladder with a cable from the robot wrapped around her shoulder. They at least had a winch where they could move the drone up to the higher walkway. Althenia found one of the higher, heavier electronic cables and wrapped the winch cable around it.

"Okay," Althenia shouted, and the drone winched itself up.

Lucinda got to the top of the ladder, followed by Natalie and Rena.,

"Something is still alive around here," advised Althenia, who had her rifle ready and took point as they again walked down the walkway past a still smoking tower, some of which had half-burnt bug corpses in it.

Althenia looked down.

She saw one of the security robots still fighting with a couple of bugs. It was missing the big left-hand arm but still took a swipe at the three bugs around it, who pushed forward only to rush back when the right arm swung into action.

She then heard Althenia shout.

"Contact."

A couple of plasma shots were fired.

She looked up as the security robot collapsed under the plasma bolts. Another stepped forward and she used her powers to push it off the edge of the walkway. She could see more on the bridge and used her power to push them off. Nausea came back, but at least the bridge was cleared, so they continued down past the doors and onto the bridge out of the sphere. As they reached about fifty meters from the hallway, there were eight security robots walking towards them. Rena and Althenia kneeled into a rifle fire position, took focus on one, and started firing. Lucinda, seeing that the robots would be on them too soon, put up a shield to try and slow them down, but as soon as one of the robots hit it, she felt a metallic taste in her mouth.

"Get back," shouted Natalie.

Lucinda stepped back, feeling a bit woozy as the robot shot went straight past Rena and into the first robot, sending it tumbling back and falling. The first robot then tried to push the helper robot off of itself as Natalie shouted, "Get down!" They hit the ground as an explosion was heard. Natalie had set the self-destruct on the robot, which created a nice, neat explosion. Fortunately, their spacesuits protected them from the shockwave and the flying shrapnel. Once the sound had cleared, she stood up and found that just one of the robots was trying to stand. Before she could say anything, Althenia fired her rifle, hitting the robot, causing it to collapse. They walked through the wreckage, and Lucinda felt a sense of hope despite still feeling unwell. They were now almost to the wormhole room.

*****

Sylvia lay in bed and smiled to herself. They had decided to allow Althenia to visit her, but she was currently in a containment suit. Her presence after the successful completion of her mission made her feel much happier. Sylvia needed the good news after being stuck in bed for so long. She was able to get out and about but had to use a wheelchair.

To be honest, it was a shock that she could no longer move her legs and she was still taking it in. She also found her psychic powers had diminished greatly. She had enough maybe to move a bottle or glass, but anything more than that and she had found herself worn out and tired.

Despite Ava's best efforts, sometimes she just wanted to lay in bed and let the day go by without her so she could sleep her life away. Althenia had been going over her mission and despite it sounding like a full debrief, Sylvia found herself enthralled and asked a lot of questions about the bugs and robots. Natalie came in also in a full containment suit, something that the starship team would have to wear for one more week.

She went up to them.

"Sorry to disturb you."

"No problem," replied Sylvia. "How is Lucinda feeling?"

"A lot better. A rest away from the starship, and she is up and about. I thought you would want to see this. One of our observatories managed to capture this earlier today." Natalie put the laptop up on a table next to the bed and pressed a button.

On the laptop, it showed a rather grainy and shaky image of the starship before slowly heading to the moon where it hit in what seemed like slow motion, sending clouds of moon dust up and around. Once the dust had settled, which took some time, it revealed a starship sitting there and looking still somewhat intact.

Sylvia looked sad for a moment. "I wonder about those people—or would it be better to call them entities?—in the ACS system. Are they gone?"

"Well, there is a mission planned to check on the spacecraft. We hope to establish a base there, so we can check that and continue to study the starship."

Natalie smiled as she continued, "Who knows? Maybe we could adapt and build our own and hopefully, if we encounter an inhabited planet it will go better than it did for Earth."

Sylvia smiled at the thought and lay back as Althenia held her hand encased in a containment glove.

Sylvia stroked her hand. She couldn't wait for this quarantine to be over.

Printed in Great Britain
by Amazon